The Christmas Market

The Christmas Market

LINDA MCEVOY

First published in the UK in 2024 by Bedford Square Publishers Ltd,
London, UK

bedfordsquarepublishers.co.uk
@bedsqpublishers

A CIP catalogue record for this book is available from the British Library.

ISBN
978-1-83501-138-6 (Paperback)
978-1-83501-139-3 (eBook)

2 4 6 8 10 9 7 5 3 1

Typeset in 11.25 on 14pt Garamond MT Pro
by Avocet Typeset, Bideford, Devon, EX39 2BP
Printed and bound in Great Britain by
CPI Group (UK) Ltd, Croydon CR0 4YY

For Kate, my bright shining star.

1

My nails dig into the skin of my palms and my feet are glued to the floor as I watch Gabe force the creaky sash window up as far as it will go then empty my linen sack of treasure onto the filthy street below. The precious fabrics I've been gathering for months and the hats I've designed and created from scratch. My ideal man, my cool lead singer with the Hozier hair has morphed into my waking nightmare and he's blaming me. And Christmas, of course. It's only mid-October but Gabe always manages to channel his inner Grinch before we make it to Halloween.

I should stamp straight over there and shove him out that bloody window. But I'm too much in shock. To hell with him anyway, I need to get outside and rescue my hats. Or *my* Christmas will be cancelled this year.

I'm taking a stall at the Galway City Christmas market in December. It's one of the best in the country and I was lucky to get in. But Gabe's not impressed. I found fairy lights and a string of tinsel in my favourite charity shop and I left these sitting on top of my oatmeal linen sack. I store my fabric and the hats that I'm working on in there and I was going to use the lights and tinsel later to start a mood board for my plans. But Gabe can't stand Christmas. And he hates twinkling lights.

'I'm not having Christmas tat all over the flat!' he bawled as he spotted my stash. Now the nightmare before Christmas is playing out in front of my eyes.

Amélie from the flat next to ours must have heard the commotion; her husky French accent calls after me as she follows me down the stairs. 'Is everything all right, Jas? I heard shouting again.' You'd think she'd be used to it by now.

'Sorry, Amélie, I have to get outside. Gabe just threw a fortune's worth of fabric and six months' work all over the bloody street.'

I pull back the cherry-red door and a blast of icy wind whacks me in the face. The smoke-grey clouds above threaten to open up and carry me and my discarded treasure off into the Corrib and all the way out to Galway Bay. But I'm a woman on a mission and I stride purposefully ahead. Straight into a leaf-filled puddle. In my pink fluffy socks. I wouldn't mind but I know this puddle. I curse this puddle every morning as I lift my Docs and leap right over it.

Amélie places a hand on my shoulder and urges me onward as she edges past me and around the murky pool. She stares for a moment at a creamy waft of antique lace floating from the wing mirror of a white HiAce van. She reaches out and disentangles the delicate fabric then folds it into a perfect square. 'We need a sac, a bag…' She dashes across the street and persuades a young male passerby to part with his Bag for Life. Amélie has soft blonde curls, rosebud lips, and cobalt eyes. She could probably persuade him to cut out his heart and offer it to us if she wanted to.

We scurry along the street grasping what we can from mucky puddles and grimy windscreens. A high-pitched whine catches at the back of my throat as I spot my green velvet bucket hat dangling from the handlebars of a mountain bike. My perfect creation, my lucky charm. Thank God, there's something left to salvage. Of my work that is. There's definitely nothing left to salvage between Gabe and me.

*

I'm back upstairs again, emptying the Bag for Life onto the kitchen table. I managed to retrieve most of my stuff, with Amélie's help. Gabe didn't even bother to come down. He's sprawled on the armchair with a face as long as his rangy legs.

I lean my palms on the worn pine table top and stare down at my bedraggled pile. 'I can't do this anymore.' I shake my head as I groan. Most of my pieces are still intact. But there's muck and debris everywhere and I wonder if those stains will ever wash out.

Gabe slumps in his chair and thrusts his lower lip. 'I had a shit night last night,' he says. As if I said nothing at all. As if I was the one in the wrong. 'You should have been there. I need you to keep me on track.'

'One night.' I grit my teeth. 'One bloody night. I'm *always* there.'

'Yeah, well, you weren't there last night and I was crap. I couldn't focus and I kept forgetting the words. They told me that's it.'

'What? What's it?'

He drags himself up and leans over me with a sullen pout. 'The lads. They kicked me out of the band, and it's all your fucking fault.'

This doesn't exactly come as a big surprise. Pretty much everything bad that has happened over the last few years has been my fault. That's the gospel according to Gabe. But I've finally seen the light. I've got to get out of this place. And I need to leave that boy behind.

2

I'm on my way home now, back to Ballyclane. I offered to work a month's notice but Della said there was no need. I told her about Gabe and my fabrics and she was almost as upset as me. Viva Vintage is a special place and Della works hard to make sure that everything in her shop is unique. She's been gathering scraps and offcuts for years and in March, for my birthday, she curated them carefully into an oatmeal linen sack and presented them all to me. Velvet, silk and antique lace; buttons, bows, flowers and threads. All the raw materials I need to make my dreams come true.

I've been working at Viva Vintage since I moved to Galway, nine years ago. Mam took me and my sister, Cathy, to the Christmas market as a pre-Christmas treat. I fell in love with the city as soon as I stepped off the train. Cathy was in her final year of teacher training and I had just finished school. I had no clue what I wanted to do. I wasn't academic like Cathy, and I knew how hard Mam had to scrape. I worked in Mullins supermarket and scrimped until the following May. Then I packed a bag and stayed on a friend's couch until I got my own place. Half of the Midlands go to college in Galway so it wasn't a stretch to find somewhere to crash. I worked in a bar for the summer until one day in September I was walking towards Sea Road and I spotted the sign. I stopped at this window every day on my way to work and I went inside almost every day I had off. Della didn't even ask for a CV. 'I've seen you,' she said, 'gazing at my garments as though you've found your soulmate. I can tell we're going to be friends.'

'It's not the best timing,' says Cathy, as I watch the windscreen wipers swoosh away the driving rain. 'You're welcome to stay with me and Brian instead.'

For Mam, she means; it's not the best timing for Mam.

I lean my head against the side window and peer out into the unrelenting grey. 'I'd like my own room for a while. It's been a shit year and I was really looking forward to home.'

She presses one hand to the back of her perfectly straight bob and focuses on the road ahead. 'It's just that Mam has been on her own for so long. All through the pandemic.' She takes a measured breath and carries on, 'And now she has Donal, and they're so good together—'

'And I'll be in the way.'

Cathy doesn't roll her eyes but she might as well, I know she's not impressed. She and Mam kept trying to get me to move home during Covid. Mam was on her own and Gran passed away near the start of it all. But I wasn't ready then, still holding fast to the hope that Gabe and I might work things out. We both got the pandemic payment and I dreamed we'd get closer and more creative and fix everything that was wrong. I could have built my own fashion empire with all the time and energy I poured into fixing that man. Until I finally realised it was me that needed to change.

Now the pandemic is over and everyone's getting on with their lives. Mam has got a man, Cathy's got a promotion, and I've got no home, no partner, no job. And, according to Cathy, even my lovely mother doesn't want me around anymore.

'I'll just crash with Mam for the first week and see how it goes. Donal's not living there, is he?'

'Not yet, but he stays over every weekend.'

There's silence for a while and I realise that I'm holding my breath. It's a thing I do when I get a bit stressed.

We pull off the motorway and tear into the Plaza food court, slicing through the sideways rain. The place is heaving with soggy travellers and we zigzag through the fast-food queues and head for the Bewley's Barista bar at the end. We bag an empty table near the door then we sit hugging our warm KeepCups and Cathy asks me seriously if I have a plan. Cathy's always had a plan: Brian, college, becoming principal of our local primary school. I think she'll be taken aback when I announce that, actually, I do. I've had this plan for a while. I just couldn't get the headspace to follow it through.

I set my cappuccino down and run a hand through my hair to tame my bedraggled curls. Then I rap the table with my palm and declare, 'I'm going to make hats, reclaimed vintage hats'. I stare across at my sister as she sips her latte and widens her eyes. It's clear she's waiting for more.

'I've been making them for a while. I took courses online during the pandemic so I know what I'm doing. And Della gave me loads of fabric from her collection, all sustainable, and gorgeous, of course.'

Cathy looks interested now. She lowers her coffee and nods. 'That sounds great, Jas. You could definitely do that; you were always creative.'

'Really?' I'm surprised at how wobbly I feel that Cathy believes I can do this. She's so focused and together I always feel she just thinks I'm a mess.

'Absolutely, remember when we were teenagers, you'd take the most basic outfit, pull out Gran's sewing machine, and put your own twist on it. You could make anything look cool.'

I sit up a little straighter now. I'm not sure Cathy's version of cool is the same as mine but I'll take it. Della said pretty much the same, and she's a punky Helen Mirren, iconic.

'Gran's sewing machine is part of the plan, and hopefully, her wardrobe too, if Mam is okay with that.'

Cathy nods again, and this time she adds a smile. 'I think she will be. Maybe your timing is not so bad, after all.'

I throw her a quizzical look and she carries on.

'Mam's been talking about clearing out Gran's place for ages but she hasn't been ready to face it. I've offered to help but she keeps wanting to wait. This could be just the nudge she needs.'

Cathy's right about that, I can feel it. I was really close to my gran, two peas in a pod, Mam used to say. I begged Gran loads of times to let me raid her wardrobe but she was young at heart and upcycled and re-wore most of the contents herself.

'You can have them all when I'm gone,' she used to laugh, swirling her tea dresses and asking my advice on what she should wear to the dance. She and her friends were having a better social life in their seventies than anyone else in the town. That bloody pandemic hit everyone hard but sometimes I think it hit them hardest of all. At least I still have time.

'As long as you're not after the house,' Cathy quips, bringing me back with a land.

'Ha, ha,' I play along. 'Just the sewing machine and anything else I can use for my hats.' I consciously unfurrow my brow. Is Cathy really asking if I'm thinking about taking over Gran's house? Or maybe she's just assuming that something so ambitious could never be part of my plan.

Gran's house, Mam's home place, lies right at the heart of the town. A narrow three-storey building perched on the edge of the Square. It's a beautiful Georgian square and most of the houses are huge. Gran's is down at the back corner and is half the width of the imposing mansion straight across on the other side. That belongs to the Hamiltons. Hard-nosed property developers, and the wealthiest family in town.

Mam comes out to meet us as soon as we pull up outside. It's only when I see her that I realise how much I've missed her. She and Cathy look so alike but Mam is softer round the edges and just being near her makes me feel safe. She wraps me in a hug and then I tear up the stairs with my suitcase before Cathy has time to protest. So, nobody has time to warn me that my room doesn't exist anymore. The space is still there, I presume. But there's no way to get in, just a full-length shabby chic mirror where my bedroom door used to be.

'Oh, sorry, love, you're in here. I should have said.' Mam opens the door to Cathy's old room.

I stare at the pale lemon walls and the giant Westlife posters over the bed. I don't even get to ask before Mam grabs hold of my arm and gives an excited coo.

'Come and have a look at what I've done. Donal did the work but I designed it all. It's absolutely fabulous, you'll see.'

I'm whisked back out onto the landing and straight through Mam's room into what used to be mine. My haven, my oasis, my world. It is fabulous, she's right. But it's a bloody walk-in wardrobe now. I feel like I've been rubbed out.

I lie on Cathy's bed that evening and message Shane. I should have messaged him days ago but it's hard to admit he was so right. Shane is my best friend since school and it's putting it mildly to say he wasn't fond of my ex. He always said Gabe didn't appreciate me and only cared about himself. Gabe never wanted him around and one night when we were all very drunk at the same party, Shane, who can't sing a note, stood against a wall and belted out 'Fake' by the Frames while pointedly staring at Gabe. Gabe's friends had to hold him back from going after

Shane, and the next day, he said it was time for me to choose.

I still messaged and FaceTimed Shane all the time but I made sure to hide it from Gabe. I pick up my phone and start typing.

Hi, Honey, I'm home.

Where? Ballyclane?

Yep.

With or without?

Without. Permanently.

Shane hits FaceTime immediately and I accept.

I'm waiting for 'About time' or 'What took you so long?' but he just beams and says, 'I'm proud of you, Jas.'

'For what? For taking six years to cop myself on?'

He offers lots of nice platitudes about how it probably wasn't all bad. Then he adds, 'He only loved you if you did everything his way. That's not real love.' Then he grins.

'But it can't be easy letting go of a flaming hot Rock God, I suppose.'

'Easier than you'd think,' I say, and I smile as I realise that it's true. I always thought that if Gabe and I broke up I'd be wiped out. But there's no heartbreak, no devastation, all I can feel is relief.

3

I'm at Gran's house now. I told Mam I'd go and have a look, see how much work there is in clearing the place out. Quite a lot by the looks of things. Mam's house is warm and cosy and bright. Gran's was too when she was alive but she didn't have Mam's neat streak and she hardly ever threw anything out. No wonder Mam couldn't face it alone. It still feels welcoming to me, though, and I get a sense of Gran here as though she's been waiting for me to come home. I'm not sure how to broach my plan with Mam, me moving into Gran's. She seems so happy to have me back but we haven't talked about what happens next. It was nice just chilling on the couch last night with a big pot of tea, hearing about her new, happy life. She's going to join me in an hour or so. She has to cancel an appointment first but she says it doesn't matter, she's thrilled to have me back, and everything else can wait.

I trace my fingers along the old Singer 201. I have my own machine but Gran worked on this for over fifty years, sitting right here, facing her front-room window. Even with her head bent in concentration, the woman never missed a trick. She knew everyone in town and anyone who needed a garment altered or a dress made for a special occasion came to her. She was the queen of upcycling before anyone had heard about climate change.

The sun is shining bright this morning and the Galway grey fades from my memory as I sit at her work table and gaze out onto the town's historic Square. It's weird being back after all this time. Gran's house, my home town, and my old school just down the road. I can see the arch over on the other side of the Square where Shane and I used to sneak off to smoke. I draw back the net curtain to take a better look. Only I can't see much as my view is obscured by a stranger in shades peering straight in. He's waving at me now. Some people have no shame. I scrape back my chair and storm out into the hall. I presume he's gone on his way but I pull open the front door just in case. I rush out and wallop straight into a broad white T-shirt instructing me to *Just Breathe.*

'You're not Bernie,' the stranger grunts as though I'm the one in the wrong.

'No, I'm not.' I reel back and set one hand on my hip. 'But who may I ask are you? And more to the point, what are you doing lurking around my gran's?'

His face – a very handsome face, I have to reluctantly admit – breaks into a broad smile. He takes off his sunglasses and peers down at me with twinkly grey eyes.

'Lurking? I'm hardly lurking. I was about to ring the bell only I didn't get a chance.'

I feel light-headed and I realise that I'm holding my breath again. I grab on to the door frame and gaze into that very fit chest. Was this guy looking for a way to piss me off when he opened his wardrobe this morning? *Just breathe.* I'm doing my bloody best.

'Are you okay, you look a bit off?'

I stretch myself up to my full height and jut out my chin. 'I'm perfectly fine but you still haven't said who you are.'

He takes a step back and holds out a hand. 'I'm Niall, Niall Hamilton, from over the road.' He nods towards the mansion on the opposite side of the Square. I'm supposed to meet Bernie here this morning.' He narrows his eyes and studies me. 'Are you little Jas?

The bloody cheek. I give him my fiercest glare.

'Sorry, I mean, Cathy's little sister… Cathy's sister, Jas?' He lowers his hand, looking embarrassed now. And so he flipping should, I'm five foot six and twenty-eight years old, I'm nobody's little anything anymore.

His phone pings and he frowns as he scans the message. Seriously, this guy is getting ruder by the minute.

'Ahem,' I clear my throat. 'You asked me a question, so yes, I am Jas, Bernie's daughter. My mam owns this house, it used to be my gran's.'

'Sorry, yeah.' He points distractedly at his phone. 'Bernie just sent me a text postponing our meeting. I'm a bit early. I thought I saw someone inside and I presumed it was your mum.'

He peers over my shoulder and I stare at him hard. Does he think I have my mother hiding down the hall?

I take a firm hold of the door as I step back inside. 'Well, if that will be all,' I say in my most officious tone. I sound like a butler so I haughtily add, 'I'm a very busy woman and I need to get back to my work.'

Shit, I sound like the housekeeper now, I just can't pull this off. I often wonder who I might have been in a former life and now it seems abundantly clear. Niall Hamilton would have been Lord of the Manor, or at least the heir, and I would have been the flipping scullery maid.

He holds up his palms and backs away but I can see he's stifling a grin. Glad to have been of some amusement, I'm sure. I shut the door and lean against it then blow out a long hard exhale. I haven't seen Niall Hamilton since secondary school. He was four years ahead of me, in Cathy's class. A quiet, dark-haired boy that I barely gave a second glance. I think he was tall even then but I don't remember him taking up quite so much space. What was he doing here? And when did he get so hot?

4

Mam arrives an hour later with a roll of black bags and a bucket of cleaning supplies. Looks like I'll be scrubbing in this life too. I shove up my sleeves and accept my fate, at least I'll be earning my keep. Mam's cleaning out kitchen cupboards and I'm mopping the floor when I decide to ask about Niall.

'You had a visitor earlier,' I say. 'Posh lad from over the road.'

She laughs. 'Niall's not posh. And he's been very helpful,' she adds, although she doesn't say how.

'They're bloody loaded, the Hamiltons. His dad built half the town.' I swipe my mop across the tiles. 'And as far as I remember, his uncle fleeced the other half.'

She climbs down from the wooden countertop and drops her cloth into the worn Belfast sink. 'He's nothing like his uncle.'

'That floor's wet,' I remind her. You'd split your head on Gran's tiles.

'He was in Cathy's class at school. He's a very sweet boy.'

I pull a face. He's a bit big for a boy and he didn't seem that sweet to me.

I head out into the hall with my mop and we don't say any more until we break for a pot of tea. Mam lets out a sigh as I pour her a cup.

'This place needs so much work.' She shakes her head as she looks around. 'I don't know where to start.'

I narrow my eyes as I set down the pot, I thought we already had made a start. But maybe that's not what she means, I suppose it does need more than a clean. Gran poured most of her time and talent into her dressmaking, and anything left over went into her social life. There's little or no insulation and the windows rattle with the faintest breeze. There was always a fire going when Gran was alive but there's no central heating and now the place does smell a bit damp.

Mam takes a sip of her tea and starts to butter her scone. She lowers her knife and goes on, 'It needs a major overhaul and a heap of money too.'

I wasn't planning to say this yet but it seems like it might be the time.

'There are grants going once the house has been vacant for over two years. It can't be that bad, Gran managed fine and she was really happy here.'

'It's too much work for me.' She shakes her head. 'I don't think I can take that on.'

'Maybe I could?'

Mam nearly chokes on her scone.

'I don't mean buy the place, no one would give me a mortgage. I don't even have a job.' She frowns but I keep going. 'But I could rent it from you and work on it while I'm living here. And we could use the grant to pay for the repairs. I'm hoping to start selling my hats soon and I could do alterations and upcycle clothes like Gran did.' I squeeze my fists under the table and take a slow breath. I need to sound calm and at least a bit like I know what I'm talking about. 'I could use the front room for my work and fix up the house over time.'

Mam gives me a sympathetic look. The sort of look she used to give me when I was a kid and I'd regale her with my latest crazy scheme. We should go on a family holiday to Disneyland, Florida was one. That was when I was ten and Tracey Hamilton arrived back at school with a princess tiara, bragging for months about her trip to the States. We had a weekend in Trabolgan the following summer, although I have to admit it was fun.

She tilts her head. 'I'm not sure you understand how much work would be involved, and how much it would cost.' She sighs again. 'This is a protected structure, Jas, and it hasn't had any work done in years. I need advice from someone who knows a bit more. What if you want to go back to Galway, or move on somewhere else? I know how much you loved your gran but she wouldn't want to tie you down.'

I open my mouth to protest. I'm definitely not going back to Galway, not while Gabe is still there. But Mam carries on before I get the chance.

'It might seem like a good idea now but life can change so fast. You might meet someone now that you're home. You might want to have children. There's no garden, only a tiny yard. There's no parking and there's a busy pub just around the corner. It's hardly ideal.'

I splutter a cough. I'm barely home a day and she has me settled down with a brood.

'It sounds ideal to me. I don't have a car, I have zero interest in getting a new man, the last one was bad enough. And I'm definitely not ready for kids.'

'Well, what about your business then? Don't you want to focus on that? I know you've made all those gorgeous hats but you haven't really told me your plans.'

I haven't had the chance. I thought I'd have weeks mooching around Gran's before I'd put forward my case.

'I've made some hats, not as many as I'd hoped thanks to Gabe, but I'm planning to make a lot more. I've been looking through Gran's wardrobe for fabric, I hope you don't mind.'

'Of course not, she'd want you to,' she says with a nod.

'Della gave me lots of fancy pieces but Gran had really good wool and felt and tweed. If you don't object to me cutting her stuff, I can make beautiful hats from her clothes.'

Mam's eyes well up and I bite my lip. I'm a heartless bitch threatening to rip up her mother's precious things.

'That would be lovely, pet, you'll be keeping her memory alive.'

I breathe a sigh of relief. 'I'm hoping to have a decent batch ready for the market,' I tell her.

'What market?'

I swallow the last of my scone and roll my eyes with a smile. 'What market do you think? The Christmas Market in the Square, of course. I'm going to ask Cathy if I can take a stall.' I thread my fingers through my chestnut curls and then stretch out my arms like a cat. I'm running the reel in my head. Me in my green velvet bucket hat with my creations laid out on display. Mulled wine and twinkling lights and a steady stream of customers queuing up to admire and pay. 'It's how I plan to launch,' I proudly declare.

Mam says nothing but I watch her wince.

'What? What's wrong? Have I left it too late to book a stall? I'm Cathy's sister, for God's sake. Surely the queen of Christmas will find a way to squeeze me in.'

Mam scrubs at her scalp and blows out a breath. 'I'm not sure there is a market this year, pet. I do know Cathy's not involved.'

My mother has lost the plot. Gran's house, my proposal, it must all be too much. Cathy has been organising the town's Christmas market for years. She started helping as soon as she got her job at the school and they elected her chairperson the following year. She's the most focused person I know and she never lets anyone down. Mam has got to be wrong, there has to be some mistake. I've been slaving away all year preparing for my big reveal. It may not be a big city market like Galway but when it comes to Christmas, Ballyclane always punches above its weight. A stall at the market here is how I plan to launch my new start. New business, new life, new Jas.

5

I cycle over to Cathy's later that evening. I'm fairly tired as I tore into the cleaning for the afternoon. I park my bicycle under the kitchen window and let myself in the back door. Cathy's sitting at the table looking a bit peaky herself. I notice dark circles under her caramel-brown eyes. Cathy, Mam and I have similar colouring. Mam says we have a bit of Spanish blood in us as Gran's ancestors hailed from somewhere down near Kinsale. She did try to explain about the Spanish Armada but I switched off as soon as Cathy got all excited and said she'd studied that at school. I look at her more closely now and I see that her honey-toned skin has taken on a faint green tinge. Cathy is one of the healthiest people I know so this really pulls me up.

'Are you okay?' I ask. 'You look a bit pale.'

'I'm fine, just tired.' She smiles. 'How was your first day back? Did you and Mam go to Gran's?'

'We did.' I nod. 'It was a mixed bag, to be honest.' I grab a glass from the cupboard and turn on the tap. I lean against the sink, sip some water, and then I start to unload. 'It was strange going through Gran's stuff but we got a lot done and I found some wonderful fabrics for my hats.' I plonk down on a chair facing Cathy and come straight to the point. 'I was hoping to take a stall at the market to show them off. But Mam says you've cancelled Christmas this year.'

Cathy widens her eyes and gives me a look. 'That's a bit harsh.'

I raise my palms in surrender. 'Sorry, I'm just a bit disappointed. And I don't understand. You always organise the market. I know there's a committee but you do most of the work. Why not this year?'

She places a hand on her stomach and lowers her eyes. 'Because I'm pregnant,' she says.

Christ. Now it makes sense. Cathy has had two miscarriages and she and Brian desperately want a child. There's a fair bit of administration in organising a small-town Christmas market but most of the work is lugging tables, sweeping streets and cleaning up the mess. And Cathy is always at the heart of it all. This year she has to put herself first.

'How many weeks,' I ask. She lost both her babies at eight weeks so I'm keeping my fingers crossed.

'Fourteen weeks on Wednesday,' she says and I sigh with relief.

'You shouldn't have driven all the way to Galway,' I tell her. 'If I'd known, I would have taken the train.'

'It was fine,' she reassures me. 'Just no heavy lifting and definitely no stress.'

Now I understand why she left the bigger bags to me. I did wonder if she was making some sort of point.

'That rules out the market then,' I agree.

'It does for me but there are ten weeks left until Christmas, it could still go ahead.'

I FaceTime Shane again as soon as I get home.

'You won't believe what's happened!' I flop onto the bed and prop myself up.

'I've known you for most of your life, there's not much left to shock me with.'

'Feck off, not me. Cathy.'

Shane widens his eyes in mock surprise. 'What has she done now? Put too much sugar in her tea? Given the kids extra homework for the weekend?'

'She's bloody well cancelled Christmas! Well, the Christmas market anyway.' I feel bad complaining, I know Cathy has a good reason and I can't tell Shane what it is yet. But I need to vent to someone.

'Oh, no.' Shane knows how important this is, I've told him all my plans. 'What are you going to do?'

'Well, according to my sister, it's easy, I'll just organise it all by myself.'

He snorts a laugh. 'Sorry, it's just being organised is not exactly your strength.'

'I've gotten better,' I huff. Shane spent our school days following me around with my phone, my bag, my leaving cert timetable. Whatever I'd left behind. 'The biggest problem is that there's not a lot of time. They usually start working on it at the end of the summer, not halfway through October.'

'I'm not saying you couldn't do it but do you really need a market?' He rubs at his cheek. 'Your hats are great. Can't you just post pics on Insta, set up some reels… Hey, maybe you should start a blog. Hat Girl. No wait, I think that's gone. Jas Hats?'

'Gone too, at least in Australia. See, I am organised, I'm already planning all that for the New Year. But I want to see some reactions first, for real. I want to watch people's faces, I want to see them touch the fabric, look at themselves in the mirror when they try on a hat. I want to get how it makes them feel.' I squeeze my fist against my chin and hunch forward. 'I know they're good in my head but I need to feel it in my bones.'

I stay in my room pondering for a while. Donal has my spot on the couch so I'm giving Mam and him a bit of space. I've only met him once before and he seems nice. He has a distinguished look about him: grey hair, neat clothes, and kind eyes. But he keeps smiling at me and trying to make conversation like he's desperate for me to like him from the start. I can't work like that; I like to take my time so he'll just have to wait. I told them I had a lot of work to do for the market and I made my escape.

I grab a notebook from Cathy's shelves – she always has spares – and root through my bag for a pen. I need to make a plan. Shane suggested I take a stall at another Christmas Market in one of the nearby big towns, but I don't see the point. If I was going to launch somewhere else, Galway would be my first choice. Gabe wouldn't be seen dead near the market; he'd consider himself too cool. But I really want to do this at home. I want to prove to the Tracey Hamiltons of this town that I'm on my way to being somebody after all.

I lie back on my pillow and picture the scene in my head, the one that plays on a loop whenever I pass by our old school. Shane and I on our class trip to see *Pride and Prejudice* performed outdoors at Oakwood Court. Striding arm in arm up the yew-lined avenue, gazing at the neoclassical mansion basking in the September sun. Shane asked me if I felt like Lizzie when she first set eyes on Pemberley. Before I got to reply Tracey Hamilton turned around and called at the top of her voice to everyone else in the line, 'Ooh, it's Jas's first trip to Oakwood. Hey, lads, let's have a whip round after the show, buy the council kids a bit of greenery, I don't suppose they have trees in Emmet Park.' Then she glared at me as though I was a piece of dirt that she needed to scrape off the bottom of her shoe. She's lucky that Shane held me back. 'Rise above it,' he would say whenever she'd start, which was practically every day. I painted her face on the bottom of my Docs with Tippex and whenever she made her smart comments, I'd grind my foot into the nearest patch of dirt and imagine it was me grinding *her* down instead of the other way around.

I'm going to work my ass off on those hats, I decide. They're going to be class. *And* I'm going to organise this bloody Christmas market if it kills me. I'll show them all. I pick up my phone and call Cathy. I'm going to need her big orange folder and her list of names. She might have been chairperson, secretary and treasurer all rolled into one. But she had a team of willing helpers and I'll need to get them on board.

I'm back in Cathy's the next evening, leafing through her folder. There are detailed instructions for everything. My sister leaves nothing to chance.

'A lot of that is pre-pandemic,' she tells me. 'The last few years we tried to keep it small.'

'I'm all for that,' I say. 'No beer tents and plastic tat. Just quality, sustainable crafts and local home-made food.'

'You won't get a licence for alcohol anyway, not at this stage.'

I pause at a section with Traffic Management highlighted in yellow. And a bundle of emails printed off, between Cathy and the local council.

'You might be a bit late for that, too,' she says. 'It took ages last year to sort out. One of the businesses objected, they said we were taking all their parking spaces. I wouldn't mind but we brought so many extra people into town that they did a roaring trade.'

'There's always one.' I click my tongue. 'I suppose I should check if anyone wants to help before I make a start.'

Cathy contacted her helpers back in August, as soon as she took her pregnancy test. She didn't explain why, it was way too early, she just told them she couldn't take charge this year. She offered her big orange folder and her willing advice to whoever might like to step up. All she got back were messages telling her how great she was at the job and how they hoped she'd change her mind.

She sends a WhatsApp now suggesting a meeting tomorrow evening. There's never much happening on a Wednesday so she's hoping they'll all be on board. They use a meeting room down a lane off the Square and Christy who is also on the Tidy Towns committee has a key. Half an hour later we have confirmations from Christy, Maura and Nadia and we're all systems go for seven o'clock down the lane.

6

I dismount my lavender bicycle and wheel it through the arch. Wow, this place has changed. The once shabby ruins and derelict outhouses have been transformed into a row of whitewashed cottages on one side and tasteful stone-fronted shop units on the other. The lane, which is really more of a road, forks off so that there are two narrow lanes with one long unit running down the centre. They join up again on the other side and lead down to a beautiful walled garden. It's edged with amber solar lanterns and wouldn't look out of place in a corner of Oakwood Court. On either side of the stretch that leads into the garden, there's room for parking and there seems to be a one-way system running around the centre unit. I had no idea there was so much space, never mind that all this work had taken place to restore it. Shane and I used to skive off behind the arch to smoke cigarettes and bitch about our enemies, mostly Tracey Hamilton, but I never copped it had so much potential.

I lean my bike against the wall of the long rectangular building that runs down the middle and I take my folder from the front wicker basket. The units to my right are in darkness but the lane itself is lantern-lit and there's a warm glow filtering through the voile-curtained window where I've parked my bike. The teak door is slightly ajar so I give a quick rap and wander in. Cathy is seated at the top of a long pine table chatting to a small, white-haired man holding a tweed cap and sporting a bright yellow hi-vis.

I wave my hand in hello. 'It's toasty in here. Who pays the heating bill? Santa Claus?'

'Ah, we have our very own Santa Claus.' Christy gives a chuckle. I know he's Christy because he has a name badge stuck to his hi-vis telling me so. Looks like I'm dealing with a seasoned committee hack here. 'Sit down, love,' he instructs me, 'and have a drop of tea.'

I'm taking my first sip when Maura and Nadia arrive. Maura was an air hostess in her younger days and she still has that look. Perfectly coiffed hair and a neatly tied silk scarf. I know her of old and clearly she remembers me too. I can tell by the way her nose wrinkles as though she's caught a bad smell. Christy chooses this moment to remark on how different my sister and I seem.

'Sure, I wouldn't know you were Cathy's sister at all with your fine head of curls and all your style.'

Maura makes a half-strangled noise, somewhere between a snort and a sniff. She can't argue with the curls but I'm sure she has plenty to say about my style. Cathy is still in her pale grey work suit with a crisp white blouse. I'm actually very subdued in a button-down burgundy midi, crochet pink hat, and pink and silver scarf. And my feet are under the table so she can't see the Docs that I've embellished with tiny silver stars. The theme of the meeting is Christmas after all.

'They were always chalk and cheese,' Maura remarks with a tight little smile, then takes a seat down the end across from me, as far away as she can find.

Nadia is much warmer with bright blue eyes and blonde hair scraped back off her face in a bouncy ponytail. She beams as she comes over stretching her hand. 'It's lovely to meet you, Jas. I'm so happy we are going to have a Christmas market after all.'

Nadia volunteered to help last year as soon as she arrived from Ukraine. She lives with her mother in what used to be a tourist hostel on the outskirts of town. Ballyclane doesn't get many tourists so now it houses Ukrainian refugees. It's a nice place to stay for a few days but it must be hard living there long term, sharing a kitchen and bathroom and never knowing when or if you'll be able to go home. Nadia's a qualified preschool teacher and spent market day face-painting and telling Christmas stories to the little ones, which went down a treat. I know Cathy felt particularly bad about letting her down.

Cathy gives a small cough. 'Hopefully, there will be, that's what we are here to decide.' She sets her elbows on the table and joins her hands under her chin as though she's about to say grace. I cross my fingers under the table and hope that what she has to say will be gracefully received.

'As I've already informed you all I can't be involved this year.'

Nadia and Christy look crestfallen. Maura's eyes blaze but she only gets as far as 'Well, I really—' when Cathy raises her palm to call a halt.

'I'm pregnant, Maura, and I'm under strict instructions from my doctor. I'm sure you wouldn't want to put my baby at risk.'

Maura clutches her scarf with a face like she's just been slapped.

'That's great news, love.' Christy beams as Nadia darts over to give Cathy a hug.

Cathy settles everyone and clears her throat again. It's about to get interesting now. 'As you know,' she starts, 'I was hoping someone might be able to take my place earlier.' She sweeps the table with a sympathetic smile. 'But I do understand that it's a very daunting task. That's why I'm delighted to tell you all that Jas has offered to take on the role.'

Christy gives a cheery thumbs up and Nadia claps her hands. Maura's jaw is hanging and there's a look of horror on her face but she doesn't say a word. I have a feeling she's biding her time.

I open the orange folder, although I'm not really sure where to start. I take a slug from my reusable water bottle and decide to come clean.

'I should start by saying that I don't have much experience with this sort of thing.' Maura raises her eyebrows and I can hear her voice in my head. *Tell us something we don't know.* She doesn't say the words, though, and I continue, 'But I have read Cathy's folder and she has everything clearly laid out.' I open the page marked insurance and glance around the group. 'I think it might be too late at this stage to plan for the Square.' I don't wait for a reaction, I just cut to the chase. 'You normally have the insurance and the traffic management in hand well before now. I phoned the insurance company this morning. It would be way more expensive this year, premiums have gone through the roof.'

Maura smiles smugly as though I've just made her night. Why did the woman come at all if she's determined to be such a Grinch?

'I propose we look at alternative locations. Somewhere that won't involve relocating traffic and ideally somewhere with insurance cover in place. Does anyone have anywhere to suggest?'

Maura pushes away her teacup as though she suspects it might be spiked. 'I thought that's why you were here, Jasmine. When Cathy said you wanted to take charge, I'm sure we all hoped you had some sort of plan.'

I'm sure she hoped exactly the opposite but I give her my sweetest smile.

'It's Jas, thank you, Maura,' I say. 'I am going to put together a plan. But this is my first meeting and I'm hoping we can work as a team. You all have so much valuable experience and it's important that I respect and make the most of that.' That should shut her up. I hope.

Christy mentions the town hall and Nadia suggests a room belonging to one of the local schools. The parish held a fundraiser there for the first group of Ukrainian refugees and she says it's cosy, although it might be a bit small. The town hall is much bigger but quite run-down and it's on the corner of a busy junction so not as accessible or child-friendly as we would like.

We arrange to meet again the following evening and Christy says he'll lock up and come early tomorrow to switch on the heating and let us all in.

I volunteer to check out the possible venues and I have one idea of my own that I haven't mentioned to anyone yet. I want to think it through and have the vision clear in my mind. If I have to battle with Moany Maura, I'll need to be fully prepared.

7

I'm in Gran's this morning working on my hats. Mam's a bit worried that I'll settle in and scupper her plans to sell, so I've promised to keep a low profile and leave every day by five. I've pulled the net curtains and set my own machine up alongside Gran's. I'm finishing off a rust felt fedora and then I'm going to take a break. I smile as I remember Gran in that coat. It was hard the first time cutting through the material but I know she'd love this hat.

I cross the Square and make my way down the lane. It's unusually sunny again for October and the place is a flurry of activity. There's a florist with a bright blue door and an array of autumn flowers in terracotta pots. There's a line of older ladies in leggings filing into what looks like a yoga studio after that. I can see rows of mats on the floor through the wide bare window. The unit at the end is partly why I'm here. It has ivory timberwork and Coffee Spot painted in black above the door. Cathy says they serve the best coffee in the county so I've come to check that out.

I get my Americano with oat milk and wander out into the lane to have a proper look around. I walk down to the garden and take a seat on one of the wooden benches near the back. Apple trees line the gravel path, there's an enormous pear tree down the end, and a gorgeous acer towards the front is glowing russet and gold. I close my eyes and fast forward to twinkling lights and holly berries and the warm woody spice of mulled wine wafting through the air. I'm getting Christmas market vibes and I really feel that this could be the place.

I drain my coffee and shove my cup into the bottom of my dusky pink tote. I've arranged to meet Christy for a quick scan around the town hall. He used to be the caretaker and he still has a key. Christy seems to have a key for every building in the town. He's waiting at the door with a friendly wave and a cheerful smile and I'm glad he's on my team.

One walk around the enormous hall confirms what I already knew, this isn't what we need. It's drab and grey and would take forever and a small fortune to glam up. There's no parking at all and it's on the busiest stretch of road in the town. We lock the heavy black door and continue along the street and around the corner. We stroll along a leafy road for about a quarter of a mile until we reach the school that Nadia suggested. There's plenty of parking here as the playground is just across the road. Christy calls into the office while I take a look around outside. He comes back a few minutes later with the key to the hall that is attached to the side of the school. It's very pretty with a row of narrow arched windows and I'm sure it would look wonderful with Christmas garlands and festive lights. But it's not large enough to hold many stalls and the only outside space on this side of the school is a metre-wide strip of tarmac flanked by a very high wall. I realise that I've set my heart on the lane garden now and I'm finding it difficult to picture the market anywhere else.

I break the news to Christy that I have somewhere in mind and he agrees to accompany me for a look. He frowns when I lead him through the arch.

'Are you thinking of our meeting room? It's not much bigger than the school hall.'

I shake my head and point to the garden. 'The meeting room would be a good backup if the weather is bad but I'd prefer to aim for outdoors. We could hire some market tents like you normally do for the Square. It would be far more sheltered down here. There would be parking in the Square and along the street, and it's right in the centre of town, so most people could walk.' I can feel my excitement building and I turn to see what he thinks.

He tugs at his cap and then pinches his chin. 'The only thing I wonder,' he says, 'is why didn't we think of it before.' He breaks into his usual smile and I breathe a sigh of relief. Then we continue down to the garden to take a better look.

'We'll have to price the insurance and get permission from whoever owns the land,' I say. 'Hopefully, it's somebody with a bit of Christmas spirit and we can persuade them to come on board.'

Christy sits down at one of the picnic tables and gives me an encouraging wink. 'I'd say we'll be all right; I know the very man.'

I clap my hands in glee. I could hug Christy right now, he's like my personal Christmas elf.

'You probably know him yourself, he's not much older than you. And he's very friendly with Cathy and Brian.'

This is getting better; my plans are looking good. I'm about to ask for a name when Christy narrows his eyes and peers over at the cottages on the other side of the lane. 'Sure, there's the man himself.' He stands up and points to a workman hammering a slate on a roof. A very fit workman in a plain white T-shirt and dark denim jeans.

I'm wondering how this lean, muscular roofer happens to own all this land when Christy strides over and shouts hello. The guy pulls off his yellow hard hat and turns around. It's Niall bloody Hamilton, the lurking stranger, my peeping tom.

He seems genuinely pleased to see Christy and climbs down his ladder for a chat. I'm still standing by the picnic table when they both turn and walk over towards me. I only realise that I'm scowling when Christy asks me if everything is okay. I pretend to shield my eyes and mutter something about not expecting to need sunglasses at this time of year. But I can see a smile twitching at the corner of Hamilton's mouth as he gives me a perfunctory wave.

'This man never takes a break,' Christy chuckles and he plops back down on the bench. 'We're very lucky to have caught hold of him at all. I'm not sure if you know each other—'

'We've met,' I cut in. 'I was lucky enough to catch him earlier in the week too.' I don't add that I caught him sneaking around and spying through my gran's front window.

Niall gives an easy shrug. 'I think we might have gotten off on the wrong foot. Let me buy you a coffee, please, to make up.' He turns to Christy before I have a chance to refuse. 'I'll take that break now and we can have a chat. What will you have? My shout.'

Christy orders tea and I say, 'I'll have an oat milk latte, thank you very much.' If Niall owns this land, or more likely, knows the person who does, then I'll bite my tongue and play along. For now.

He comes back with our order and a plate of oat and raisin cookies too, then he and Christy start discussing pergolas. Niall seems to be making plans to build one when I give Christy a frantic nod to remind him that we have other issues to discuss. They can have next summer to build their pergolas; we need to focus on Christmas right now.

'Sorry, Niall,' Christy interrupts. 'Jas has a proposition to put to you.' Niall raises his eyebrows but doesn't say a word. He just watches me and waits.

Christy carries on, though. 'She's a great woman for the ideas, and a real community spirit, just like her sister.' I haven't mentioned to Christy yet that the reason I want the market is to launch the sale of my hats. 'And she's into all that sustainable, eco-friendly stuff like yourself. I'd say you and Jas are really going to hit it off.'

I splutter into my latte and then try to gather myself and ignore Niall's self-satisfied smirk. If he thinks I've come back to Ballyclane to keep him amused, he can bloody well think again.

I set down my coffee and arrange my most serious face. 'I want to save the Christmas market.' I feel my cheeks warm as it dawns on me that this sounds totally over the top. 'What I mean is, Cathy isn't able to be involved this year, and the market wasn't going to go ahead. So, I'm going to take her place. Not her place, exactly, I'm no Cathy.' I'm rambling now so I try to wind up. 'But I'm going to do my best.'

'That sounds great, Jas,' says Niall, and I feel my shoulders relax. He actually looks impressed. 'Cathy had mentioned a while back that she couldn't do it this year,' he continues. 'I was hoping she'd change her mind—'

'We all were,' Christy cuts in.

'But then I was out with her and Brian the weekend before last and she told me her news, so—'

'Excuse me?' My mouth is hanging open so I force myself to close it and give him a questioning look.

'Oh, don't worry, I haven't said a word to anyone. But I think it's out now.' He grins. 'She did tell Maura, after all.'

Niall Hamilton knew my sister was expecting a baby before I did. My sister told Niall Hamilton the most important news of her frigging life before she told her own family. Well, okay, she told Mam almost straight away, but I'm her bloody sister, after all.

8

'You told Niall Hamilton you were pregnant before you told your own sister.' I cycled over to Cathy's as soon as I left Gran's at five o'clock. She's not long in from work and she's resting on the kitchen armchair with her feet propped up on a stool.

'You weren't here, Jas. I did phone a couple of times to fill you in but you seemed to have so much drama of your own going on that I decided to wait until I could tell you in person.'

'But the Hamiltons? Seriously?'

Cathy looks at me like I've lost the plot. 'Calm down,' she sighs. 'First, I don't understand why you're saying the name like it's some kind of insult. Secondly, we told one Hamilton. Niall is a lovely guy, and he's Brian's closest friend—'

'Since when?'

'They were always friendly but I suppose since the pandemic they've gotten much closer. Brian found it really tough trying to teach the kids from home, especially the leaving cert students. You know how conscientious he is.'

I nod. Brian teaches honours maths and physics as if it's his life's vocation. If his students don't do well, he takes it as a personal failure. Having to teach them through a computer screen must have been hard.

'Anyway,' Cathy goes on, 'Niall noticed he seemed very stressed one day when they met up in the supermarket. He suggested Brian go running with him.'

'Brian goes running?'

'He does now. They started very slowly. I'm sure it must have driven Niall crazy – he's been running for years. But he was really patient and they built up the pace over time. They go running together at least three evenings a week.' Cathy stretches her legs and rubs her stomach. 'Switch the kettle on, will you? I get a bit nauseated in the evenings and I could do with a ginger tea.'

I feel conflicted as I root in the cupboard for teabags. When Cathy revealed she was pregnant I told myself I would be a better sister, look out for her, and keep her stress levels down. But I can't let this go.

'He's still a Hamilton. His cousin was an absolute bitch to me in school and I heard his uncle swindled half the town.'

Cathy sighs. 'Freddie Hamilton is a chancer and his wife and daughter are horrible snobs. But they moved away years ago after he lost all that money. Niall's parents had nothing to do with that. In fact, I know they spent a lot of their own money trying to help the people Freddie let down.'

I hand her the ginger tea and pour some milk into my own brew. 'I suppose,' is as much as I can concede for now. Niall's mam was a regular at school events and I have to admit she was always kind.

'And Niall wasn't even around when all that was going on,' Cathy adds. 'He went travelling after college. He only came home just before the pandemic hit.'

Travelling, huh? Well for some. I suppose he went straight into business with his father's building company when he finished touring the world and sowing his wild oats. I don't say this, though. Instead, I put forward my new best self and offer to make Cathy some dinner as it looks like Brian is still off on his run.

Cathy looks pleased, if a bit surprised. 'Thanks, but that's okay, there's a veggie stew in the slow cooker. Brian made it this morning.' She eases herself out of the armchair and glances out of the window. 'You're welcome to stay for dinner, he should be home soon.'

I look at the kitchen clock and shake my head, 'Sounds lovely but maybe another time. I'm meeting Shane for a drink and a catch-up and I need to have a shower first.'

I'm looking forward to that. I haven't seen Shane since I got home. He's a nurse over in the local hospital and he's been flat out all week. Tonight is his first night off.

I leave Cathy setting the table for dinner and I'm wheeling my bicycle out of her drive when I'm knocked sideways by a backwards jogger and both me and my bike land in a heap on the grassy verge. WTF? Who the hell jogs backwards anyway?

Niall bloody Hamilton, that's who. He's looming over me in skimpy shorts spluttering apologies when Brian jogs up insisting it's all his fault. I don't think so, Brian.

'Are you all right, Jas? It's my fault,' he goes again. 'I started lagging behind and Niall was just trying to keep me motivated for the home stretch.'

I wish I could think of a biting comeback to make it clear I know exactly who's to blame. And I have the scars to prove it. But I'm winded, and the heel of my hand caught the tarmac and it's stinging like hell so I'm all out of wit. I'm also facing straight into the offender's tanned muscular thighs and finding it very hard to focus on anything else.

9

I'm back at Mam's and I've cleaned myself up and nursed my wounds. Well, Mam nursed my wounds. What's the point of living at home as a fully grown adult if you can't let your mammy mind you a little bit? So, my hand has been soaked in diluted Dettol, covered in Sudocrem – Mam's cure for everything – and wrapped in a waterproof bandage. To be honest, it's only a minor graze and I'm going to dull the pain with alcohol anyway. But it's been nine years since anyone has taken care of me like that and the whole process was really quite sweet.

I'm calling over to Shane's parents' house as soon as I'm dressed and ready. They live three doors down from Mam and he's crashing there tonight so we can meet for a drink. He lives in Portville now. He bought an apartment three years ago, around the corner from the hospital. I'm still getting my head around the fact that my best friend is a property owner. It's no mean feat for anyone of my generation but he says the mortgage is less than what he would pay in rent, and he spent six years living at home to save the deposit.

Shane is almost the boy next door and I know both our mams harbour a secret hope that we might become more than just good friends. But I don't think about him that way, and even if I did, I wouldn't go there. He's too important to me as a friend to risk messing that up.

Of course, Tracey Hamilton used to constantly jibe that Shane only hung out with me in the hope of getting into my pants. Her words, not mine. Shane hated her almost as much as I did and I'm glad to hear that she's no longer around. I was well able for her. We both were. But she was a nasty scab that refused to heal and I'm relieved she's not here to irritate us anymore.

He's waiting in the doorway looking very cool in a navy shirt and skinny jeans. His dad gives me a wave from the hall but Shane is straight out of the door, pulling it shut behind him. His parents could talk for Ireland and once they start there is absolutely no shutting them up. So, even though I'm very fond of them both, I totally understand his haste. I can call back for a chat later in the week. Shane and I haven't had a proper catch-up in a very long time and I am seriously in need of a drink.

He links my arm and gives it a squeeze. 'Gallagher's?'

'Gallagher's,' I agree.

We clink our Coors and settle into the red-leather couch. Shane fills me in on his work: crazy hours, bananas workload, and harrowing patient tales. But he seems to take it all in his stride. I fill him in on the saga of Gabe and I watch his eyes glaze but who else can I tell this to? I desperately need to vent.

'Christ, this is long overdue,' I say. 'Can't believe we haven't seen each other since last Christmas, can you?'

Shane looks a bit subdued. 'Considering what happened at the party, I could hardly visit you and Gabe.'

I give a friendly shove into his shoulder. 'What? Serenading my boyfriend by calling him a fake? I'm well over that.' I shrug. 'Anyway, turns out you were right, I should've listened to you years ago.'

'Yeah, but,' Shane mutters, 'it wasn't him I was serenading.' He chews at his lip. 'It was you I was trying to convince.'

'Well, you succeeded. I dumped him, didn't I?' I pick up his empty beer bottle. 'Another one?'

He sinks back into the soft leather looking like I've taken a weight off his chest. If I'd known he felt so bad about insulting Gabe I would have told him to get over that months ago. It was Shane belting out of tune and at the top of his lungs that my boyfriend was a waste of space that finally dragged my head out of the sand.

As soon as I come back with our beers and sit down, he blurts out, 'Anyway, you don't need to worry because I've met someone now.'

I'm not sure what he thinks I've been worrying about. Shane is a good-looking lad and never short of girlfriends. Although they don't tend to last all that long. He's not usually too keen on talking about them either so I sit up straight and give him a questioning look.

'Someone special, you mean?'

'I think so.'

I take a slug of my beer and give him an encouraging nod. 'Come on, tell me more. How long have you been seeing her?'

He slumps in his seat. 'I'm not actually seeing her. I'm thinking about asking her out but it's complicated.'

I stare at him wide-eyed. 'What's complicated about it? You ask her, she says yes.' I shrug. 'Worst-case scenario, she says no, you move on.' I shake my head then it occurs to me that Shane is good-looking and popular and has probably gotten used to women asking him out or at least making it obvious that they are available if he decides to ask them. 'What's the problem? Is she playing hard to get?'

He frowns, 'No, it's not like that. I only know her through work and I'm not sure if she thinks about me in that way. We've been working together a lot and we've gotten close but I don't want to misread the signs.'

I roll my eyes. 'You've been with your fair share of women; you should be well used to reading the signs.'

His cheeks flush pink as he mumbles, 'I don't want to make a fool of myself again.'

I pick up his beer and fold it into his hand. 'Drink up. Either I'm tipsy on two beers or you're too sober to make any sense. When have you made a fool of yourself before?'

'The party, Jas. You know.' He shoots me an embarrassed glance and then stares down at his hands.

I throw my head back and laugh. 'How many times do I have to tell you? You did me a favour calling that idiot out as a fake.'

'I mean the way I feel about you.' He winces. 'The way I *felt*. I promise I'm over that now.'

I'm not often speechless but all I can do now is swallow hard and stare as those words sink into my brain. I don't have a clue what to say. I never saw this coming at all. I lean across and put my arms around Shane and hold him as tight as I ever have in my life.

'I'm the bloody fool,' I manage to sniff eventually. 'I'm so sorry, Shane.'

He pulls back slowly. 'It's okay, I'm over it now. It helps that I'm focused on somebody else. Kamala,' he adds. 'But I'm not ready to ask her out. Not until I'm absolutely sure of how she feels.'

'I don't know if you can ever be sure what's going on in someone else's head.' I drain the dregs of my beer and sigh. I definitely can't. It's taken me twenty-eight years to figure out my own mind and I'm clearly rubbish at reading anyone else's.

10

I'm taking a morning coffee break and I'm back in the garden down the lane. I've got my sketch pad laid out on a picnic bench and I'm drawing mind maps when I feel the first drops of rain. Damn, I was hoping if I sat here for a while, I might catch sight of Niall. Not that I'm itching to see him again or anything. Although it's possible I may have had some very bad thoughts about those very athletic thighs. I'm only human after all.

But this is the new me; I'm focused now. A businesswoman on a business mission. And Niall Hamilton is simply a pawn. I was so thrown by his revelation about Cathy and her pregnancy that I forgot to follow up on my market plan. I need to get back on track.

I dash into the coffee shop as the rain starts to pelt down. It looks like I'm not the only one hatching a scheme. I see Christy, Maura and Nadia huddled down the back.

I make my way down to join them and Nadia moves over to make room. I pull up a chair and shove my sketch pad and gel pens underneath.

'Doing a bit of colouring?' Maura nods towards the floor.

Nadia's face lights up and she tells us about the adult colouring group she joined in the library and how so many people find it helps their mental health.

'Hmph, yes, well, I thought Jas would have more to keep her occupied.' Maura sniffs. 'She is supposed to be organising the market after all.'

I reach down to retrieve my sketch pad and pens. 'I was under the impression we would be working as a team.' I force a tight smile. 'But you're right, I have been very busy. I spent yesterday checking out Christy's suggestion about the town hall, and Nadia's about the school. Then I came up with a proposal of my own which I'm looking into.' I set my pad on the table between us and click my pen. 'I was going to wait until the next meeting to ask if you have any ideas, Maura.' I tilt my head to look like I actually care. 'But seeing as you seem so keen, I'm all ears now if there's anything you'd like to share.'

Maura rearranges her navy silk scarf and scoops up her purse. 'You'll have to wait until the meeting, we can't all sit around chatting all morning. Some of us don't have the time.' She stands up, rigid as a broom. 'If you'll excuse me, I have an appointment. I'll see you all on Wednesday night.' She graces Christy and Nadia with a smile as she sweeps away. I don't even get a cursory nod.

'What did I ever do to that woman?' I groan into my coffee.

Christy chuckles, as usual. That man would chuckle his way through an apocalypse. It seems like nothing gets him down.

'Ah, her bark is worse than her bite,' he offers.

I arch my eyebrows. 'That's easy for you to say, Christy, she doesn't snarl at you. Or you,' I add as I glance over to Nadia. I notice she looks a bit sheepish, so I ask her what's up.

She stirs her tea even though her cup is almost empty. Then she shrugs. 'Maura has always been very kind to me but I think… I think, perhaps, she has formed a bad impression of you. But it's not really for me to say.'

I cross my arms with a scowl. Say what?

'She barely knows me,' I protest. 'She's really nice to you two and Cathy says she was a fantastic help to her.' I gather my things and shove back my chair to stand up. 'Just because I don't have a good job or wear the right sort of clothes or own my own house, I'm not good enough for Moany Maura. Is that it?'

We're all standing now but Nadia and Christy are quiet. They edge over to the counter to pay and I go and wait for them by the door. Maybe I shouldn't have said all that quite so loudly but they needn't think I'm letting this go. I've had people like Maura judging me all my life and they haven't broken me yet.

Luckily, Christy came prepared and we all huddle under his giant golf umbrella as we make our way out into the rain. He offers to escort me to Gran's door as his car is parked on that side of the Square and he'll give Nadia a lift home. I try to persuade them to come in, I want to quiz Nadia some more. I also need to follow up with Christy about Niall. We didn't confirm anything about holding our market down the lane. And yes, that may have been my fault. I may have briefly lost focus and whisked myself off in a huff. But I'm back on track now and I need to get hold of Niall.

But Nadia and Christy are damp and shivery and keen to get into Christy's warm Fiesta. They're bundled up inside and I'm still hopping about in the rain when Christy rolls down the window and calls out.

'I nearly forgot; Niall told me to give you his number. He's away for a few days but he says to WhatsApp him and you can start to make plans. I'll send it as soon as I'm home.'

I turn my key in Gran's lock and try to slow my breathing as I make my way down the hall. I'm trying not to picture a certain broad chest and those lean muscular thighs. Physical attraction is really not everything, I tell myself. It's not that important at all. I've already made that mistake with Gabe. Although, in fairness, a lot of the attraction there was the lifestyle. I wanted to be young and carefree and not give a damn. And it was fun for a while. But when you're struggling to eat and pay rent and your boyfriend spends most of his money on weed, it starts to wear a bit thin.

I can't see Niall Hamilton wasting his money. And I'll bet he has plenty of it too. Maybe I can get him to sponsor our Christmas market. Although, if he's anything like his uncle, he'll charge us through the roof for holding it and then sue us if something goes wrong. And if he's anything like his cousin Tracey, he'll tell the whole town we haven't got a clue, we're only selling a bunch of old tat, and don't bother to waste your time.

But I don't really know what he's like. I know he has an angular jaw and twinkly grey eyes and there's something soft about his smile that makes me feel a bit melty inside. But he always seems to be smiling *at* me, not with me, and I'm not so impressed about that. I didn't come back to Ballyclane to amuse the posh boy who owns half the Square. I'm here to make a new start and prove everyone wrong. By everyone I mean Tracey Hamilton and Maura McGuire. My family, Shane, Christy and Nadia have been great. And as for Niall, well, we'll just have to see how that goes.

11

It's Sunday afternoon and I'm out for a walk by the river trying to decide what to do. I take a detour to the playground and settle myself on a bench. I stare at my phone again. I've been staring at it all weekend. Aargh, why is this so bloody hard?

Christy sent me Niall's number on Friday night so that I could WhatsApp him. There's nothing complicated about it, I know exactly what I need to do. So why do I feel like a nervous teenager asking a guy out on a date?

This is business, I tell myself for the thousandth time. Get a grip, woman, get over yourself, and get on with it.

Dear Niall? No, definitely not. *Hi, hello, hey?* I settle on *hi,* bright and breezy, just like me. I wish.

Hi Niall, hope you don't mind me getting in touch.

Nope. Delete. I need to own this.

Hi Niall, I'm messaging about the Christmas Market. We are keen to pursue the idea of holding it in the garden at the end of the lane. Christy assures me you will be on board. Perhaps you could confirm this for me then we might discuss some details, insurance, costs, etc. I look forward to hearing from you.
Jas.

And send.

Sugar, I should have said thanks, or at least best regards, yours sincerely, anything. Not just Jas.

Niall comes back almost immediately. No procrastination there.

Hi Jas, no problem at all. I think it's a great idea. Don't worry about insurance, I have cover for events. I guess costs will depend on the type of market you have in mind. I look forward to hearing more. Well done for taking this on. Best of luck with it, Niall.

Hmm, he has insurance for events. Interesting. Wonder if he'll wangle that into his costs. Still, he does sound like he's in support, maybe he won't try to fleece us, after all.

I decide to call over to Cathy to see what she thinks of my idea about the lane. She and Brian are curled up on the couch watching a movie and it occurs to me that I've spent the entire weekend on my own. Mam and Donal are off on a minibreak somewhere down in West Cork. Shane is working through the weekend and only wants to talk about Kamala anyway, now that he's considering asking her out.

Cathy and Brian see each other every day too and they never seem to get bored. They're always in the middle of some animated conversation about politics, the local football team, or one or other of their schools. Fascinating stuff, I'm sure. God, I was so bored with Gabe by the time I left, I was losing the will to survive. If I heard one more speech about how he could have been bigger than Harry Styles if only he'd gotten the breaks, I'd have gone in one direction too. Straight out into the middle of Galway Bay and down to the ocean floor.

Cathy pauses the movie and Brian says he'll head out. He's been trying to psych himself up for a run. I sit on an armchair and pull out my notebook and pen.

Cathy smiles. 'I take it we are having a meeting about the market, the one I'm not involved in this year.'

'Sorry.' I wince. 'How are you feeling? We don't have to talk about the market if you're sick of it. We can talk about you. How's the pregnancy going, are you still throwing up?'

Cathy laughs now. 'No, I'm over that phase, thank God. And you're fine, I'm actually tired of talking about being pregnant, it's all anyone seems to want to ask me about these days. I'm going to get a glass of soda water. Can I get you anything?'

'Same, thanks, sounds great.' I open my notebook on my lap and write *Market Basics* in red across the top of the page. I've listed food, children's activities, and Christmas music when Cathy comes back with our drinks.

She glances down at my list and gives me an enthusiastic nod. 'Writing out your plan is a great way to start. It's always good to have a list.'

'I learned from the best.' I grin. Cathy is the queen of lists. She makes lists at night for what she needs to do the next day. She rewrites that list in the morning in case she missed anything before she fell asleep. Then she crosses things off as they're done. She has work lists, home lists, and goals lists. Even her holidays are strategised like a major military operation. Mam is the same. In fairness, she had no choice but to be organised. Dad ran off to England with some young one when Cathy was eight and I was barely four. Mam had to be the homemaker and breadwinner and keep herself on an even keel when she must have been going through hell.

I used to think I was more of a free spirit, someone who could go with the flow. But all I've been really doing is surfing someone else's wave. Now I need to make my own way. I tell Cathy that I'm thinking of relocating the market to the lane garden and ask her what she thinks.

'That's a lovely idea,' she says. 'But you'll need to think it through.' She sits back down on the couch and folds her hands on her lap. 'I don't want to put a damper on your plans but if you hold it outdoors there's a lot that can go wrong.'

'But you've always held it outdoors,' I protest.

'Yes, and sometimes it was a great success. Other years it was a nightmare.' She presses her palms into her thighs and gives a heavy sigh. 'We had to cancel the second year because of a storm, and another year we kept it going but we were almost washed out. Maura spent Christmas in bed with flu that year, she got so cold and wet.' She looks worried now and I notice she's tugging at her lip. 'You and Nadia will be fine but Christy's not a young man and Maura's almost seventy. One thing I've learned the hard way is that it will all go more smoothly if you can keep everybody dry and warm.'

'I suppose.' I can see she has a point but I've had this image in my head of a crisp December day, everyone wrapped in winter woollies, chatting and smiling and cradling hot chocolate. Now all I can picture is Christy and Maura shivering in a torrent of hail, and tents ripped apart by a howling gale. I'm not sure what I should do.

'Maybe you could use the meeting room,' Cathy suggests. 'I don't think Niall has any plans to rent the building out yet and he's always been happy to let community groups use it as long as they finish up by nine.'

'I guess I could ask him,' I say. But I feel a bit deflated watching my dream get washed away in my head. 'I wonder…' Another notion starts flickering in my brain. 'What if… what if we had elements of both?'

'Both what?' Cathy furrows her brow.

'Indoors and outdoors. What if we had some stalls indoors, maybe food and crafts that might get damaged if there was rain? And we could make sure Maura and Christy and anyone else that would need to keep warm were stationed inside. We wouldn't need as many tents or outdoor tables then and we could have activities and carols and some of the hardier stalls in the garden if the weather holds up.'

'That could work.' Cathy looks impressed. 'Especially if you don't book too many stalls indoors and then if the weather turns bad you can always move some in from the cold. The coffee shop and florist will be open anyway,' she adds. 'I'm sure they'll be delighted with the extra business.'

'Hmm, that's true, maybe I could wangle free hot chocolate for the workers and some Christmas plants to decorate the hall from the florist.'

'I don't see why not,' Cathy agrees. 'Elena will be thrilled with the passing trade, it'll give the coffee shop great visibility. She's only been open six months and some people in town don't even know she's there, tucked away down the lane.'

'And what about Veronica?' Veronica owns the florist near the top of the lane. It looks fabulous from the outside with turquoise timber shelves and terracotta pots filled with autumn colour. But Veronica is Maura's daughter and I've yet to go inside.

'Oh, she'll absolutely be on board. Maura always takes a stall; she makes fresh Christmas wreaths. They're a very close family and Veronica will want to support her mam.'

12

I pull out one of Cathy's cork noticeboards, some index cards, and a pack of pins. Luckily for me, she's still storing her cast-off college things in her old room and she's happy for me to use whatever I need. It occurs to me now that I not only have no home of my own, I no longer have my own room. Cathy has a spacious three-bedroom bungalow and yet here I am surrounded by her old books, stationery, and pin-ups. The place is basically a shrine.

Oh well, might as well get to work. I plan to spend my days making as many hats as I can from Gran's clothes. I want to show what I can create from garments that have been in the family for years. So many people have pieces hanging in the back of old wardrobes that either don't fit or aren't in a state to be worn. But the fabric is beautiful and the memories are precious and often it's hard to let go. I can use that fabric to create something personal and special so the garment no longer goes to waste and those heartfelt memories live on.

I intend to spend my evenings working on my market plan, and my business plan too when I have time. It's Sunday evening now and Mam and Donal are due back soon so I had better make a start. I reach for my sketch pad and draw out a map of the lane. Cathy reminded me that the meeting room has wide double doors down the back, which is ideal as we can open them out towards the garden. I hadn't taken much notice because we always go in by the side. The double doors are only used in summer when the weather is fine. But if we open them up, we can connect the indoor stalls to the events going on outside.

I need to measure the indoor space and work out how many tables we can take. Cathy had over forty stalls in the Square one year but she said it was way too many and the market lost its local feel. It ended up more of a commercial enterprise than a small-town festival vibe and that's not what I'm aiming for at all. I want to use the opportunity to launch and sell my hats. But I'm not your average business model; I'm trying to make art. And I'm using reclaimed vintage fabrics that have been handed down through families for years; you don't get more local and sustainable than that.

Our next meeting is Wednesday so I decide to message Niall again to see if I can access the meeting room in advance. We need to contact potential stallholders soon so we will have to discuss that at the meeting. I'm pretty sure Maura will have a favourites list made out and I want to be prepared. If I know how many tables we can fit in and I have a plan ready for what we need to prioritise, then I'll have a better chance of keeping us on track.

Hi Niall, any chance I could get access to the meeting room before Wednesday evening? I need to check something out in advance. Christy has a key so I could ask him to let me in if that's okay with you.

That seems all right, no need to elaborate yet. I'll see what the others think at the meeting and if they agree with my plan, I'll fill Niall in then.

Niall comes back about ten minutes later.

Hi Jas, I'll be home from Portugal on Tuesday night and I'll be working down the lane on Wednesday so I can let you in any time. Maybe about eleven, if that suits. I usually stop for coffee then.

Portugal. Well for some. No wonder he has such a great tan.

Eleven's perfect, thanks. See you then.

Great, sorted, must set a reminder for eleven on Wednesday for… for what? *I usually stop for coffee…* Hold on, am I picking up the key or have I just agreed to a coffee date?

It's Wednesday morning and I'm due to meet Niall in ten minutes. I've just added a satin band and handmade flower to a 1920s cloche hat that I made yesterday and I'm starting to get excited about showing my collection on my stall. I've been taking lots of photos, of my process as well as the finished products. In January, I plan to start a blog. But first I want to put my creations out into the world and gauge the reaction on people's faces when they view them up close.

I lay out my sketch pad on the kitchen table. I've drawn my plans for the market and I've made multiple lists. My sister would be proud. I've got my measuring tape ready and I've written down the measurements of the tables that Cathy says we can borrow from her school. I think that's everything I need. I take Gran's wicker basket from the countertop and pile my tools inside.

I make my way through the arch and towards the meeting room but I don't see Niall waiting there yet. It's not quite eleven so I continue down to the garden. I'm scanning the space and working out where things might fit when Niall emerges through a black wrought-iron gate set into the back left corner of the garden's stone wall.

I give him a wave, make my way down, and point to the gate.

'How did I miss that the last day I was here? What's behind it, a secret garden?'

He smiles that soft smile again, all dimply and twinkly and turning my insides to mush. Focus, I remind myself firmly. I'm here to do business, that's all.

'It was draped in ivy,' he says. 'I had to cut most of it back this morning, it was getting too hard to open.'

I notice that he didn't answer the second part of my question but I'm not a woman who lets things go.

'So, what does it open to?' I peer through the wrought-iron bars. All I can see is long grass and weeds and a hedge too high to make anything out beyond.

'Not a lot, it's all overgrown. There's a small cottage tucked away that I've been renovating for a while.'

'Nobody lives there?'

'Not quite yet. It's been a long-term project, this one.'

Realisation dawns. 'Ah, so you own that *too*?'

I notice him flinch as though I've given him a jab.

'Too?'

I snort. I didn't mean to but it just came out. I wave my hand to take in the garden, the cottages, the workshops. 'Well, this isn't exactly nothing.'

'I don't own all this, it's a joint venture with my dad. And the bank,' he adds, sounding serious now.

I'm not letting him away that easily. 'And you Hamiltons own the grandest house in the Square. That'll be yours eventually too.'

His face clouds over but he doesn't take the bait.

'I'll let you into the meeting room now if you're ready. I'll go and get a coffee and you can give me a shout when you're done.'

Oh shit, me and my enormous mouth, I need to tape it shut. 'Sorry, Niall, I didn't mean to offend you. Verbal diarrhoea, I'm afflicted with it. It's a serious condition, honestly.'

He laughs, hearty and loud, then stands there shaking his head like he can see I'm a lost cause.

'Let me get the coffee, please. I owe you one anyway.'

'Okay, thanks,' he relents. 'Americano please, black, one sugar.' He reaches towards my basket, slung over my left arm. 'Here, let me take that, I'll open up the room and wait for you in there.'

I'm back in five with the coffee and I decide to let Niall in on my plan. He seems enthusiastic and impressed and he opens up the double doors so we can see how things might work if we use both the garden and the room. I estimate we can fit fifteen stallholders inside, maybe a few more if people are willing to share table space. We could string fairy lights along the windows and cover the old school tables with red cloth. And borrow some holly and poinsettias from Veronica; she can have them back afterwards to sell. Someone is bound to have a spare Christmas tree in the attic and if everyone brings in a few decorations we can make the place festive for very little cash. There's a paved area over in the back right corner of the garden and we could set up our children's tent there. We don't actually have a tent, or any sponsorship money to pay for one, so I add that to my list for the meeting tonight.

Niall spots me scribbling and notes that my list is quite long. 'I'm free later,' he says, 'I could join the meeting. I'd be glad to help out.' He tilts his head. 'If that's okay with you?'

13

Niall and Christy are inside when I arrive at the meeting. They're standing by the double doors, with one slightly open, and they're talking about pergolas again. I leave them to it and wander down to the tiny back kitchen to fill the kettle and grab some mugs from the cupboard for tea. I'm on my way back with a tray when Nadia and Maura walk in. Nadia is beaming and looks fit to burst. She clearly has news, so I set down my tray and ask her what's up.

She turns and gives Maura an enthusiastic hug. 'Maura has asked my mother and me to move in with her. The hostel is getting so full and there's hardly any room. Because of Maura, we are going to live in a proper home this Christmas.' Nadia is close to tears. 'Can you believe it?' she asks.

To be honest, I am a bit shocked.

Maura looks chuffed if a bit embarrassed by the fuss. 'You'll be doing me a favour, my dear. It can get very lonely rattling around that big house on my own.'

This also comes as a bit of a surprise. Not the big house, I know where Maura lives, it's a two-storey mock Georgian on the leafiest road out of town. But I thought she had a husband. I know she had a husband – Seamus was his name. She also has her daughter, Veronica, and two strapping sons. Of course, they all have families and houses of their own now, but where's

Seamus gone? I decide not to ask, he might have run off like my dad. No point embarrassing the woman, not when she's actually doing some good.

It occurs to me that I have really lost touch with my home town. I packed my bags and moved to Galway at nineteen and never thought I'd be back. I came home at Christmas and for the odd family occasion, I could hardly miss my sister's wedding after all. But I never kept up with all that stuff Mam and Cathy go on about – whose cousin is dating who, who won the monthly Credit Union draw, and who died suddenly in their sleep. All these people who were part of my landscape growing up, they're practically strangers to me now. I tell Nadia and Maura that it's wonderful news and it seems like a great idea for them both. Then Niall and Christy emerge from their huddle and come over to the table to join us. They look like they've been hatching a plan of their own.

I take my folder and sketch pad from my basket and set them down in front of me. Niall gives me an encouraging smile while Christy pours the tea. Nadia and Maura are still chatting about the move, so I give a small cough and open my sketch pad on the page with *Agenda* scrawled in red across the top.

'I suppose we should make a start,' I say. 'We have a lot to discuss.'

Christy hands me a mug of black tea, his face a broad grin. 'I think it's a great idea you have there, girl.' He passes me the milk.

Maura's head jerks up. 'What idea is that?' She glances suspiciously over at Niall then turns back to me. 'I suppose I'm the last to know.'

I stir my tea and take a breath. 'It's just something I thought of since the last meeting. I did mention that I had an idea the other day at coffee but you had to dash off.'

'Hmph.' Maura opens her notebook and clicks her fancy silver pen. 'Perhaps you might enlighten me now?'

The woman seems determined to set me on edge. I catch Niall's eye and a vision of that T-shirt flashes in my head reminding me to *Just Breathe*. The first time I saw it, it made me so cross. Now I feel like I'm smiling inside. I keep a straight face though, like I'm taking her concerns completely to heart.

'Absolutely,' I say. 'That's why we're here.'

I outline my plan and hold up my drawings. I've been creating my own patterns for years so measuring and sketching is right up my street. Nadia gets excited when her gaze lands on the tent.

'For the children!' she beams.

I smile and nod yes.

Maura's in like a blade. 'We don't have any sponsorship money this year so we won't be able to afford a tent that size.'

I anticipated this so I'm ready for her now. 'I'm sure lots of people have old tents or tarpaulin lying around. I'll put out a call on Facebook and I can stitch something together with what we get. We can get a roll of tarpaulin fairly cheaply if we're stuck and put up a few poles.'

Maura rolls her eyes. 'Obviously, it's your first time being involved in anything like this. You can't just stick up a few poles and stitch a few sheets together.'

'I didn't say sheets. We'd use waterproof material, of course.'

'I'm sorry, Jas.' Nadia shifts uncomfortably in her chair. 'That doesn't sound safe, especially not for young children.'

I'm about to protest that Shane and I played in home-made tents in the back garden for years and we're still here, but Christy raises a hand.

'Eh, Niall and myself were just talking about something earlier that might work.'

Niall shoots me an apologetic glance, then starts to explain. 'The children's tent is a great idea, Jas.' He gives me an enthusiastic nod. 'And I'm sure we could make it work.' He pauses for a moment and looks around the group. 'But I've been planning to build a large deck and pergola in that corner for a while. I was thinking more in terms of summer or even late spring, I'm hoping to use it for small-scale events.'

Maura cuts in with a questioning, 'Oh?' and Niall comes back with a reassuring smile.

'Don't worry, it will all be low-key. I was thinking maybe some outdoor theatre, a bit like Oakwood Court but on a smaller scale.'

Bloody Tracey Hamilton crawls back into my brain and I have to force myself to stay calm. I catch Niall gazing at me with a worried expression and I consciously soften my face. The thought of Tracey Hamilton always makes me scowl. But Niall has gone out of his way to be helpful so I try to flick her out of my mind.

'A pergola, that would look amazing,' I say. 'We could decorate it with lights and Christmas decorations and Nadia could do Christmas story time there for the little ones.'

'That does sound lovely,' Maura agrees. 'My grandchildren would love that.' I notice her face soften as she mentions them. 'I have lots of outdoor cushions in my garden shed and I can bring those for the children to sit on.'

'That would be fab, Maura,' I say. 'Now, I suppose we had better decide about the stalls.' I feel bad pulling us back when everyone is so enthusiastic. But we are trying to organise a market, my list is long, and I need to get the contentious items sorted and out of the way.

Maura holds up her notebook. 'I've made a list of all the people we should contact first.'

'Great.' I reach for my phone. 'I'll take a screenshot of that and I can compare it with what I have.'

She clasps her notebook with both hands and stares me down. 'How can you have a list? You've been gone for years; you don't know anybody in this town.'

That's a bit of an exaggeration but I decide not to argue the point. 'Maybe not but Cathy knows everybody and I've gone through all of her lists. She made very detailed notes so I've based my shortlist on that.'

'How many do you think we will fit?' Christy asks.

'I think we should aim for about twenty. We can fit fifteen comfortably in here and still have space for a tree. We can set up a few stalls outside, especially if there are any stallholders that can bring their own tables and overhead cover. If we allow any more than five outdoors then they will have to be okay with us cancelling if the forecast is bad.'

Nadia smiles but Maura is stony-faced beside her.

'We had at least twenty-five last year,' she says. 'And I hoped now that the pandemic is over, we could fit more than that in.'

'Well, maybe we could have if we had started organising it earlier. But we didn't,' I point out. 'So, I don't think we can. And maybe that's not such a bad thing.' I shrug. 'Looking at Cathy's notes, it seems to me that a lot of the stalls before the pandemic were already successful businesses and quite a few weren't even local at all. That's not what we're trying to do here.' I look around the group. 'At least it's not what I'm trying to do.'

Nadia, Niall and Christy agree and even Maura doesn't put up much of a fight. We go through her list first and, in fairness, she has chosen well. Everybody on her list is local and the offerings are wide-ranging and sustainable. Stuff like home-made Christmas cakes and puddings, hand-painted cards, solar lanterns in recycled jars, Christy's wooden cribs and ornaments, and Maura's centrepieces and wreaths.

Things only go a bit pear-shaped when I mention that I would like to take a stall.

'But you're only in the door.' Maura clutches her hands to her chest. 'We're leaving out people who have been part of the market for years and you turn up and expect to take a stall in your very first year.'

Niall has been quiet for a while but he chips in now.

'None of those people offered to help organise the market or do any of the donkey work. I was there last year helping to clear up and it was Cathy, Brian and you three doing most of the work. Anyone that helped you set up and clear away is already on our list.'

Maura says nothing but Christy gives the table a good slap.

'Well said, Niall. If anybody does complain we'll tell them no one is stopping them from organising a market of their own. I think Jas is doing a great job this year and I definitely think she should have her own stall.' He fist-thumps the table now. 'I say we put it to a vote.'

Niall and Nadia's hands shoot up as Maura tuts and shakes her head.

'Don't be ridiculous, there's no need for a vote. Of course, she can have a stall.' She cocks her chin. 'I was merely asking questions. Surely that's allowed.'

14

I stand outside the social welfare office trying to decide what to say. I'm going to have to spend the next few weeks making hats so that I have enough ready for my stall. I did have a small stash of savings but I'm already eating my way through that. My only option seems to be to sign on. I don't know as much as I should about starting a business but I assume it doesn't come cheap.

I get lucky. The woman dealing with me has a daughter who started her own business making organic soaps so she understands where I'm at. She signs me up for jobseekers benefit and smiles as she tells me she has a feeling it won't be for long. She admired my indigo beret as soon as I came in and I ended up telling her my plans. She advises me to call the local enterprise office and to talk to anyone else I know who started their own business too. I tell her I took a short course online during the pandemic but I don't remember much of it now.

'It's a minefield,' she warns. 'You take all the help you can get.'

I take her advice and head to the lane after lunch. I'm hoping to bump into Niall, not literally, of course, although we do seem to make a habit of that. He seems like a guy with a good head for business so it might help if I fill him in on my plans. So far all I've told the committee is that I would like to take a stall. Maura demanded details so I mumbled something about upcycled fashion but I didn't divulge too much more. I don't know why I'm being so secretive but I feel I need the element of surprise. I'm sure Nadia has guessed; she's already noticed I wear a different hat almost every time I change my clothes. And she has complimented them all. I've just smiled and said thank you and haven't revealed yet that they are actually my own. I've Mam and Cathy sworn to secrecy too. You'd think I was launching a war.

I spot Niall and Christy carrying planks of timber down to the back corner of the garden. They must be starting the pergola already. They certainly don't waste any time.

I'm wrapped up warm in my navy duffel but there's a biting wind this afternoon and I wouldn't fancy working outdoors.

'Are you two not frozen?' I call.

Christy gives his usual chuckle and tells me that hard work is the best way to keep warm. He is well prepared with a woolly beanie and fleece-lined tartan jacket. Niall on the other hand is wearing the usual white T-shirt with only a light navy hoodie not even zipped to keep out the cold.

'I've tried telling him I'll manage the job on my own.' He shakes his head with a smile. 'But there's no talking to the man.'

'Sure, it's only a bit of timber,' Christy tuts. 'I'm well able to do my bit, and the work keeps me young.'

I'm more in awe of Christy every time I meet him. He must be close to eighty but he's always on the go. And he always has a smile. It doesn't seem like a good time to ask for business advice, though, so I let them explain their design and then I tell them I need to get back to my Gran's.

'I was over there earlier,' Niall informs me. 'Bernie asked me to take a look.' He scrubs at the light stubble on his chin. 'I was supposed to meet her a while back, remember, but, eh… anyway, I think she's still there.'

Yes, I do remember: Niall peering in the window, staring over my shoulder, taking a very good look. It turns out it was all above board, he had an appointment then and another today, it seems. My mother invited him to take a look. But take a look at what?

I give myself a mental shake, to bring myself back, and I focus on Niall. He's peering into my eyes now and it feels like he's peering into my soul. I get it, I'm frowning too hard. I'm no good at hiding my reactions, no use at pretending to be polite. Maybe I should look *that* up online, and see if I can sign up for a course.

'I hope you don't mind,' Niall says. 'It's just that Bernie asked for my advice—'

'No bother.' I swipe up my hand, cutting him short. 'I'll leave you to it, I really do have to get back.' It's true, I don't have time to hang around in the cold, I need to get to my gran's and find out what my mother has planned.

Mam and Donal are out in the tiny yard staring up at the back wall of the house. I make my way out to join them and ask them casually what they are at.

'Just looking at that crack.' Mam points to a thin vertical line running up the middle of the wall. 'Niall says it isn't that serious and all of these old houses have cracks but… I'm not too sure.'

Okay, so she's had Niall over inspecting cracks, it's possible she's going to ask him to do a bit of work. That's a good sign. Maybe she is considering my idea after all.

'The roof's a lot worse,' Donal chips in. 'Those slates need to be completely replaced. And the windows. And the doors.'

Way to put a downner on my mood, thanks, Donal. I was just beginning to have hope.

'Gran managed fine with those windows and doors,' I point out. 'The house next door is much worse.'

'I know.' Donal nods as though I've confirmed everything he just said. 'The other side of the Square looks so perfect. This bit really lets the side down.'

Mam looks embarrassed and I know I should just bite my tongue.

'The other side of the Square is loaded,' I growl. 'My gran was widowed in her thirties and had to manage all on her own. I think she did a bloody good job, and so has my mam.'

'Oh God, sorry, of course, she has.' Donal's spluttering now. I've embarrassed him and I'm glad. How dare he upset my mam.

'I just meant... I just meant it needs a lot of work.'

'That's what the grants are for.'

Mam doesn't say anything, just puts her hand on Donal's lower back and ushers him towards the kitchen door. She's following him into the house when she turns to me with that look again, like I'm a difficult child and she's trying to find a way to get through.

'Sorry, love, we have to go. Donal has a doctor's appointment and I said I'd drive. We'll chat later, okay?'

Later. Yeah. Sure.

15

Mam texts about four to say they are only leaving the doctor's now and she might stay at Donal's tonight. I wonder if she's avoiding our chat. I grab a cheese and relish toastie from Coffee Spot and decide to stay late and continue working on my hats. I see Niall down the garden still hammering away at the pergola, looks like Christy's gone home. I think about going down and sussing him out about the house but something holds me back. I suppose, really, it's between me and my mam.

I get loads of work done and I raid Gran's chest of drawers and find a fabulous midnight blue cable knit scarf. I'm wrapping it around my neck and I'm in a much better mood as I lock up.

'You're working late,' a familiar deep voice calls out.

I turn and see Niall making his way across the Square. I can't miss him; he's wearing a bright orange windbreaker and I pretend to protect my face.

'My eyes, my eyes,' I tease. 'Oh, it's you, Niall, I thought I was staring into the sun.'

'I've been called worse,' he says with a grin.

'I'm sure you have.' I can't seem to help myself.

'I've just finished work too.' He studies me intently as if he's making up his mind. 'I was thinking of going for a pint. I don't suppose you fancy joining me?'

Well, I wasn't expecting that.

Gallagher's is almost empty; I suppose it is only eight o'clock. Niall goes to get our drinks and I settle myself into a booth. He comes back with a creamy pint of Guinness and a half glass for me.

'Sure you don't want a pint?' he asks as he takes a seat on the other side of the table.

'Nope, this is perfect, thanks.'

I'm way beyond trying to keep up. I used to match the lads pint-for-pint when I started going out with Gabe. The hangovers nearly killed me and I was always broke. I copped myself on eventually but Gabe just seemed to get worse and I ended up subsidising him. I cringe at the memory of so many wasted years.

'You okay? You've gone very quiet.'

The orange jacket is off and he unzips his navy hoodie now to reveal yet another white T-shirt telling me that *It all works out.*

'I'm grand.' I smile. 'It's been a long day.'

He takes a sip of his Guinness and leans back into the red-leather banquette.

'I saw your hats this morning, they're really good,' he says. 'Sorry. Your mum wanted me to look at a bit of damp in that room. She said not to mention it.' He winces. 'Actually, she said not to look at them.' He lowers his gaze then peers up again, straight into my eyes.

I stare back. I can't decide what to say. It's nice that he thinks they're good. But she did tell him not to look. And she might have warned me he would be coming around. I'm pleased but I'm pretty pissed off too.

'I'm really sorry,' he goes again. 'I did try not to see but the damp patch was behind the shelves so I had to move some of your stuff to get a proper look. You always wear such cool hats, well, cool everything really. But that collection… it's special.'

'Special.' I'm mulling over the word. I like how it sounds, how Niall saying it makes me feel.

'You shouldn't store them there, though. Not with all that damp.'

I take a good slug of my Guinness. 'Right, thanks for the advice, I'll bear that in mind.'

I notice a flush in his cheeks and he's the one who has gone quiet now.

'It's okay.' I shrug. 'You're probably right.'

His smile is shyer now than I've seen before.

'I feel like I'm a teenager again, I keep saying the wrong thing.'

I can't help but laugh at his honesty. 'Don't worry about it, I'm twenty-eight and I do it all the time. Verbal diarrhoea, remember.'

He grins. 'Yeah, but I'm thirty-two and I thought I'd learned not to care.' He shakes his head with a jerk. 'Gah, I'm doing it again. I don't mean I don't care what you think. I mean I used to care way too much about what everyone thought of me and it got like I could barely speak at all.'

I narrow my eyes and crinkle my nose. 'That doesn't sound like you, you always seem so chilled.'

'I am now, I suppose. I've worked hard to be. Travelling really helped.' He takes a sip of his pint. 'It's much easier when nobody knows you – no judgement, no expectations. It gave me space to be me.'

I'm about to make a remark about rich kids who go travelling when it hits me that Tracey Hamilton and Maura aren't the only ones who can be too quick to judge.

I settle for, 'Where did you go?'

'I did the usual,' he tells me. 'Fruit picking in Northern Victoria, bar work in Sydney for a while. Then all over Europe: Greece, Italy, South of France, mostly just picking grapes.'

'Sounds like fun, but also hard work.'

'Yeah.' He smiles. 'I did have my fair share of fun. I went interrailing too, of course, like everybody else.'

'Of course.' I drain my glass and wonder what have I been doing with my life.

I stand up and say I'll get us another round. Niall says he usually only has one. But then he stands up too. 'One more won't do that much harm.'

I reach for my bag but he's already out of the booth.

'No, I'll get it,' he insists. 'I asked you to come and you're only having a half.'

He comes back with our drinks and I'm keen to hear more. Maybe I should head off travelling. Maybe that's what's missing in my life.

'How long were you away?' I ask.

'Five years.'

'Five years, picking fecking grapes!'

He laughs out loud, nearly spilling his pint.

'No, three years messing about between Australia and interrailing and Europe, mostly *picking fecking grapes*.' He does air quotes and grins. Then he goes serious again.

'Then I met Mel.'

'Oh?' I note the change of tone and wonder who this person is who warrants so much respect.

'I was picking grapes in Bordeaux and I met this girl taking a break for a month from a much more important job.'

'Hey, don't knock picking grapes. The world would be a much poorer place without wine.'

Niall laughs again and I ask, 'So, what did she do?'

'She worked for an organisation rebuilding homes devastated by flood and storms, in areas where communities were already struggling to survive.'

'Wow.'

'So, I volunteered, joined up, and that's what I did for the following two years.'

I'm speechless now, for a change, and wondering again what on earth I've been doing with my life.

'You spent two years volunteering, rebuilding homes?'

'Rebuilding, building. Sometimes the damage was so bad we were working completely from scratch.'

'And what brought you back here?'

Niall takes a drink and then rubs at his jaw. 'Ah, a few things. I suppose I got burnt out. It's hard work and even harder when what you've spent a year building is devastated all over again.' He blows out a breath. 'Sorry, I didn't mean to put a downer on things.'

'You're grand.' I sip my Guinness and tell him to keep going. 'I'm interested.' I nod encouragingly. 'Especially in why you came home.' I know why *I* came home. I couldn't spend one more week in the same county as Gabe. And I couldn't think of anywhere else I could go. But Niall, he's been all over. I wonder why he didn't head off on another adventure, maybe one not so demanding, especially as it sounds like he needed a break.

'Stuff happened,' he says, low and quiet. 'With Mel. Then Dad had the heart attack and he and Mum really needed my help.'

'Your dad had a heart attack?'

'Yeah, sorry, I thought everyone knew.'

'No, I'm sorry. Is he okay now?'

Niall nods. 'All good.'

'And this girl, Mel? Do you still keep in touch?'

He shakes his head and I catch a hint of regret in his tone as he says, 'We send each other a card at Christmas but apart from that, no.'

'It sounds like she was important to you.'

'She was.'

He sighs and tells me that he thought he was in love at the time. Then he had his heart broken just a little bit and he was glad to come home. I try for more but he just smiles and says it was a long time ago and he's over it now. I'm not so sure. It sounds like she still has a hold.

16

It's mid-November and less than four weeks to the market now but I feel like I have it under control. I'm going to call round to Cathy's tomorrow afternoon to go over everything. She's well past the queasy stage of her pregnancy and I think she's finding it hard not being involved.

And I found a beautiful bottle-green wool coat in Gran's collection this morning. It put me in such a festive mood. I'm going to add a velvet trim to the collar and cuffs with the same fabric that I used to make my favourite bucket hat. I want to look my best on the day of the market and I want to make sure I look Christmassy too.

I'm glad I have so much on, it's keeping my focus off Niall. Okay, that's not really true but at least he's not the only thing on my mind. I don't know what's wrong with me these days. Nothing has happened between us and he's not even my type at all.

I don't know what my type is anymore. I thought Gabe was when I first saw him perform six years ago. Leather trousers, long glossy hair, and he even had a fairly good voice. He told me he was aiming to be the Irish Paolo Nutini. Ever humble, our Gabe. He seemed to be smitten with me too, he kept telling me I was beautiful and cool. I got this idea in my head that we would make a perfect creative force: encourage each other, support each other, and build each other up. It turned out to be all one way. Gabe was only interested in supporting himself. Although, as the years moved on, he did find more time to spend tearing me down. In the end, cool hair and an okay voice just weren't enough. He didn't have much songwriting skill and he had absolutely no work ethic at all. Harry, Hozier and Paolo can rest easy, Gabe's not coming for them anytime soon.

If I think about it, Niall is nothing like that. He has been really supportive and considering everything he's achieved he doesn't seem to have notions at all. There's a solid energy about him and he has a way of putting people at ease. All that running and hard physical work hasn't done his body any harm either. Christ, I have to stop thinking about that.

I haven't seen him since we went for that drink two weeks ago, though. Well, I've seen him driving past in his jeep, and I saw his back disappearing through the ivy-draped garden gate. He did wave from the jeep, I suppose, but he didn't bother to stop. Christy says he's up the walls at the moment, everyone wants work finished before Christmas and he's got some special project of his own going on too.

He offered to walk me home after Gallagher's that night but I had my bike parked outside Gran's and I was a bit put out about Mel. I know I'm being unreasonable; I don't know their whole story. But I got a sense that she is really important and I don't need any complications right now. I'm overthinking, of course, I don't know if he's interested at all.

There's also the fact that he's Tracey Hamilton's cousin and his family is the wealthiest in Ballyclane. Tracey never lost an opportunity to diss where I came from, what I wore, how I spoke. And Niall grew up in the grandest house on the Square. I'm not sure if he's ever been through my part of town.

17

I'm on my bike on the way out to Cathy's when I see Niall running hard up ahead. I'm cycling at a leisurely pace but my heart starts beating out of my chest. He really should put on a pair of track pants. It's November, for God's sake, and legs like that are a hazard on the road. I'm awful, I know; if I heard some lad say that about a girl, I'd give them a clout. But my head's spinning now and my stomach is in flitters. I need to cop myself on.

I pull up for a minute and make myself take a deep breath. I feel he's been avoiding me lately so I'm not going to let myself act a fool. I gather my thoughts and get back in the saddle. I'll cycle slowly and keep well behind. At the speed Niall runs that won't be too hard.

I keep my eyes on the road and try not to get distracted by those shoulders, that back, and those thighs. I'm just about succeeding when he suddenly stops and turns. I almost crash into him this time; I'm so startled that I forget to brake. I manage to swerve and, luckily, I'm going so slowly that I naturally grind to a halt.

'Hey, it's you.' He gives me a wave. 'I had a feeling there was someone behind.'

I climb off my bike as two cars and another cyclist zip past.

'It's not the quietest road.' I shrug. 'There's always someone behind.'

He lowers his eyes and then looks up again, gazing directly into mine. I've noticed he does that a lot.

'I just had a feeling it was someone I knew. Do you ever get an odd sense, like maybe you're being watched?'

'I wasn't watching you.' I feel my cheeks flame and I realise I sound a bit harsh. 'I mean, I didn't notice you up ahead, I was too busy focusing on the road.' I'm telling downright lies now, something I pride myself on trying not to do. But I'm not having Niall Hamilton act like I'm following him when he clearly has no interest in me.

As if he's reading my thoughts, he blurts out, 'I'm sorry I haven't been to the last two meetings, I've had so much on. And, then with Bernie's proposition… But I think that's out of my reach.'

'Sorry, what?' I lay my bike down on the grassy verge and take a step back. What on earth is my mother propositioning to Niall?

'Yeah, to be honest, I thought it best to give you both a bit of space, to talk it out and think it all through.'

'Right, yeah, of course.' I haven't a clue what he's talking about but I'm not about to let on.

'I will try to make the meeting next week.' He bites his lower lip and I picture myself tracing my finger where he's left a small dent. 'And maybe we could go for a drink afterwards?' His eyes are back studying mine.

'Sure, yeah, that would be nice.'

I climb back on my bike and wave as I cycle ahead. Nice! Nice! Where's my sparkling wit and cracking comebacks? I'm buying that man a pair of track pants for Christmas. He needs to cover himself up. He's turning my brain to mush.

I make my way into Cathy's trying to figure out if Niall has asked me out on a date. Maybe he just wants to talk a bit more about the market. Or possibly Mam's plans. I have to admit it annoys me the way my family share all their secrets with him before ever saying anything to me. I don't suppose that's his fault, though. And he did seem to care how I felt.

Not that I can feel much when I don't have a clue what it's about. I'm guessing Gran's house. Mam did say she was asking his advice. She might be taking my idea seriously after all.

It's a full house when I open the back door into the kitchen. Cathy said to come for afternoon tea but I thought she meant just her and me. Mam, Donal and Brian are seated around her pine kitchen table and there's a mountain of food on display.

I leave my basket with my market notes on the countertop and pull up a chair.

'Smells good,' I say as I lift the lid off a tureen of soup. 'Bit more than afternoon tea.' There's a huge roast chicken, a big dish of veggies, three types of spud and a basket of warm crusty rolls.

'Blame Brian.' Cathy grins, rubbing her belly which is beginning to show a bit now. 'He's determined we get into the habit of healthy home-cooked meals before the baby comes.'

I nod agreeably as I grab myself a roll. Brian pre-cooks dinner every morning and Cathy takes a packed lunch to work based on her classroom food pyramid chart. Then she encourages all her pupils to do the same. I'm not sure their habits could get much healthier than that.

'We dropped in for a quick chat earlier.' Mam smiles. 'And, well, as you can see, we're still here.'

'The more the merrier.' Brian looks proud as punch. I suppose it would be rude to point out that I had a meeting in mind. It also might not be the best time to insist Mam comes clean about her plans and what exactly she's propositioning to Niall. I decide to sit back and enjoy the feast. Mam spent the last few weekends with Donal, and during the week we usually just chill on the couch after work with a plate of pasta or takeaway fish and chips.

We have a lovely evening, I haven't eaten or laughed as much in a while. Cathy is glowing and I've never seen her and Brian so relaxed. Brian looks like a guy who has everything he ever wanted and he's so happy he seems fit to burst. Mam and Donal keep exchanging soppy glances and Mam has her hand resting on Donal's right arm. They're like a scene from a Christmas movie, the happy ending where it all comes together and it's a wrap. Except, there's me in the middle, the cliché messed-up little sister, sad pathetic singleton, always the odd one out.

Maybe I'm being too dramatic. I'm not that much of a mess these days. I'm working hard at building my business, I'm organising the town's Christmas market, and I may even have been asked out on a date. By a handsome, eligible businessman, no less. And from what Niall said earlier my mother may be coming around to my plans. If she's asking his advice and he's giving us space to talk it through, just the two of us, then it must mean she can imagine me taking on Gran's house.

I help Cathy and Brian clear up after dinner then take my apple tart and tea into the living room where Mam and Donal are watching *A Place in the Sun*. They're flicking through episodes and they settle on Alicante, then Donal gives Mam's hand a light squeeze. I'm watching them fondly, thinking how lovely this is at their time of life, when Mam fires the first of her grenades.

'Doesn't it look gorgeous, Jas?' she starts. 'All that sunshine and so close to the sea. Just what Donal needs now that he's been diagnosed with arthritis.'

She had mentioned his arthritis after another doctor's appointment last week.

'We've booked a trip for the end of January. We're thinking of looking for an apartment south of Alicante, near where we went for our holiday last year.'

An apartment. And it doesn't sound like she means just to rent. We've spent quite a few evenings watching reruns of programmes selling property in Spain. I thought we were just escaping the Irish winter in our heads. I didn't know Mam was considering it for real.

18

Mam and I are back home now. I couldn't get my head around what she and Donal were saying and I needed space to think. Cathy and Brian joined us in the living room and everybody seemed to have something to say. Mostly about Gran's house where I was planning to set up my business and possibly even live. I know I haven't been around much the past few years but it feels like I've been written out of their lives.

I cycled home at a furious pace, and there may have been a bit of screaming into the wind. I didn't see any other cyclists or pedestrians so I don't think anyone heard me, although I might have terrorised a black cat.

'We haven't fully decided anything yet, Jas.' Mam closes her eyes and pinches the bridge of her nose. She's perched on her olive-green armchair and I'm curled on the matching couch hugging one of her oversized velour cushions. She looks tired and I feel bad that I've put a damper on her dreams.

'Donal will be retiring in June,' she says. 'He's always wanted to buy a place in Spain. And, after everything he's been through, I think he deserves a bit of happiness now.'

She's right, I know. Donal's wife died four years ago but she was sick for a very long time. And it sounds like he was devoted to her from everything I hear. He didn't plan or expect to meet anyone else until Mam's friends made her come along to an open day at the golf club encouraging women to join up. Donal was the tour guide and coach for the day and he and Mam really hit it off.

'I'm thinking of going part-time at the supermarket so that we can have more time together and I might even retire a bit early if I can make enough money from selling the house.'

Boom. She means Gran's house, of course. The one solid thing I have left of her and the memories we shared. And the one chance I have of building a future here in Ballyclane. When I sit at Gran's sewing machine and look out onto the Square, I picture myself here. I *feel* myself here, years from now, happy and successful and surrounded by my fabulous hats.

I think about reminding her of my plan to set up my business in the front room. If she got the grant we could fix the place up and let out the floors upstairs. Maybe I could even live there myself if I can make enough money to cover paying her a decent rent. But I know I'm not being fair. Mam has worked so hard all of her life and she has always put me and Cathy first. Now she finally has something for her, a chance for happiness and a bit of time to relax.

I climb off the couch and give her a hug. 'It's okay,' I say. 'I'm behind you whatever you decide.' I feel her whole body relax and I tell myself it will all work out. I managed nine years in Galway on my own steam; Gabe was more of a hindrance than a support. And I don't really need Gran's house to work from. I can always set my machine up in Cathy's old room. If I have to, I can do a lot of business online.

It's not really me, though, I prefer the personal touch. The memories appeal to me, and the idea of being based in a beautiful, historic Georgian square. I'd catch so much passing traffic there too and the location has an authentic vintage vibe. But it looks like that's not to be so I decide to focus on Mam and I tell her I'd love to hear more about her and Donal's plans.

'Donal was fairly high up in the council,' she says, 'so he has a good pension and a lump sum. He's going to buy the apartment and he says he's happy to support me if I'd like to retire.' Mam shakes her head and frowns. 'But you know that's not me. I've always been independent. And, yes, it's been hard but I like having money of my own. I've never needed to depend on anyone and I'm not about to start now.'

She doesn't mention that she could never depend on my dad but I know from Gran that he never helped out at all. Just took off to London with some girl half his age and nobody has heard from him since. It doesn't bother me. Good riddance. But it makes me rage when I think how it must have affected Mam.

'You and Donal are fairly serious then?'

'We are.' Her face softens as she says the words.

I lean back into my cushions and decide I could come around to the idea of an apartment in Spain. If Mam is still going to work part-time then it's just a bolthole, somewhere for them to spend time together. It can't be easy for Donal having to share his spot on Mam's couch with a fully grown adult daughter with no home of her own. Hopefully, they'll have a spare bedroom for guests, I could do with a holiday in the sun.

Mam takes a deep breath and sits up straight. She seems to be steadying herself. 'Donal has asked me to move in with him after Christmas.'

Looks like it was time for the next grenade.

I shoot upright so suddenly that I hear my neck crack. I thought the plan was that Donal would move in here. Eventually, that is, but not really anytime soon. Now Mam's telling me she's moving out. So, where does that leave me?

'Donal's house is more practical for us,' she goes. 'A bungalow will suit us better as we get older, especially with his arthritis, you know. And he has alarms and security cameras and gates, it'll be far more secure when we're away.'

Looks like I'm not going to be housesitting so. What's the next bombshell headed my way?

'What about here then?' I ask, 'Your house, our home?'

'I haven't given that much thought yet,' she says. She might as well say she hasn't given me much thought. I suppose that's my own fault. Mam doted on me growing up, Cathy really looked out for me, and whenever I was getting a hard time at school, especially from Tracey Hamilton, Gran was my rock. Then I decided Ballyclane was boring and Galway was cool, and Gabe was the love of my life. I haven't been around much these past nine years, apart from Christmas. I'd never miss Christmas at home.

I press my lips together so hard they're likely to bruise. 'I suppose I'd better start looking for a new place to live.'

That's a joke, but I'm not laughing at all. There are no places to rent, no places to buy. This country is in the middle of a housing crisis and has been for years. And it seems to be getting worse by the day. Even if I had money, which I don't, I'd find it impossible to get anywhere decent to stay.

'Oh, there's no rush, love, I'm hardly going to throw you out.' Mam smiles now as though it's really no big deal. 'I don't expect you'll settle here anyway, Ballyclane was never your scene.'

Since when did Mam say things like scene? I guess she's just quoting me.

'But Cathy did say you're welcome to stay with her and Brian for as long as you like. And I'm sure she'll be glad of the help when the baby comes along.'

Aargh, I feel myself sinking inside. So, this is what my life has come to now. I love my sister to bits but I don't want to be her live-in babysitter. And I doubt that she wants me under her feet. Where would I put all my fabric and my sewing machine? I can't imagine Cathy will want needles and pins strewn around with a small baby crawling about. I'm not even sure how soon they start to crawl. I really don't have a clue.

19

'You can always crash on my couch, you know.' Shane sits in the window seat in Coffee Stop and I peer past him and out at the relentless rain. I pull so hard at a clump of my hair that it's in danger of being ripped from my scalp. I'm not sure how to respond to that offer without coming off like a total cow.

'Do you really think that's a good idea, what with all the serenading and stuff?'

He arches his eyebrows, set to protest, but I find a better alibi just in time.

'And what about Kamala? It's hardly going to help your chances if you move another woman in. It is only a one-bedroom after all.'

He ignores the Kamala point and shoots straight to the first.

'It's almost a year since that happened, Jas. I'm over it, I promise. I'm not even sure why I told you. I think, maybe, I was a bit pissed off that you never copped on.'

I get that. And as Shane is being so honest, I figure it's time for me to come clean as well. With him, and with myself.

'I love you to bits, Shane, you're my best friend. It's not that I never found you attractive. Have you looked in the mirror, you muppet?' I reach over and scruff up his hair and he gives me a big soppy smile.

'But I know if we went there, it would just mess everything up. And then where would we be? I'd never have gotten through school without you. I might still be with Gabe if you hadn't been there to keep pointing out what a prick he was, even if it did take me way too long to hear. And I'd be lost back in Ballyclane if I didn't have you around.'

Shane sighs. 'I suppose I thought it might be nice to have a relationship with somebody I actually like.'

Shane's last girlfriend turned out to be a self-centred cow. She was stunning and I think he was flattered when she hit on him. But he's too nice for his own good and she walked all over him in the end and then two-timed him with somebody else.

'We wouldn't be human if we didn't both think about something more now and again but I don't want to risk what we have for some friends-with-benefits situation, and I think we both know that's all it would be. You deserve better than that. You need to make better choices, that's all.'

He widens his eyes. 'We both need to make better choices, Jas. And you deserve better too.'

I nod and my brain conjures up an image of a hot, handsome runner speeding away as I pedal furiously behind on my bike. I might deserve better than Gabe but Niall is definitely out of my league. Then I see Shane's hand waving in front of my eyes. He does that a lot to bring me back, he's gotten so used to my ways.

'But it's nice to hear that I'm not completely un-fanciable.' He grins. 'And I suppose you're right. It wouldn't look good if I move you in before I get around to asking anybody out.'

I take a slug of my coffee and wave my index finger. 'Yeah, about that, mister, get your skates on, before Kamala ups and meets somebody else.'

He grabs hold of my finger, laughing, and says, 'Did your mother never tell you that it's very rude to point.'

We're practically hand wrestling and creased up with giggles when I look up and see Niall peering in through the rain. I let go of Shane's hand and my gaze follows Niall as he walks past the window and then I watch as he comes through the door. He gives a quick wave and cursory nod towards Shane. I look over my shoulder as he makes his way past and it's only now that I see his mam and Maura having coffee and cake down the back.

My giggles have gone, replaced by a frown, and Shane is quick to pick up.

'That's Niall Hamilton,' he says, stating the obvious, of course. 'The same Niall Hamilton who's helping you with the market. And giving your mother advice about your gran's house.'

'Mmm.' I lower my gaze and try very hard not to turn back around.

'You like him,' he adds, furrowing his brow.

'I do not!' I feel the heat rise through my veins. 'I mean, of course, I like him. He's been very helpful. And polite.'

'Polite?' Shane splutters a mouthful of brownie and nearly chokes on the word.

'What's wrong with polite?'

'Nothing, polite is great.' He looks over my shoulder and I have a feeling he's sizing up Niall. 'But I can see by your face that you like him for a lot of reasons, and the least of them is that he's always polite.'

20

I climb off my bike and make my way across the Square. I'm twenty minutes early for the meeting but I want to get myself prepared. Mostly for Maura, if I'm honest, that woman makes me feel like I'm back at school. But if I lay out my notes, set up the tea, and take plenty of deep, deep breaths, I should be able to cope.

I have a key now – Niall gave me a spare. And speaking of Niall, I spot him straight ahead chatting to a guy up a hoist. They are putting up the Christmas lights and I feel a warm buzz in my chest. I love the town lights, they're madly multicoloured fun. It'll be another couple of days before they're switched on, the same night as the tree that stands proudly in the middle of the Square. They used to get turned on earlier but the committee is keen to make things more sustainable, so now they wait until the first Friday in December and all the lights are LED and will only be on for a few hours every evening after dark. It's a good compromise, I think. I do my best to keep my lifestyle green but in the middle of winter, when things can seem bleak, we all need a bit of Christmas cheer.

Niall makes his way towards me as I lock up my bike and I hope that means he's joining us at the meeting after all. Christy and Nadia are lovely but when Maura gets on a roll, I feel Niall, at least, is on my side. In fairness, she is always kind to Nadia and now she's taking her into her home. And Christy puts a positive spin on just about everything so I don't think he even notices Maura's cutting tone. It's only directed at me anyway. I'd love to know what exactly it is that annoys her about me or whether is it something she thinks that I've done.

'Hey,' Niall says in that deep, husky tone. I feel my shoulders relax, something about his voice soothes my strung-out nerves.

'Are you okay?' he asks. 'You look like something's getting you down.'

I knead my forehead to ease out my frown. God, where do I start?

'I'd just like to get through one meeting without Maura giving me grief.'

'I've been thinking about that,' he says, and I feel a small skip in my stomach at the idea that he's been thinking about me. 'You and Maura seem to have gotten off on the wrong foot for some reason. How would you feel about trying one or two team-building exercises before we start the meeting?' He ignores my wide-eyed horror and adds, 'We used them a lot on the rebuilding programme that I worked on and I think they do really help.'

We're at the door now and Niall unlocks it and stands back to let me go in. He wanders down to the kitchen to set the tray for tea and I wait until his back is turned, then I try to practise some of the breathing exercises that Della showed me. I look at the clock on the wall and see that it's ten to seven and I have ten minutes to sort myself out. I don't know what's wrong with me this evening, I don't normally let Maura get to me like this. But Mam had an estate agent out this afternoon to look over Gran's and her own house in Emmet Park. On top of that, I called Della at the weekend and stupidly asked her if she had bumped into Gabe. I don't think she wanted to say anything but she didn't want to lie to me either, so she told me he came into the shop pointedly holding hands with some girl. Then I met Cathy on her way home from work today and she said Maura's been telling anyone who'll listen that I'm only involved in the market because I want to make sure I get the best spot for my own stall. It's one thing after another and I feel like I'm starting to spin.

Niall comes back with the tray and as soon as he sets it down, he turns and takes hold of my hands. 'Close your eyes and breathe, Jas,' he says gently. 'In for four… hold… out for eight. Just take it slow.'

I don't even question it, him giving me instructions, holding my hands. I just let go. I keep breathing, slow like he says. And he keeps hold of my hands. He smells earthy and woody and I'm inhaling peppermint too. I begin to feel myself steadying, my feet more solid on the ground. Even if I do start to fall now, I know he won't let me go. I hear a car engine outside. Luckily Christy's old Fiesta is loud. I open my eyes and Niall lets go of my hands and gives me a soft, encouraging smile as he pulls out a chair for me to sit down.

Maura's Toyota rolls up just as Christy is coming through the door. I wanted to ask more about the team building but it's clear I won't have the time. Christy is close to bouncing, rubbing his hands, and beaming early Christmas cheer. Tonight's meeting is to plan the annual fundraising quiz so I'm guessing he has some good news.

He waits until Maura and Nadia file in behind then he gives us the scoop.

'We're all set to go, Saturday week in Gallagher's. Dermot says he'll sort the posters and raffle tickets and throw in a couple of spot prizes as we haven't tapped him for sponsorship this year.'

'That's fantastic, Christy.' I give his arm a squeeze as he sits down next to me. I was worried we might have left it too late to organise a fundraiser but Christy, as usual, insisted it would be grand. 'If it's any sort of success it means we can afford to hire some proper outdoor tents.'

'Oh, it'll be a success, all right,' he assures me. 'You leave that to Dermot Gallagher. No better man. And sure, we can all rope in family and friends.' He gives a small sigh. 'I might even be able to persuade the wife.'

'How about you two – Maura, Nadia?' Niall asks, and I'm guessing like me he has spotted Maura's anxious frown.

Nadia looks excited and says she would love to be part of a team. 'I don't go out very much but a quiz sounds so much fun.'

'Will you come this year, Maura?' Christy asks. 'You didn't make it the last few years but you used to love them one time if I remember right. Maybe, if I can persuade my wife to join us, you and Nadia and me and Lizzie could make up a team.'

'Maybe,' Maura says quietly, clearly not ready to commit.

Niall finishes pouring out the tea and announces that he has a suggestion to make.

'As we're talking about teams,' he says. 'I was hoping we could do a team-building exercise. I know it might not be what everybody's used to but I've used them a lot, in work and in sport, and I promise you they do really help.'

Maura's frown deepens, Nadia looks puzzled but intrigued and, of course, Christy is the first one on board.

'What do you have in mind,' he asks, rubbing his hands again with glee. 'Team huddle? The haka?' He chuckles. 'I'm not sure Maura will be up for that.'

Niall smiles and shakes his head. 'We might save that for the day of the market. No, I was thinking more along the lines of a sharing exercise, something to help us get to know and understand each other a bit better. I'm thinking if we start our meeting with one small share each it will help us to bond more as a team.'

That might be what *he's* thinking but I'm thinking this guy has completely lost the plot. I'm not sharing anything with Maura

Maguire, definitely not anything she can use as ammunition, for sure.

Christy is up for it, though, and asks what sort of stuff Niall would like us to talk about.

'Anything really,' he says. 'But ideally, something that matters to you, something we might not already know, something it might help you to share.'

'That sounds very personal,' Maura protests. 'I thought I was here to help put together a market, not talk about my private life.'

Niall nods understandingly and says, of course, there's no pressure to say anything personal at all. It can be something small, maybe about her garden or Christmas or anything really. 'Or,' he adds, 'if you prefer not to take part, it's absolutely fine just to listen as well.'

Christy offers to go first but Niall says that as it's his idea maybe he should start us off. He also reminds us that everything we say should remain confidential, of course. I'm expecting something about his business or running, although a small part of me is hoping it might be a snippet about Mel. I'm definitely not expecting this.

'I'm glad I came home when Dad got the heart attack,' Niall begins. 'After what my uncle did, after what he put my parents through, and so many other people in the town, I wanted to stay away, to go as far away as I could and pretend it wasn't anything to do with me.' He looks around at each of us in turn. 'It took me a long time to get over the embarrassment and the shame but I've learned that you can't let other people define who you are. You have to stand on your own terms and make yourself proud before you can expect other people to like or respect you too.'

Feck. So much for sharing a snippet about Christmas or the garden. I had no idea he felt like that. That he felt ashamed and embarrassed and wanted to hide. And then just to open himself up to us all. I have no clue what to say or how to follow that.

Maura visibly softens and leans towards Niall. 'That was a terrible time for you all, especially your parents. But nobody blames anybody but Frederick for that awful business. It was very hard on his poor wife and daughter too.'

Niall blinks slowly and I catch a trace of a wince. Maura doesn't seem to notice, though, and just continues to give him sympathetic nods.

'Well, that's my dark secret.' Niall sets his face in a smile. 'Christy, would you like to go next? Like I say, no pressure, it can be about anything at all.'

Christy tells us that his youngest daughter went off to Canada this summer and his wife, Lizzie, is taking it hard. 'She misses her something terrible,' he says. 'She'd be better if she could take her mind off it but I'm finding it impossible to get her out of the house.'

'That is difficult,' Nadia says. 'Family is so important. You must miss her also.' Nadia's brothers are still fighting in Ukraine so I know this really affects her too.

'Ah, I do, but sure, I'm happy to see her enjoying herself. She's always sending photos on WhatsApp and she's having the time of her life. And it won't be forever, she's on a career break and she's only planning on staying a couple of years. But I can't seem to get Lizzie to see that. Katie is the baby of the family and Lizzie and Katie were always very close.'

'Would it help if I had a word?' Maura asks. 'Mine all went abroad for a year or two at least. And they're all back home and settled now. It might reassure her to hear that it's just something young people do these days. And with FaceTime and Skype and all that, it's not like it was in our time at all.'

'That would be great, Maura, if you could,' Christy says. 'And maybe you could ask her to come to the quiz, tell her you need her on the team. She's brilliant at the Arts and Literature round, never has her head out of a book.'

Maura doesn't say yes but she gives a small nod, so it's not a no either. Well done, Christy, I think.

Niall offers to have a word with Lizzie too. 'I went travelling for five years and I didn't know if I'd come back, but the pull of home is strong and I'm glad now that I did. I'm sure your daughter is having a great adventure but she'll be missing you both and she'll appreciate you even more when she gets home.'

Then he turns to Nadia who is sitting straight across from him and asks if there is anything she would like to say. 'You don't need to unless you want to,' he adds. 'We all understand you have already been through so much.'

Nadia's blue eyes mist and she lowers her gaze. 'I lost my boyfriend,' she says quietly. 'He was killed at the start of the war.' Tears stream down her cheeks as Maura immediately turns and wraps her arm around her and gently rubs her back. 'I don't like to talk about it, only to my mother. And I told Maura too.'

'I'm so sorry, Nadia,' I say. I want to go over and give her a hug but I'm half-afraid Maura will push me away. And it does seem like she is a great support. She's wiping Nadia's tears with a tissue and Nadia looks up and goes on. 'I haven't really gone out much since I came here. But I have a job now at the crèche and I'm helping with the market, so I feel like I am starting to have a life. My mother tells me that Olek would want me to have a life.' She turns to Maura. 'I would really like to go to the quiz and I would like to be part of your team.'

This meeting is not shaping up the way I expected. I was preparing for yet another battle and here, Niall has everyone sharing and bonding and Maura seems to be the glue holding it all.

Maura swallows and then nods and gives Nadia a smile. 'I would like that too, dear.' She glances around at the rest of us and it looks like she has decided it's her turn.

'As you know, I lost my Seamus three years ago this Christmas. I won't pretend it hasn't been hard. Seamus loved Christmas. I used to love it too. I loved baking and decorating and having all the family over for Christmas dinner. But I couldn't face it these last few years. I went to my daughter's but it wasn't the same without him and I couldn't wait for it to end. I kept up with the market because that was never Seamus's thing, he was always too busy with work, so that was something I did that didn't make me think about him, at least not all the time.' She stops and closes her eyes for a beat. 'The quiz was hardest of all. You all know how my Seamus loved a quiz. I couldn't face it without him.' She turns to Nadia now. 'But I think it's time. When I see how brave Nadia and her mother have been, having to leave their family and friends and face their future in a strange country without any idea what that might mean, it makes me want to try harder to be brave too.' She gives Nadia a smile. 'Maybe I'll start with the quiz.'

Christy gives a quiet clap and Niall tells Maura that's great and he's sure she and Christy and Nadia, and hopefully, Lizzie, will make a good team. Then he turns to me with a tilt of his head and asks if I would like to go next. I'm not feeling too sure but it doesn't seem like I have much choice. Everybody else has already shared, and when I say shared, I mean been honest and brave and open, which has come as quite a shock. It occurs to me that Niall knew what he was doing when he decided to go first. He really set the tone.

There's so much I could throw out there. Gabe, Gran's house, the worry about starting a business when I've no money and possibly even nowhere to live. But, for some reason, that's not what I say. I curl my fists on my lap and stare hard at the middle of the table, desperately avoiding everyone's eyes.

'I hated my time at school,' I tell them. 'I did my best to act like I didn't care, that nothing they said... she said... got me down. But it really, really did.' I bite down on my lower lip. Then I remember to take a breath and focus on the long slow exhale. That's it, that's as much as I'm able to give. I can't believe it's out. I've never even admitted it to myself.

21

'That was brave of you this evening,' Niall says as he hands me my pint. I've decided tonight I need more than a glass. As usual, there's only a handful of customers, so we've nabbed a booth straight across from the fire. He peels off his hoodie and almost strips off his T-shirt in the process and I catch that grounding woody scent.

'Are you kidding?' My eyes widen for more than one reason as I reach for my drink. 'Nadia lost her boyfriend, Maura lost her husband, Christy's without his daughter, and your uncle shafted your whole family and half of the town. I just had someone be a bit mean to me at school, it doesn't exactly compare.'

'Being bullied is one of the hardest things to get over, Jas. Believe me, I know.'

'You do?' I narrow my eyes in question as I pull off my dusky pink baker boy hat and run a hand through my messy curls. Niall always seems so together, so solid. I can't imagine anyone bullying him. 'Did you get shit thrown at you in school too?'

He swallows a mouthful of Guinness and sets down his pint.

'No, school was fine. I did have a slight stammer when I was younger but I never got more than a bit of friendly teasing from the other kids about that.'

'What then? Home?' I don't really know Niall's dad but everyone says he's a gentleman and his mother always seems so kind.

'God, no, my parents are great.' He pauses for a minute as if he's deciding whether he should say any more. Then he does.

'My uncle Freddie was a sarcastic prick. And his wife, Jacinta, was just as bad. They never said anything if my parents were around. It took me a while to realise that. But if either of them got me on my own they'd make fun of my stammer and try to convince me that it meant I was stupid and everyone was laughing at me behind my back.'

'Bastards,' I spit.

'Yeah. As I got a bit older, I came up with reasons to avoid going to their house and if they came to ours, I'd make some excuse to go out. My mum started to notice so she asked me about it and I ended up telling her the truth. She was great and took it all in her stride. She told Dad and we barely had anything to do with them after that. She brought me for counselling and to the best speech and language therapists she could find. I was lucky. My parents listened and they had money to pay for the right help.'

I smile as I watch him take another sip of his beer. 'You sound like Christy. Always the glass half-full.'

He grins. 'I'm glad you think so. Christy was born looking on the bright side but it's not my natural state. I've trained myself to think that way. Choosing to see the positives, being grateful for the good things that come. It's taken a bit of work but it's been worth it.'

I glance around the almost-empty bar, nine o'clock on a Wednesday is not prime drinking time in Ballyclane. 'That sounds like something I need to work on too,' I say. 'I might start by thanking Dermot for his help. And while I'm at it, I'll get us two more pints.'

I'm chatting to Dermot and he's filling me in on the plan for the quiz when who walks in, only Shane.

'Hey, I didn't realise you were around for the night,' I say. He didn't mention it earlier when we had lunch.

'I'm on a late shift tomorrow so Mam insisted I stay for dinner. And then I just decided I felt like a pint.'

He calls out to Dermot for another Guinness and insists on paying for my round. I'm on my last twenty until I get my jobseeker's tomorrow so I happily accept. I'll pay everyone back when I make my first million and anyway, I just told Niall I'd try to be grateful for the good things. Might as well start with these pints.

'You look good.' Shane comments and I see him glance over towards Niall. I'm only wearing a plain navy midi dress that he has definitely seen before. I have added an antique silver pendant and a lick of the Charlotte Tilbury lipstick that Della bought me last Christmas.

'Thanks. Are you meeting up with someone or do you want to join me and Niall?'

'Just out for a quiet pint,' he says as we stand watching his Guinness settle in the glass. 'But yeah, might be good to meet this guy you seem so taken with. See if he's up to scratch.'

'I'm not taken with him!' I give him a dig and he retaliates with a gentler version of the same.

'Well, he looks pretty taken with you,' Shane says and I turn to see Niall frowning as he watches our spat. Dermot tops up the last pint and I grab mine and Niall's and leave Shane trailing as I make my way back to the booth.

'These are courtesy of Shane,' I say as I set down our drinks. 'My best friend and self-designated minder.' I grin as Shane shrugs off his navy reefer and flops down opposite Niall.

'Right. Thanks. Good to meet you, Shane,' Niall says politely, although the expression on his face reads confused.

Niall and I chat about the quiz and he asks if he can be on my team. Before I get a chance to say yes or think about who might make up the rest, he suggests Cathy and Brian.

'Teachers are great at quizzes.' He grins. 'And it's perfect as the teams are usually made up of four.'

'Nurses are pretty good too,' Shane quips. 'All those years studying science.'

'You should come.' I grab hold of his arm. 'Bring a team. Does Kamala like quizzes?'

'I don't know,' he says quietly. 'I guess I could ask.'

'There you go,' I give his hand a squeeze as I stand up. 'It's the perfect opportunity to ask her out.'

I scooch past Shane and pop out to the loo. When I come back, I nudge him further along the booth and take his seat opposite Niall. Then I notice that Niall's draining the last of his pint.

'I'll see you next week at the meeting, Jas,' he says. 'Or hopefully before.'

'We do seem to have a way of bumping into each other,' I say as I force a smile. I'm a bit put out that he's leaving so soon, or at least leaving without me. I knew we would only have a couple of drinks, it's the middle of the week, and it's Niall. But I was hoping that this time he might walk me home.

'Shane says his parents live on your road and he'll be going your way, so I guess I may as well head off.' He hesitates for a minute then adds, 'Maybe we could get lunch sometime? Things are a bit hectic for me this week but I'll text you and we could arrange to meet up next week or maybe even over the weekend. If you like?'

I swallow and nod. I could kill Shane right now but at the same time, I don't want to make a scene.

'What did you say that for?' I glare at Shane as Niall walks out of the door.

'What? That I'll be going your way? It's true. Anyway, I thought you weren't interested. That's what you said.'

'I never said I wasn't interested.' Okay, I did say I wasn't taken with him but I realise now that wasn't exactly true. I purse my lips tight then tell Shane, 'I'm not sure how I feel but I'd at least like the chance to find out.'

'Well, if he's put off that easily, maybe he's not worth the bother,' he huffs.

'This is coming from someone who has fancied a colleague for months and can't find the balls to ask her out.'

I knock back the rest of my pint and make my way to the door. Shane follows behind and we fall into step as we head up the road for Emmet Park.

'What else did you two talk about while I was gone?' I ask when we get to my gate.

'Not much. The quiz. His bitch of a cousin.'

'What did you bring her up for? She doesn't even live here anymore.'

'Yeah, well, she made your life hell when we were at school.' Shane scowls.

'That's hardly Niall's fault. What did you say?'

'Just that there was a Hamilton in our year at school and we weren't exactly fans.'

'Right. Thanks, Shane. Thanks a bunch.' I leave him standing at my gate and storm up the path to my door. As I close it behind me, I feel bad. Shane and I don't often fall out and if we do, we normally just have it out and end up turning the whole thing into a laugh. The only time I stayed cross with him was after he sang 'Fake' about Gabe. But after a couple of weeks, he apologised and I had to admit he had a point so even that didn't last long. I think about texting him, he really didn't say anything that bad. Then it occurs to me I didn't ask if he said we weren't fans of Tracey, or was it the Hamiltons per se? Aargh, maybe I'll just go to bed.

22

It's Mam's birthday tomorrow, the seventh of December, and I'm over in the lane to pick up a fresh Christmas wreath. I suppose a bunch of flowers is more usual for birthdays but Mam always hangs a wreath on her door. She mentioned at the weekend that Veronica has fabulous fresh ones on display in the window of her shop. She smiled wistfully and said she couldn't afford one as they are fabulously expensive as well. I've been squeezing in some alterations alongside finishing off my hats and I made a bit extra last week. I do feel guilty about collecting jobseekers and working, but the woman at the welfare office said it was okay to earn a small amount and I'm not making enough yet to get by. I'm planning to sign off in the new year anyway and go full steam ahead with my hats and maybe some other upcycling jobs too.

When I get inside, I see Maura talking to Veronica at the counter so I turn to examine the wreaths in the window and let them get on with their mother-daughter chat. I'm meeting Niall soon for lunch and I don't want to risk Maura putting me in a mood. They seem to be having a stand-off about something so I decide to risk getting spotted and I lower the hood of my duffel to listen in. I'm not normally very nosy but I feel I'm in battle with Maura and I need all the ammunition I can get.

'I don't think it's a good idea, Mother,' Veronica says, and I can hear the concern in her voice. I edge a bit closer, wondering what Maura has planned. There's another woman behind her scanning bouquets on the counter and luckily for me, she's not small so she's camouflaging my presence pretty well.

'Hmph, well, I *do* think it's a good idea,' Maura's voice rises. 'As it happens, I've already invited her to stay.'

'All I'm saying is that in this case, the apple doesn't fall far from the tree.'

Maura huffs and puffs and the woman behind her backs away and makes for the door. I'm wondering if I should do the same, grab a coffee, and come back when they've finished their tiff. But Maura's on a roll and when I hear the next sentence, I realise that I absolutely should stay.

'I don't like what you are implying, Veronica. Jacinta is one of my closest friends. That business with Frederick was all just a dreadful mistake. He simply invested unwisely. And Jacinta assures me that he has learned from the experience.'

Veronica rolls her eyes, then she spots me waiting so I give a hasty shake of my hand to say don't worry about me and I go back to studying the wreaths. Don't stop now, for God's sake, I need to hear what this is all about.

'Mother,' Veronica continues, 'if he was sorry, he'd have stayed here and at least tried to pay people back. Instead, he's off sunning himself in the Canaries and selling property, what's more. I just hope he's not up to his old tricks.'

'There's no talking to you,' Maura tuts. 'But you can surely agree that what happened wasn't Tracey's fault. And as fond as I am of Jacinta, she and Frederick never had much time for that poor child. And now they've left her alone in Dublin to fend for herself.'

Veronica's shoulders sag and she rolls her eyes again as she glances towards me. 'She's twenty-eight, Mother. And she's married now. She's hardly a child.'

Maura twists as she sniffs an unwelcome guest. I grab the nearest wreath and give her my best effort at a smile. I'm hoping it says I'm only here to make a purchase and I have zero interest in her personal affairs.

I don't think I succeed, though. Maura strides past me with a withering look. Then just before she exits, she turns and says in her haughtiest tone, 'I think Tracey is a very brave young woman to come back to Ballyclane after everything she had to endure at that school.'

23

I head over to Coffee Spot to meet Niall. It's been a week since our post-meeting pint in Gallagher's and I was beginning to think he'd forgotten his suggestion about lunch. Then he texted on Monday apologising that he was laid up with a dose all weekend. I decided to play it cool and told him I was pretty tied up myself but could fit him in on Wednesday afternoon.

He's sitting in the window seat and he's almost finished his Americano when I arrive clutching my holly berry wreath. He's wearing a grey T-shirt and navy zip-up hoodie and I'm baffled as to how he can make the simplest of clothes look so good. Of course, that has a lot to do with what's underneath but I'm trying hard not to focus on that. He didn't offer to walk me home last Wednesday night so I'm going for bright and breezy and nonchalant. I'm definitely not going to let myself drool.

'Sorry,' I say with a smile. 'Am I late?'

'Not at all.' He takes my wreath and lays it beside him on the window bench. 'I was early. It's been a busy morning and I needed a shot of caffeine in my veins.'

We order French onion soup and toasties and I ask him what he's working on now.

'That personal project I was telling you about, behind the back wall.'

'Ah, the secret garden behind the lane garden. I've been wondering what the mystery is behind that gate.'

'Not so much a mystery as buried treasure,' he grins. 'Buried deep under years of overgrown hedging and ivy, that is. But I'm nearly there now. I'll take you for a look after lunch if you like.'

I shrug off my navy duffel and peel off my gloves. 'I'd love that,' I say. 'I've got my trusty Docs on so I should be able to stomp my way through.' I don't mention that I'm also wearing my favourite ditsy floral dress so I hope it's not too overgrown.

'I've got it all cleared now,' he reassures me. 'And I laid a gravel path to the door. I've been working on the cottage any time I had spare over the last couple of years and I'm hoping to move in before Christmas if I can.'

Our food arrives and we chat about the quiz while we eat. Christy has asked Brian to do quizmaster as Dermot will be too busy pouring pints. Brian is well used to running quizzes, he organises one for the school every year and usually gets roped in for the athletics fundraisers too. He and Cathy are putting together the questions and they've nabbed Donal and Mam to tot up the scores. I'm sure Maura will try to have me disqualified for having so many family members involved. But Niall's more concerned about who else is going to make up our team now that Cathy and Brian are ruled out.

'I could ask Shane to join us,' I say. Then I realise I've spoken before I consider how that might play out. Shane wasn't very friendly to Niall last night, Niall didn't seem too impressed with him either, and I don't fancy playing referee. 'If he can get Kamala to join us, that is. We'll need two, obviously. It will only work if there are two.' I'm babbling again now, not sure how to backtrack. But maybe it might all work out. If Shane asks Kamala, and Kamala comes, then Shane will be made up and I'll be free to focus on Niall.

Niall studies me carefully as he considers my suggestion. 'Do you think he'll want to ask this Kamala, is she a friend or is she something more?' He looks as though he feels a bit awkward asking so I laugh and confess, 'I've never actually met the woman. At the moment I think they're still only friends but Shane did say he would like them to be more.'

'Hmm.' Niall looks unsure. 'To be honest, I got the impression he's a bit hung up on you.'

'Oh no, not anymore.' What is the matter with me, why did I have to say that? I should have gone with a straightforward *no.*

'Not *anymore*?'

'Long story, not that interesting.' I reach for my duffel. 'Come on. You promised to show me the mystery house. Let's go.'

Niall is growing more attractive by the hour but Shane is my best friend and I'm not about to discuss how our friendship seems more complicated these days. I find it hard enough to get my head around as it is. Sometimes, I'm inclined to agree with our mams and his three sisters who all seem to be rooting for us to make a match. He is good-looking, funny and kind and I can absolutely see how someone would believe he's the one. I'm just not sure he could be the one for me. I don't even know what that means but I guess I'd hope for more of a spark. The sort of spark I feel now when I look into Niall's serious grey eyes. I swear he can see into my soul.

He unlocks the padlock on the wrought-iron gate and holds it open as I make my way through. I hadn't realised he was so security-conscious but then I see a heap of expensive-looking tools piled up against the wall. I hang my holly wreath on the handle of an electric lawnmower and take a good look around. Niall has been busy all right. All the overgrowth has been cleared but there's still lots of life considering the time of the year. The garden has been laid out in gravel paths with lawns, evergreen shrubbery, and flowering winter plants. I don't know the names of any of these but they all look beautiful to me. There are also lots of trees although I'm not sure what these are either as they are mostly bare. There's even a covered timber pergola to the side of the cottage with an enormous rectangular picnic bench. He must be planning to hold a party here at some stage, I guess.

'Wow,' is all I can say.

'You like it?' Niall looks pleased although I can still hear a question in his tone.

'I love it. I can't believe there's so much ground here, there must be a third of an acre, at least. It's like its own little world tucked away.'

He takes me along the gravel path that cuts across the end of the plot. It leads to another high black wrought-iron gate and beyond that is a long narrow lane which seems to be the last part left overgrown.

'That's my next job,' he says. 'It comes out around the middle of Beechwood Road.' That's the long leafy road where Maura lives, the poshest address in our town.

'You get your pick of the two most coveted postcodes then?' That would be Beechwood and the Square. Niall laughs, he's learned not to rise to my bait.

'Would you like to see the cottage?' he asks. 'That's where I've done most of the work. It was my grandparents' but nobody has lived there for years.'

We walk up the winding gravel path that leads to the glass and timber porch, the timberwork a soft blue-grey. The interior is what I would picture if you asked me to design my dream home. Oak floors and worktops, warm white walls and cabinets, and a soft floppy couch and chairs in gorgeous denim blue. I'd add a few splashes of colour, maybe a pop of pink or lime green, but it's a work in progress, as Niall says.

We sit at the kitchen island and I tell Niall how I wish I could do the same with Gran's house. Not exactly the same, of course. I'd have a work area and shop downstairs, live on the second floor, and if I needed to, I'd rent out the top. I've drawn up the plans in my head and made a few sketches on paper too. Niall looks taken aback.

'I had no idea, Jas. I thought Bernie was keen to sell. And I thought you and Cathy wanted that too.'

I take a sip of the sparkling water he poured for us and then prop my chin on my hands. I feel deflated all of a sudden. Maybe it's seeing what can be achieved and realising how unattainable that is for me.

'Mam is going to sell. The sign goes up this afternoon. It'll probably be there when I get back.' I'd happily stay here for the rest of the day, maybe lie down on that big floppy couch. I can't bear the thought of going back to Gran's now knowing that it will belong to somebody else soon. And even while I'm trying to work, there will be strangers coming in to view.

'I did mention my ideas,' I say. 'But I don't think she took me seriously. I think she assumes I'll take off again, that I'll get bored of Ballyclane.'

I see a flicker of something spark across Niall's face – worry, disappointment, concern. I'm not sure what exactly, I'm not great at reading the signs, but I get the feeling that he'd like me to stay.

'Will you, do you think? Get bored?'

'No. I'm loving being back. Especially being in Gran's. I miss her so much.'

I haven't said that out loud since she died. I don't think I've even said it to myself. Now it hits me with a force that I do. It's not just the house, her workshop, my hats. It's Gran. Tears start flooding down my cheeks and I lower my face hoping my hair will cover them up. Christ, what is wrong with me, Niall must think I'm a mess. But before I can wipe them away and cop myself on, he's beside me and I'm wrapped in his arms and he's stroking my hair and telling me it will be okay, and just to let it all out.

'For what it's worth,' I hear him say quietly, 'I really hope you stay.'

I brush away the last of my tears and raise my face to offer him a thank-you smile. He bends his head towards me at the same time and suddenly his lips are on mine. He holds my face in his hands and I wrap my arms around his neck and kiss him urgently back. I can feel the want in his touch but then he takes hold of my shoulders and slowly pulls away.

He presses his lips to my forehead and strokes my cheek, tracing the tracks of my tears. 'I'm sorry, Jas, I've wanted to do that for such a long time but I shouldn't take advantage when you're upset.'

Take advantage, please, I want to plead. But I won't, not if he's having second thoughts. If it was up to me, we'd be already up those stairs or maybe even here on the floor – I spotted a fake sheepskin rug.

Then I realise that he's right, my head's all over the place and I don't know what I'm at. I absolutely fancy Niall but my heart feels like it's breaking over Gran. And, if I'm honest I am a bit jealous about this place. I know he's worked hard and done a great job and deserves all the success that he has. But part of me feels absolutely shattered that I don't have a chance for the same.

24

Niall offers to drive me to Emmet Park, as I'm not ready yet to face Gran's. I need to get my head together and process – everything is happening too fast and I'm struggling to get my world under control.

'I'm so sorry, Jas,' Niall says again as he indicates to turn into the estate.

I peer out of the side window at the row of uniform three-bedroom semis and picture the memories I'll lose when Mam sells up and moves on. Hopscotch on the footpath, kicking a ball around the green, and cycling endlessly up and down the road outside my house and Shane's. We started on our trikes and we kept it up until our leaving cert year. I thought about selling my lavender Triumph when I was frantically trying to scrape money for Galway. But I'm glad I kept it now that I'm back. That and my sewing machine are pretty much all that I own.

'It's okay, Niall. It's not like any of this is your fault. Mam needs to move on with her life. I just need to figure how I'm going to move on with mine.'

'I think it *might* be partly my fault, though,' he says. 'I wish I realised before that you were interested in taking on your Gran's place.'

I turn my head to face him and his eyes sear straight into mine.

There's worry, apology, and a flicker of fear and it feels like he's laying himself bare.

'I told your mum she should sell.' He blows out a shaky breath. 'She asked me what I thought about her renovating the place. She even asked me if I would take the job on.'

'And you said no?' My eyes are narrowed slits, my lips a thin, bruised line.

He reaches for my hand and I pull away hard. He lowers his eyes and stares at the space in between.

'I know that must be difficult to understand. It's what I do and I would love to work on your gran's.' He waits for a response but I'm not in the mood to oblige.

'The thing is,' he goes on, 'Cathy came to see me. She knew Bernie was trying to make up her mind and that she had asked me about taking on the job. She said she thought your mum wanted to sell but believed she should hold on to the property for you two – you and Cathy, that is.'

'And what's so awful about that?' I blurt out.

Niall stifles a wince. 'Cathy was worried that it would be too much for Bernie, that it would tie up her time and money for years. She said she had sacrificed enough and it was time she put herself first.'

I nod my head and stare down into my lap. I'm clasping my hands so hard my knuckles are white. I know Cathy's right, of course. But I'm not ready to say that out loud. So, I clamp my lips tight and wait for Niall to go on.

'Cathy asked me to emphasise the negatives and the things that could go wrong with such an old building.'

'So, you convinced Mam to sell.'

'Yes. I'm sorry, I thought I was doing the right thing at the time.'

I look up again and this time I'm the one meeting his gaze. 'Did you offer to buy?'

He looks a bit thrown, and there's a flicker of hurt, but I keep my eyes fixed on his as I wait.

'Most of my money is tied up with the lane and I wouldn't be able to raise what it's worth.'

'So, what, you thought you'd wait? Let the market play out, and if nobody else wants to take on a run-down old corner shack, you'll go in for the kill.'

Niall's face goes white. It's clear he thinks I'm a bitch and he's one hundred per cent right. What the hell is wrong with me? I'm acting like a bitter old hag; I'd put Maura to shame. I've spent too long listening to her and Tracey Hamilton in my head. It feels like they've taken over my brain.

'I'm sorry,' I say, 'I'm not being fair.' I lower my face into my hands and try to hold back my tears.

'You're hurt, Jas. People say angry things they don't necessarily mean when they're upset.'

He looks hurt now too, though. And this makes me feel even worse. I give him an embarrassed shrug and push open the passenger door. 'I need to think all this through,' I say, then I close the car door as gently as I'm able and lift one hand in a hesitant wave. He blinks slowly back and his dark brows furrow in a frown.

'See you later, I hope.' I watch his mouth form the words through the glass.

Later. I'd almost forgotten about that.

25

I've managed to pull myself together, just about. I'm sitting in the meeting room close to the three-bar electric heater and waiting for the others to arrive. It's three days to the quiz and three days and one week to the actual day. The day of the market, that is. I'm starting to panic now, there is so much to do. Everyone I meet has promised to come to the quiz and we've booked two large outdoor tents based on the proceeds that we're hoping to raise. This means we can fit a lot more stalls, which is great. But also quite scary, as it will be far more to manage on the day. I've spent all afternoon ringing people on our waiting list and they are all delighted to be in. But Cathy reminded me on Sunday that we need at least two people overseeing everything on the day, especially as we have a lot of activities for kids. She also said that as I'm the committee chairperson, one of those people should be me. How come I didn't think of that before I stupidly put up my hand and volunteered?

I'm trying to figure out how I can operate my stall and keep an eye on everything else at the same time when Maura and Nadia rock in. I could do with a reassuring word from Niall first or even just a big Christy smile. Maura seemed taken aback by my revelation last week but I don't think she believed me in the end. She was quiet for five minutes then she seemed to decide I was spouting rubbish and went back to her usual scowl. And then there was that baffling remark she made on her way out of her daughter's florist shop. I might have been overly harsh with Niall today, but nobody could have given Tracey Hamilton a hard time at school. That girl had rhinoceros skin.

I haven't heard any more about her possible visit so I'm hoping Veronica has managed to make Maura see sense. She gives me a nod and asks me how many stalls we have confirmed. I tell her we have twenty-five and she concedes that is good news and she's pleased it will be a proper Christmas market after all. Maybe we'll manage to get through this meeting without our usual stand-off, for a change.

Nadia is absolutely buzzing about her story time. She's been practising her skills at the crèche and her mother has offered to help keep an eye on the children's area too. 'It will be so good for her to be involved,' she says. 'She loves children, she was a teacher also before the war.'

'That's great,' I tell her. 'And we'll need to get some face paints this week. Cathy has asked some of the transition-year students at Brian's school to help you with that. They're delighted, they'll enjoy it, and it will look good on their President's Award applications too.'

'I'll bring Nadia over to Portville tomorrow and we'll get some at the party shop,' Maura offers. 'You can reimburse me when you collect the money for the stalls.'

I'm about to reply when Niall and Christy arrive in.

'Sorry, we're a bit late,' Niall says, and his cheeks take on a faint flush as his eyes meet mine. He holds my gaze and carries on. 'We were just down the garden having a look at where to run wires for the plugs.'

I hadn't even thought about that. Christy tells me his daughter, Mags, is an electrician and she is going to meet them in the morning and give them a hand to make sure everything is safe. There are a couple of outdoor plugs by the wall and they can run extension leads from there if we need more. Niall also says he can run a lead from his cottage for lights around the pergola and a patio heater for Nadia's story hour in case she gets cold.

I go through my notes with everyone and fill them in on the stalls I've booked and also the map I've drawn of where everything might go. I've made a few copies so I pass one to Maura and ask her to take a good look.

'You and Christy have a lot more experience and you know most of the people involved so you probably know best which stalls will work better where.'

She looks a bit surprised but also quite pleased and we spend a good half an hour working on the plan. I mark any changes on my original and say I'll redraw the map tomorrow and we can go through it again next week to be sure. Cathy has warned me to be careful who I put beside each other. They used to operate first come first served and one year it led to all-out war. Two mortal enemies ended up sharing a table because someone on the committee had double-booked. They kept moving each other's stuff to make room for their own and after a few too many mulled wines, things nearly came to blows.

The mulled wine will be non-alcoholic this year as it was too late to get a licence but Christy told me on the quiet that some of the stallholders bring their own flask with a drop of brandy or port to add in. He chuckled that they are only trying to keep themselves warm, and I have a feeling he plans to do the same.

I ask if anyone has anything else they need to bring up before we go. I think we've covered everything and, anyway, we'll see each other again Saturday night at the quiz. It doesn't seem like anybody does but Niall doesn't hang around to find out. He scrapes back his chair and stands tall and tells us he has another meeting and has to rush off. I leaf through my folder and then glance around the rest of the team, checking in with everybody else except him. He's obviously not going to suggest a post-meeting pint in Gallagher's. I probably would have said no but I'm weirdly disappointed that he doesn't plan to ask. I gather up my things and watch him walk out of the door. He turns as he's pulling it closed and I see that his eyes hold just as much confusion as my heart.

26

Della FaceTimes me when I get home. I'm a bit knackered and ready for my bed but Della is a total night owl and never calls before ten. I could use a friendly chat right now and she always gives great advice, so I hit green straight away.

'Jas. Darling!'

Della is the sort of woman who calls everybody darling. Well at least, everyone she likes. I don't mind, now that I'm used to it, it's actually quite sweet.

'Hi, Dels, how are you, how's the shop going?' I flop onto the wicker chair beside my bed and watch Della's face light up even more.

'Fabulous, darling! Busy, busy, busy. And your little friend, Amélie, has been such a super help.'

'Amélie?'

Della and I went for goodbye drinks before I left Galway and I asked Amélie from the flat next door to come along because she had been so kind after that awful afternoon with Gabe. She and Della hit it off straight away, which didn't really come as a surprise. They're both gorgeous, utterly stylish, and obsessed with vintage fashion and couture. What did come as a surprise is that Amélie is in Galway working as a photographer for some fancy Paris fashion magazine. She's been travelling all over Ireland shooting images of vintage collections and seeking out sustainable designers to feature in her mag. She was blown away when she saw my hats and even suggested I let her take some photos there and then. Considering the state of them and the fact that most of my best work had also blown away, I was way too upset to get my head around a shoot.

'Yes, darling. She's been taking photographs of my favourite pieces and she's going to use my shop as the location for her next project. My God, I could be famous yet. This could put Viva Vintage on the map.'

Della sounds so excited and I'm happy for her. It seems the universe really does work in mysterious ways and I'm glad I was the one who set all this in train. A small tinge of disappointment creeps through my brain that the timing wasn't better for me. I know Amélie offered to photograph my work but filthy and bedraggled isn't exactly the vibe I'd hope to convey. Maybe I'll give her a call in the new year, if the market goes well, and ask her if she's still interested in taking a look then.

'You look tired, darling,' Della says. 'Has it been a long day?'

I venture a smile although I'm pretty sure it doesn't reach my eyes. This feels like the longest day I've had in my life. And considering some of the marathons I went through with Gabe that's saying a lot.

'You could say that.' I drag myself up from the chair and flop cross-legged on my bed. I lean back against the headboard and exhale a jaded sigh.

'You've been through a very difficult time, darling. You're bound to feel worn out.' Della eyes me kindly, her expression full of concern.

'Galway feels like a lifetime ago,' I tell her. What I really mean is Gabe feels like a lifetime ago. I love Galway and I always will but I know for sure now that I've absolutely given up on him.

Della tilts her head and waits a beat before she says, 'I get the feeling this might have something to do with another boy.'

Boy? I suppose now that I consider it, I did think of Gabe as a boy. He definitely had the whole 'toddler throwing a tantrum' vibe nailed pretty well. But Niall? Despite my weariness, confusion and upset, I feel a heat working its way up my body and I'm sure Della can catch the shake in my breath. Niall is most definitely a man. Oh, Christ.

'A bit,' I concede. 'But not just a guy' – I opt for the most neutral term that occurs – 'it's also my family, my business, my home.'

Della nods and keeps her kind eyes focused on me as she waits.

'I feel like, no matter how hard I try, everything keeps slipping away. Every time I think I know what I want and try to reach out, it seems like I'm about to get somewhere, and then just when it all feels so close, everything, everyone, pulls away.'

I feel a warm tear trickle down my cheek and I hurriedly swipe it aside. I don't want Della to think I'm a sap. I need to stop feeling sorry for myself and learn to cop on.

Della looks surprised and also concerned. 'I thought your family were always supportive of you, Jas. Your mum and your sister seemed so lovely and kind when they called in to the shop.'

Della met Mam and Cathy a few times. I wasn't great at making it home but Mam and Cathy, and often Gran too, made regular trips on the train. It occurs to me then that Della is absolutely right. My family has been nothing but supportive and they have always been there for me even when I wasn't there for them. I'm a selfish cow and I need to stop constantly putting myself first.

'They are. They are,' I reassure her. 'I think I'm just tired.' I decide not to say anything about Gran's house, it feels disloyal to Cathy and Mam. And I don't know where to start about Niall so I opt to focus on the least confusing item on my list. 'I think I'm just overwhelmed by all the work organising this market. And, apparently, I have to supervise on the day so I've no idea how I'm supposed to manage my stall.'

Della goes to respond but I'm on a bit of a roll. 'And we're having this big fundraising quiz night on Saturday in Gallagher's,' I tell her. 'I'm hopeless at quizzes. The quizmaster is a teacher – Cathy's husband – so I can just imagine the questions. I won't know the answer to a single one and everybody will think I'm a fool.'

By everybody I really mean Niall. He's so intelligent and wise. And he's been to college. And his best friends are Cathy and Brian, two of the most studious people I know. I barely opened a book in school. And if I did, I closed it again pretty fast. I couldn't focus, couldn't concentrate, my brain was forever flitting off and landing someplace else.

'Oh, you poor pet, that does sound hard. I think you're right, you're obviously very tired. You need to get a good night's sleep and then none of this will seem so bad.' She purses her lips and gives a determined nod of her head before she goes on. 'And I'm sure nobody will think you're a fool, darling. You're one of the brightest people I've ever met.'

That brings a small smile to my face but I still shake my head to protest. Della has more to add, though, and she says to leave things with her for a day or two, she might have a way to help out.

I tell her not to even consider abandoning Viva Vintage on a Saturday to come help with my stall. She shushes me with a wave of her hand, beautifully adorned with an array of antique silver rings.

'Just leave it with me, darling. You need backup and I have the perfect knight in shining armour in mind. Although, I think the correct term is Dame.' She laughs. 'But that certainly doesn't fit.'

I'm totally confused now and I'm starting to sink on my bed. I need to close my eyes and hope this nightmare of a day stays out of my dreams. But it wasn't all a nightmare and there is one small part that I can't, and don't want, to forget. All those years kissing

Gabe, and quite a few teenage flings before that… none of them ever made me feel like I did when Niall put those gorgeous soft lips on mine. He didn't linger nearly long enough, though, one more dream pulled away. I give myself a shake and focus on my iPhone screen and Della's fabulously made-up face.

'I'll be fine,' I tell her in my most determined voice. 'Honestly, I'm making a big deal about nothing and you're right, I am just really tired.'

She gives me a smile and a wave and repeats, 'You leave it with me. Goodnight, darling.' And she's gone. Like a beautiful fairy godmother disappearing in a puff of white smoke.

27

It's Cathy's birthday today so I call round after work to bring her the present I've made – a silver grey cloche hat with a deeper grey satin band. Mam loved her birthday wreath and I'm hoping Cathy will be equally chuffed with her hat. It's understated and classy and will look perfect with her hazelnut bob. She lays the brown paper parcel on the kitchen table and sits down to unwrap.

'It's beautiful, Jas.' She looks genuinely impressed. 'I must call into Gran's and see your collection. If they're all as special as this, you really will be in demand.'

'I'm storing them in your room now,' I tell her. I still don't feel right calling it mine, especially as I'm surrounded by all her old college stuff, not to mention her posters of Westlife and Adele. My Garbage, Lorde, and The Frames obviously ended up in the bin when Mam decided she needed a bigger wardrobe.

'Probably a good idea,' she says, 'Gran's can get a bit damp. Well, I'd love to have a peek, if you don't mind.'

'Sure, that'd be good.' I nod, although my stomach flips just a teeny bit. I haven't shown anyone the pieces I've made since I came home. I'm not sure why. I am really proud of them but maybe I'm not confident yet that other people will feel the same. Hearing Cathy say the word *special* reminds me of Niall. He did see some if only by chance, and he used the same term.

The only people that ever called me special were Gran and my mam. My teachers were patient enough but my school reports generally said that I was flighty, distracted, unfocused, and not academically inclined. Cathy told me once in a row that I was an absolute ditz. I had to look that one up and I wasn't impressed. When I complained to Shane he laughed and said she did have a point but it was endearing and sweet.

But I'm not unfocused anymore, I know what I want, at least when it comes to my hats. And I'm going to prove them all wrong, especially that bitch Tracey Hamilton who told me practically every day of my teens that I was nothing but trash.

Cathy asks me then how I find it working in Gran's. She's been meaning to drop by but, she says, it used to make her feel sad when she went in after Gran died so she's been putting it off.

'I always expect her to walk through the door or come down the stairs,' she tells me. 'And then I feel so down when it hits me that she won't.'

I realise that I haven't thought much about how Gran's passing might have affected my sis. I've been more focused on myself and on Mam. But I know Cathy called in almost every day all those years I was away and I get it now that it must have been hard to face that Gran wasn't there anymore. I suppose it was easier for me. I'd already gotten used to her not being around and I was the one who went away.

'I still feel her there,' I say. I hope Cathy doesn't think I've lost the plot but I need to tell somebody this. 'Sometimes when I'm working or just sitting in the kitchen, I get a feeling like she's over smiling at the sink, filling up the kettle for tea, humming one of her songs.' Gran was always singing and she always had a smile. She was bright and chirpy and forever flitting about like a colourful little bird.

'It's a nice feeling,' I add. 'A comforting one. Like she'll always be there with me, watching over me, keeping me safe.'

Cathy comes round to my side of the table and wraps me in a hug. 'You'll miss that when you move on,' she says. And even though I know she means to be kind, it's a knife through my heart. Does she really not want me to stay?

'You mean when Mam sells?'

She settles back in her chair and thinks for a moment before she replies, 'Well, no, I meant when you start selling your hats. I presumed you were thinking of moving back to Galway, or maybe even Dublin or Cork. Won't you need to be based in a city to get the sort of business you'll need?' It hadn't occurred to me that Cathy or Mam would think that.

'Not really,' I say. 'I can advertise online. Everything is on Insta or TikTok these days, although it changes by the week. But I'll put pics up on whatever platform works best. I plan to set up a website and I know a well-connected fashion photographer – she works for a top Paris magazine. I'm going to ask her if she'll feature me in a shoot.' I'm totally winging it now, I don't even know the name of Amélie's mag and I haven't asked her if she'll consider taking some pics, never mind placing me in a spread.

'Wow, Jas, that's incredible. I'm really impressed.'

'And Della will take some of my collection to display in her shop.' I haven't asked Della this either but I'm pretty sure she will. 'She's going to be in the magazine too so her place will be famous all over Europe. She only stocks really high-quality pieces, and her customers know that so they're generally happy to pay.'

Cathy sits shaking her head very slowly but her face is alive with a smile. She seems to be struggling to get her head around it all but she also seems genuinely happy to be hearing my news.

'So, you really are planning to stay? Here in Ballyclane?'

I thought I'd already made that clear but I nod my head

firmly and tell her, 'Absolutely, yes. I just need to figure out where.'

She looks serious then, and narrows her eyes, and says, 'Don't worry, Jas, we'll sort something out.'

28

Shane crashed at home again last night. He said his Mam was pestering that she doesn't see enough of him and she worries that he's working too hard. He came home for dinner and stayed over as he's on a late shift today. He texted me last night to ask if we could meet up before work and I have a feeling that's the real reason he stayed. Things have been a bit cool between us since that night in Gallagher's with Niall, and Shane absolutely hates when we fall out. He's always been a big softy that way.

I call over bright and early so that we can go for a jog. The new me is going to be healthy and focused and in January, I'm going to start Couch to 5K plan. The ground's a bit frosty, though, so I think maybe we should ease in with a stroll. We head over to the riverbank, there's a really nice walk all the way along with a low stone wall and silver-dusted green fields off to the side. I ask Shane if Kamala is coming to the quiz.

'I don't think so, sorry. I think she has to work.'

'You *think* she has to work. What's going on, Shane, have you even asked her to come?'

'Um.' Shane burrows his hands deep into his hoodie pockets and twists his mouth in a wince.

'Maybe I should call over tomorrow,' I suggest. 'The bus goes right by the hospital and I could say I was visiting someone and just popped in for a chat.' I'm delighted with my plan. I'll get us our missing team member and I'll also bag Shane a date. 'I could say that we are really stuck and will she please, please help us out. It sounds like she works way too hard anyway, so if she likes you enough to say yes surely somebody will switch shifts.'

Shane slows his pace and stares hard at the ground. 'Just leave it, Jas, please.'

'Ah, for God's sake, this is pathetic. Why won't you just ask her out?'

'Because she's not real!' he blurts. 'Well, she is real. There is a Kamala and I do work with her and we are really good friends. But I'm not attracted to her and even if I was, she's married to Jayne.'

My jaw drops about a foot. 'WTF?'

'I'm sorry, Jas. I just wanted to put you at ease. I thought if I said I was really into someone else you'd accept that I'm not still hung up on you. Which I promise I'm not.' He rubs at his forehead and gives me a mortified look.

Just when I was beginning to think I should trust people more, it turns out I was right all along. But I didn't expect lies from Shane. We've been best friends all our lives and he's never let me down. At least, not until now.

He stands in front of me, silent, waiting for me to speak. To tell him it's okay, that I do understand. But it's not, and I don't. I moved home to sort out my head and now everything feels even more confused. I need time to process this. All thoughts of jogging have disappeared. If it wasn't so bloody cold, I'd hop over the stone wall and lie down on the grass for a nap.

'Say something,' Shane finally pleads.

'I don't know what to say,' I tell him because I don't. 'Just give me some time.'

We walk home in silence and shrug our goodbyes. But I give him a wave and a smile as I push open my front door. I may be upset and confused but I can see it's even harder for Shane.

I make my way down the hall to get some breakfast. Mam's in the kitchen and she holds out a plate of buttered toast.

'Cathy called me last night,' she says. 'She tells me you're planning to stay.'

'I am.' I reach for a slice. 'But don't worry, I'll be grand. Even if you do sell here soon, I've plenty of offers. I'll find somewhere to crash.'

She looks serious now and flops down on a chair. 'Listen, Jas—' she starts but I'm not in the mood. I don't want to think any more about how everyone else is sorting out their life and casting me aside. I'm going to focus on my own future, and that means getting back to my hats.

'I need to get to work, Mam,' I cut in. 'I have so much to do before the market next week and I want to make a start.' I grab another slice of toast and dash upstairs to get dressed.

29

It's Saturday night at last and Shane calls for me before we go to the quiz. He knocks on my bedroom door and stands in the door frame looking embarrassed and lost. I climb off the bed and walk straight over to give him a hug.

'It's all right, you soft muppet, I do understand.' I'm not really sure that I do, it's hard to get my head around. Does he still fancy me or not? But however hard this is for me I'm guessing it's a lot worse for Shane. And we've been best friends way too long to let one silly white lie tear us apart.

I take a last look in Mam's full-length hall mirror before we head down the stairs. I'm wearing my navy polka-dot Kooples dress that Della found for me at a bargain price online. And my black lace-up heeled boots instead of my usual purple Docs. I've even gone all out and put on some make-up, I'm not sure why. I have this niggling feeling inside that I'm going to need armour tonight. Shane was downtown this afternoon and he thinks he may have spotted Tracey Hamilton whizzing past in the passenger seat of a shiny black Merc. I've had a pain in my chest since I read his text. Hopefully, it was just a horrible mistake.

Shane pulls open the heavy oak door and my eyes are on stilts when I see the crowd that's inside. Every single booth and table is occupied and Dermot's passing round spare stools with a Julia

Roberts' grin. I can practically see the bank notes whizzing in his brain. Shane tells me to look for a seat and asks me what I want to drink. There's half a gymnastics team leaping around my stomach and I don't think I can face Guinness so I opt for red wine.

Shane makes for the bar while I scout out a spot. We still don't have a fourth team member and I can't see any sign of Niall. If it's just me and Shane then I'm pretty confident we're definitely coming last. The bar is straight across from the door, so I'm about to make my way through the crowd to see if there are any seats down the back when I hear a voice behind me that sends the gymnasts doing cartwheels and bouncing off my chest. I spin around and just as I do somebody jostles past Niall practically shoving him into my arms. I have to grab hold of his biceps to stop myself reeling back. The gymnasts crash-land on the floor of my stomach and I look up to find Niall's usually grey eyes now smouldering black. He loops one arm around my waist to steady me and then apologises, although I'm not sure for what. For almost knocking me to the ground or for turning my insides to slop.

'I've been trying to call you,' he says, and his brows wrinkle in a frown.

I pull my phone out of my duffel pocket and yes, I do have three missed calls. I must have pocket-clicked silent by mistake. I shrug as lightly as I can then I realise I'm still clinging hard to Niall's left arm. I pull away and tell him we'd better grab a few stools off Dermot as it looks like we're too late to bag a table or a booth.

'That's why I was calling you, Jas.' He does that lower lip-biting thing again and my pelvic floor takes on a life of its own. I give myself a mental shake – as if I wasn't already shaken enough – and then I strain to catch Niall's words over the cackle of the crowd.

'We should have a booth down the back,' he says. 'An old friend of mine is in town. She said she'd get here early as she has another friend coming to the quiz. She hasn't told her she's here yet because she wants her visit to be a surprise. I think we'll find her hiding somewhere down the end.'

My lips form themselves into an involuntary pout. On the one hand that means we have our fourth team member and somewhere to sit. But my chest clenched in a knot when I heard the word *she* and I'm not sure how I feel about sharing Niall with this other woman even if she is just a friend.

'Before we go look for her,' he says, 'I want to explain.'

That sounds good to me but then I hear an almighty shriek. A mass of blonde curls, porcelain cheeks, and radiant smile bounds towards me and buries me in a hug.

'Ma chérie, ma chérie.'

I'm over the moon but I'm speechless with shock. I don't get a word in anyway as lovely Amélie is still babbling and I hear something that sounds like, 'And you already know Niall.'

How do you already know Niall, Amélie? seems more to the point. But I don't get to ask this either as Shane picks this moment to land over clutching his beer and my glass of red wine. Amélie retreats from our hug and flicks back her golden hair. Shane nearly drops his drink and, even worse, mine. The poor lad looks like he's been hit by a train then sprinkled with pixie dust and brought back to life. And I swear to God I can see Taylor Swift's 'Love Story' playing out in his head. If he wasn't over me before tonight then he's definitely over me now.

I catch Niall's eye and he looks even more gobsmacked than I am. He blinks hard as if he's struggling to reset his brain. He glances over to Amélie and then back again to me.

'Jas,' he says, sounding like a Garda sergeant about to break some awful bad news. 'I can see you already know each other... but... Jas, this is Mel.'

WTF. Amélie's brows pinch and she takes a step back. She's obviously blindsided that I might have heard of her as Mel. Niall is usually the one to smooth the awkward situations but for once since I've met him, he seems at a loss. I ignore the pounding in my chest and I don my brightest smile and suggest he goes to the bar before they run out of beer. Then I ask Amélie if she's managed to hold us some seats.

'Ah, yes, and I've made some new friends. They are keeping our table for us.' She threads her arm through mine and I finger the soft silky fabric of her cherry-red dress.

'This is beautiful,' I say.

'I bought it from Della. Oh, I have to thank you so much for introducing us. She and I have become the best of friends.'

I'm about to say you're welcome when we arrive at our table. Christy and his wife, Lizzie, and Maura and Nadia are ensconced in the next booth and they've covered our chairs with their coats and batted away anyone eying up our spot.

I have so much I want to ask Amélie. Is she the mystery knight in shining armour that my fairy godmother promised to send? When did she get here, where is she staying, and how exactly does she know Niall? But Christy and Nadia are buzzing. Christy is so happy to finally have Lizzie out, he's all introductions and quiz strategies and I can barely hear myself think. And Nadia and Amélie are chatting like old friends as they sort out the coats. Shane is just standing there with a soppy smile on his face like his world has turned into a pink fluffy cloud and he's happy to go along wherever it floats. I take a giant gulp of red wine and plonk down on one of the chairs.

Shane sits down next to me, leans in close, and whispers, 'Who is she? I think I'm in love.'

I tip my head back and smile. I'm about to tell him he'd better join the queue when Amélie takes a seat across from us and Niall arrives back with their drinks. He's bought a pint for Shane and another red wine for me too.

'The bar's a bit manic so I thought I'd better get them in.'

'Cheers.' Shane accepts his pint with a big, grateful grin as if Niall has somehow become his latest best friend. Clearly, everything looks rosier under an Amélie haze. I'm not sure how long that will last when I tell him I think Amélie is Niall's former girlfriend and I'm wondering if she's here to reclaim what she lost. I'm wrapped up in that thought and I try to drag myself back to focus on making conversation and preparing for the quiz. Then I look over to see Maura waving frantically and calling someone to join her. For some reason, Niall, Shane and I all turn at the same time to see who she's so keen to welcome into the fold. I'm not sure which of us is more shocked, although I'm guessing that would be me.

I drain my first glass of red and make a grab for the next. I don't normally drink wine but nothing about this evening has been normal so far and I've a feeling it's only going to get worse. If I can get hold of a bartender, I'll be ordering a bottle. I might even ask if there's any chance they could hook me up to a tap.

'Tracey, Tracey, pet. Over here.'

My nemesis strides through the crowd channelling *Gossip Girl*'s Blair Waldorf only with cropped red hair. Her eyes flick to our table as she sweeps past and I catch the downward curl of her mouth and the vicious glint in her eye. Message received. Watch out, Jas McAdams, Tracey Hamilton hasn't come back to Ballyclane to make amends. What has she come back for, though? I'm not even sure I want to know but I'm pretty sure I'm going to find out.

Amélie breaks the tension by introducing herself to Shane. I had told Shane about the lovely French girl who came to my rescue after Gabe, and how we had fast become friends. And I had told Amélie that my best friend in Ballyclane was a very cute boy. I even suggested I might introduce them sometime. Looks like that time has come.

In fairness to Shane, he holds it together, asks interesting questions, and even manages not to drool. It's clear that he's smitten, though, and that's hardly a surprise. Amélie's so bloody stunning I'd nearly fancy her myself. And she doesn't just look like an angel, she acts like one too.

Finally, Shane asks the question that's been on the tip of my tongue, only I've been biting it back.

'And how do you know Niall?'

Niall's eyes flick to mine and it feels like he wants to tell me something. He did say he wanted to explain. But Amélie starts first. She only gets as far as, 'Ah, what a story that is,' when Dermot booms through his microphone asking for some hush. And the veteran quiz freaks start flapping their arms and warning everyone to shush. This isn't Shane's first rodeo so he waves us into a huddle then leans his forearms on the table and clutches his pen. He seems to have designated himself team leader and I look up from under my lashes and try to sneak a glance at Niall. I haven't a notion about quizzes and my main interest right now is bagging another glass of wine. But Niall is leader material personified and if it came to a contest as to who would claim Alpha Male, then as much as I love Shane my money would be on Niall. But he seems out of sorts and his head seems elsewhere. He keeps shooting me meaningful looks. Of course, I've no idea what they mean. Probably something like, I'm sorry that I kissed you and I'm sorry you're a prickly, grumpy mess, but my beautiful sweet ex-girlfriend is back now and I definitely won't be kissing you again.

The quiz whizzes past in a blur and we do well on the first four rounds. No thanks to me. Shane gets all the science questions and he's pretty good at general knowledge too. Niall knows his history and both he and Amélie have read a truckload of fancy books. But fair play to Brian, he finally comes up trumps with a round of music and film. I thought it would be all Mozart and obscure foreign stuff. But there's indie, punk, and rom-coms, and those old Hollywood musicals that Mam and I watch all the time and I ace every question he calls out.

My head was buzzing after I finished the second wine and I caught another nasty sneer from Tracey as she watched me finish my glass. So, I ordered another round and switched to sparkling water for myself. And a pint of tap water on the side for everyone on the team. I could happily drain a vineyard right now but I'm not having Tracey Hamilton watch me get pissed. She's only waiting to catch me off guard.

All that liquid has me dying for a pee, so I make my way out to the loo. Luckily there's no queue, two of the cubicles are occupied but the one at the end is still free. Mam and Donal are nearly finished totting up the scores and I suppose everyone is staying put to hear where their team has come. I have a quick pee, then I'm washing my hands and checking my mascara in the mirror when the cubicle door behind me pulls open and Tracey sashays out.

'Well, if it isn't Raggedy Jas.' Her lips curl down in what I'm beginning to think is a permanent sneer. Then she cackles like a classic wicked witch. 'I hear you're unemployed now and homeless too. And I very much doubt you have a man.'

I'm about to clap back but she barely draws breath. She sweeps her icy blue eyes up and down the length of my body and adds, 'And you're still wearing that cheap second-hand trash. No wonder my cousin and your pathetic hanger-on – what's his name? Shane – only have eyes for the blonde.'

'Feck off, Tracey, I'm not in the mood.' There was a time I would have wanted to shove her back into her cubicle or at least say something smart. But I'm worn out caring what everybody thinks of me, and Tracey Hamilton is last on that list. I suddenly feel absolutely exhausted and all I want to do is go home. I pull open the door into the corridor, make my way out into the beer garden, and keep going until I reach the back gate. I don't even have my duffel and I'm freezing but I start walking as fast as I can and I warm up a small bit as I pick up the pace. I jog down the lane behind Gallagher's and take the bridge over the riverbank that leads into our estate. It's not the safest route at this hour of the night but I'm not thinking about that. I'm not thinking about anything really, I'm just struggling to breathe, keep my head from exploding, and trying to make my way home.

30

As soon as I get in the door, it hits me that I'd better text Amélie. I haven't even asked if she has somewhere to stay. I'll tell her I felt unwell and had to dash off but she's welcome to crash here and I know Shane will see her safely home.

She's back straight away. It seems Nadia told them I was feeling iffy and needed to go. I'm a bit baffled as to how Nadia figured this out but at least it covers my tracks. I'm about to repeat my offer of a bed, or at least a pull-out couch, when Amélie messages me to text her tomorrow when I'm feeling up to it. And she's sorted for a bed as she's staying with Niall.

She's staying with *Niall*. She's *staying* with Niall. *Of course*, she's staying with Niall. Just when I thought things couldn't get worse. I forgot this is me, Jas McAdams. Welcome to my so-called bloody life.

I tag her text with a thumbs up. I haven't the energy to reply and, seriously, what am I supposed to say? Cool, have fun, don't do anything I wouldn't. Or maybe, please, please don't take my man. Pathetic. He's not even mine anyway. Probably never would be even if Amélie hadn't rocked up. Might as well face it, Tracey Hamilton has a point. Homeless, unemployed, an anxious runaway wreck. Not exactly prime girlfriend material, especially not for the likes of Niall. But she can feck off with her Raggedy Jas remark. I'm wearing bloody Kooples tonight. Either the evil bitch still has zero fashion sense or she's completely fecking blind.

I climb upstairs, pull off my lace-ups, and crawl into bed. I don't even bother to undress and my make-up can stay where it is. I just want to bury myself under the covers and hide away from the world.

As if he's reading my mind one last time, Niall messages to ask if I'm doing okay. And if I'd like to go for a walk or maybe a drive out to Oakwood tomorrow to talk. Talk about what, Niall? Amélie? Mel? I think I can figure that story out for myself. I don't need your pity or sympathy or apologies that the love of your life has shown up and I'm surplus to requirements again.

I'm good, thanks, I shoot back.

Okay, let me know if you change your mind. I'm here, anytime. Btw we won the quiz, thanks to you!

Mam is supposed to be staying at Donal's tonight and I don't want her thinking she needs to come home to check up on me or bring me a medal for finally getting something right, even if it was just a few lousy quiz questions. So, I send her a text.

Sorry to run off, got period cramps and needed painkillers and a hot-water bottle fast. She can't really argue with that. For safety, I add, *I'm fine now and tucked up in bed.*

I need the house to myself tonight. I can't be dealing with anyone asking me what's wrong. I wouldn't know where to start. I give up on the idea of going straight to sleep and head downstairs to Mam's vodka stash instead. I pour myself half a tumbler and grab a can of Seven Up from the fridge. Then I head back upstairs with Spotify on shuffle and I flop down on Cathy's pale pink carpet and mix myself a much-needed drink.

31

I wake up the next morning still fully dressed. There's a big ass woodpecker inside my head and my mouth feels like a furball ringed with glue. At least I learned one thing useful last night. Red wine and vodka don't mix. I reach out and lift the pint glass of water that I filled when I went down for more booze. I can just about lift my head. I hit shuffle again on my phone and pray for some comforting words, musical chicken soup. But the messed-up universe that has become my world decides that's not what I need. And before I can hit silent or fling my phone at the wall, Glen Hansard is roaring at me to redeem myself at the top of his godforsaken lungs.

'I want to, Glen,' I roar back. 'But I'm still trying to figure out how.'

Everything feels wrong and I know most of it's my own fault. I keep running away and holding everything inside and expecting my life to magically improve. None of which is working and I feel completely alone. Maybe it is time for me to trust the people who have earned it, ask for their help, and have the courage to go after my dreams. I'll start by talking to Mam and Cathy again about Gran's house.

As if on cue, Mam texts to say that Donal is cooking Sunday lunch later at his place and they'd love me to join them. It won't be until about three o'clock and she'll drive over to pick me up.

That sounds good and I should surely be human again by that time, so I text back that I'd love to and add three kisses too. Hangovers always make me feel soppy and in need of a hug and my mam does the best hugs, so I'm all in.

I set my alarm for one o'clock, take a good slug of water and a couple of Ibuprofen, and bury myself under the covers to sleep everything off. By the time Mam arrives at two thirty, I'm showered and dressed and reasonably together. I've even held down some tea and a full slice of toast. I also messaged Amélie to ask if she'd like to join us for a traditional Irish feed, but she's out at Oakwood with Shane this afternoon. Apparently, they fancied a walk.

I'm pretty sure that's not all Shane fancies but I haven't a clue what's really going on. I thought Amélie was supposed to be with Niall. First, she's best friends with Della, then she's Niall's rekindled flame. Now she's off doing I've no idea what with my Shane. I think I've been hanging around second-hand shops for too long looking for inspiration. This feels like life imitating art with me as the unwanted cast-off. Amélie has moved in as the high-class couture piece everyone's been craving all along and while I have *some* potential, I'm still a raggy work in progress and nobody seems to care enough to invest.

Glen's words telling me to redeem myself reverberate in my brain and I remind myself that Niall did actually text me last night to invite me out to Oakwood today. And I declined. And Mam is here now giving me sympathetic looks and asking me if I'm feeling any better and if there's anything else she can do. She's already donated a quarter bottle of vodka, even if she doesn't realise it yet, and now she's supplying Sunday lunch. So, I tell her a hug would be great and that's really all that I need. She looks absolutely delighted and wraps me in a warm, soft embrace. And I realise that I'm at least partly telling the truth. It may not be *all* that I need but it is definitely what I do need the most.

We spend a lovely afternoon and evening at Donal's. His bungalow is spacious and the garden is a perfectly manicured lawn with lots of green shrubbery. There's even a little pond. The house is full of dark wood and heavy furniture, though, and I'd say Mam won't be long brightening it all up with gallons of off-white paint. I'm pretty sure that heavy black leather will be going straight to the charity shop too. Mam's very attached to her comfy green couch.

Donal's son is visiting from Kilkenny for the weekend with his wife and two small kids. They're friendly and welcoming and very sweet to Mam. I'm glad to see that they don't seem threatened by the idea of her moving in and they're not giving her any wicked stepmother vibes. Then I remember my own outburst at Donal over his comments about Gran's house and the disappointment etched on Mam's face. I know he was only looking out for her and I tell myself that from now on I'll be more supportive of them both.

It turns out that Donal has another son and two daughters, all spread out in various corners of the country – Donegal, Mayo and Cork. No wonder there's no spare room for me when Mam moves in here. Not that I would take it anyway but I did wonder when they didn't offer if Donal didn't want me around. I decide to start my redemption process by being nicer to Donal and appreciate that he's good for my mam.

32

Amélie called me last night all excited, like a child on her first trip to Lapland. I never imagined anyone could be so hyped up about visiting boring old Ballyclane.

'Oh, *chérie*, it's truly magical, the Christmas tree in the Square, the lights, the ambience. And isn't Niall's parents' house beautiful? It was so kind of his mother to insist that I stay there even though they're away for the next few days.'

'Um, it does look very grand,' I say. 'Although, I've never actually been inside.' Oh my God, she's already been welcomed into the hallowed ground. Of course, she has. His parents probably met her when she and Niall were together before. No doubt his mother has been lighting candles to Saint Anthony and praying for her miraculous return.

'It's like a winter wonderland,' she cries in that gorgeous husky, breathy tone. 'Lily has decorated every room but it's so tasteful and elegant, I feel like I'm in a beautiful dream. She gave Niall a key for me and told me to use the whole upper floor as they keep that for guests.'

It strikes me as odd that Lily would insist that Amélie stays there and not with Niall. But then Amélie did break his heart once and maybe she wants him to take his time and be sure that won't happen again before he gets too close.

Lily, Amélie, Niall, even their names seem in sync. A perfect

Christmas family, obviously meant to be. What's his dad's name? Jack? Hmm, maybe I can get him onside. God, my head's all over the place again. I can't even be cross with Amélie; it would be like being angry at an overexcited kid on Christmas Eve. And even though I'm miffed that she's already embedded herself in Niall's family home, I'm also finding it easier to breathe now that I know she's not nestling up on his denim blue couch or climbing those painted oak stairs. I still feel like the mystery cottage in the secret garden is our special place and it's the one thing I'm not ready to share. I seem to be sharing just about everything else with Amélie since she arrived. I'd like to hold on to something, some tiny fragment of Niall, before I have to let go for good.

We've arranged to meet in Coffee Spot at eleven then I'm going to take her back afterwards to Gran's to see some of my hats. I've brought a few of my favourites in for the day to see what Amélie thinks. I'm determined to put all of my muddled-up emotions to one side for the rest of this week and focus on my most important goal – my brand-new business, my hats. The market is next Saturday and I don't want any distractions. I remind myself again that this is the reason I came home. I want the day, my stall, my creations to be a success and I can't let anything or anyone get in the way.

Amélie is waiting in the window seat, wrapped up in a cream padded jacket with a big fluffy hood. Her teeth are chattering and she's hugging an enormous mug of hot chocolate with marshmallows like it's the only thing keeping her warm. Her cheerful smile beams wide as she spots me coming through the door. It's clear that she has absolutely no idea of the heartache she has caused.

'Oh, my goodness, *ma chérie*, your country is so beautiful but how do you bear this cold?'

'Ah, you get used to it,' I say with a shrug as I pull out a chair. You really don't but now that I'm home I feel a strange loyalty to this place, my place. Emmet Park, the lane, the Square. Elena is clearing the table next to ours so I order an Americano with oat milk, peel off my duffel, and sit down.

'But it's so wet, so damp.' She shivers. 'It's colder in Paris in the winter, but, this, this gets into your bones.'

She's right, of course. Half the country is crippled with arthritis. It's no wonder Mam and Donal want that apartment in Spain.

'And Galway is even wetter,' she goes on. 'I try to tell Della she should move to the South of France. She could open another Viva Vintage there, maybe in Cannes or in Nice. I'm sure it would be an enormous success.'

Oh God, please don't take Della too, I think. I haven't been back to Galway to see her yet. But I'm planning to soon. Maybe after Christmas with a batch of my hats. I don't say this, of course. And I don't need to as Amélie adds with a laugh, 'She will never leave Galway. She tells me it is the best city in the world. Perhaps she is right.' She smiles. 'If only there wasn't so much rain.'

Amélie tells me then that Della has told her all about our Christmas market down the lane and how I'm supposed to oversee everything and that means I won't have time to focus on my own stall.

'And so, I am here to save you, *ma chérie*.' She grins. 'Just tell me what to do.'

There's a big grey rock lodged in the pit of my stomach and part of me wants to be a bitch and snarl, 'Feck off back to Galway and stay away from my friends, my town, my Niall.'

But there's a reason everybody falls in love with Amélie and I can't help but love her to bits too. She's not just a ridiculously stylish beauty. She's sweet and honest and kind, and she's travelled halfway across the country to offer me her heartfelt help.

We finish our coffee and hot chocolate and also the delicious warm buttered croissants that Amélie insisted on ordering for us too. She reaches for the black camera bag perched beside her on the window seat. Then she lifts the neck strap over her head, grips the bag firmly with both hands and tells me that it's time for us to get to work. We make our way out through the arch and across the Square to Gran's. Amélie seems surprised that I still call the house Gran's when she's been dead for more than two years. But she manages to ask kindly so I share my secret that I still feel her there and that as long as I can keep working and maybe even living in her home, a part of her will always be with me, smiling and humming and encouraging me on.

Amélie adores Gran's house. Mind you, she seems to adore everything about Ballyclane apart from the damp cold seeping into her bones. If it wasn't for the fact that Della has already told me that she is definitely moving back to Paris this Christmas, I'd wonder if she's planning to set up home. I get a queasy feeling in the depths of my stomach as a fleeting image of Amélie planting lavender in Niall's cottage garden flashes through my mind. I'm sure being a visual person is helpful for working on my hats but sometimes I wish I had a remote control for my brain and I could switch the blasted thing off.

Amélie brings my focus back to exactly where it needs to be as she tells me about all the fabulous ideas filling up her head. She takes shots of the dried wildflowers on the deep window ledge behind Gran's Belfast sink. She focuses her camera on the old Singer 201 and my portable Brother set up alongside. Then she follows me through the house settling on all the precious pieces that have given me so much inspiration – the Narnia wardrobe at the end of Gran's brass bed, the creamy white louvred screen in the second bedroom that Gran hand-painted around the edges with her favourite flower, sweet pea. And, of course, Gran's beautiful clothes. Gran would take the train to Dublin at least once a year and bring me with her when I had a day off school. We'd scout all the best second-hand shops, especially her favourite, Jenny Vander. Then we'd carry home her haul and she'd make all the garments even more magical with her own special touch.

Amélie tells me it's important to have personal photographs like these when I set up my social media, whether that's Instagram, TikTok, or a blog. Or whatever the latest fad is by the time I get around to doing all that. She tells me that she'll also use the snaps she takes for an article in her magazine focusing on me and my hats. This sounds a bit far-fetched to me but it's sweet of her to suggest that it might be a possibility so I smile and say that sounds like a dream. Then she reminds me that we still have to capture the most important images of all. My hats. She wants me to model some now but I'm not sure. I haven't even washed my hair this morning and I'm still a bit wrecked from overdoing it on Mam's vodka on Saturday night. I suggest we leave that for another day and Amélie considers this and agrees. We need more models, suitable clothes and jewellery, and an elegant timeless location to set the scene. I already have the perfect place in my mind.

She hooks a selection of hats on Gran's pretty flowered screen and takes some photographs of those. Then just before we leave, she sits behind Gran's Singer and takes multiple shots of the Square through the tall front window.

'People like to see the view from other people's windows,' she tells me. 'And you have a very special room with a very special view. If I were you, Jas, I would never let this wonderful house go.'

I realise then that Amélie is just like me in that way. She doesn't see the cracks or the peeling paint or if she does, she doesn't care. She sees the beautiful bones of the place and feels the creativity and the love that filled its beating heart for so many years. She's still sitting at my work table gazing out on to the Square but I feel like she has just wrapped me in a warm hug and passed a sunbeam of strength to help me carry on.

33

I take Amélie back through the lane and down to the walled garden to show her where I would like her to set up her shoot. She's twirling around, admiring everything – the stonework, the pear tree, the now-finished pergola – when her eyes land on the black wrought-iron gate.

'Ah, that must lead to Niall's cottage.' She tilts her head and stares. 'Lily phoned last night to ask how I was getting on. She's so kind. She told me all about Niall's cottage and how it's a very special place. Just like Niall.'

I swallow hard. I'm not sure what to say. There's a kaleidoscope of mixed-up thoughts whirring around my brain. Amélie hasn't been to the cottage yet. It was his mam, Lily, who told her all about it. Not Niall. And the yearning in her voice when she said *just like Niall.*

'You and Niall?' is all I can manage. I'm not sure how much I can ask without feeling obliged to share my own yearning too.

'I have had two great loves in my life, Jas,' Amélie begins.

'And one of them is Niall?'

She smiles a sweet, wistful smile and it's clear the answer is a yes. I'm guessing the second is fashion or photography or a mixture of the two but I don't get to ask. Amélie is still gazing tenderly at the gate when it opens and who comes strolling through, only Niall.

He looks surprised and a small bit confused to find us both seemingly waiting at the entrance to his world.

'Amélie, Jas, I really need to talk to you both.' His eyes are smoky grey and smouldering and I can't help but feel that he's holding too much emotion inside.

Amélie looks at me and I look at Amélie. We can both guess why he wants to talk to her. I'm surprised they're not already wrapped around each other and doing a lot more than talking by now. Although, in fairness, Niall does seem to like to take things slow. I'm struggling to figure out why he wants to talk to me and I'm sure Amélie is equally at a loss. Probably the market or even Gran's house but we have a meeting on Wednesday to finalise everything about the market so surely whatever it is can wait until then.

He nods at me then peers into Amélie's eyes with that way that he has. If she wasn't such a sweetheart, I'd want to shove her aside and stand right in front of him yelling, 'Me, me! Stare into *my* eyes instead!' But I don't, of course. I just lower my gaze and start backing away when Niall looks over to me and says with a catch in his tone, 'Jas, I really need to talk to you too. Can I call over to you later? Please?'

Amélie frowns and crinkles her nose and looks at me more with interest than accusation, which is kind of her, I think. I'm not sure I would be so generous myself.

'Sure, yeah, I'll be in the Square until five.' I'm trying to stop calling it Gran's. I'm hoping to talk to Cathy about holding on to the house, and if she agrees I might even come up with a plan to persuade Mam. But until then I need to keep a bit of distance in case it doesn't work out. There's only so much loss that my heart can bear in one week.

Amélie gives me a wave and follows Niall into his garden. The garden that I was clinging to as our secret place. I purse my lips hard and remind myself again that nothing about Niall was ever really mine. It just felt like it was for one exquisite, fleeting kiss. But Amélie's here now and it seems like it all belongs to her. And probably always did.

34

I FaceTime Shane when I'm back at my worktable, staring out on to the Square like Amélie did before she drifted off into fairy-tale land with Niall. Shane has been on night shifts since Sunday evening and he's covering extra hours until next weekend. He's probably shattered and the last thing he needs is a grilling from me but I need some clue as to what is going on with Amélie and Niall, and if there's anything at all going on between her and Shane. He can surely fill me in about that.

Shane tells me he has ten minutes exactly before he has to dash out to work. It's winter flu season and the hospital is completely overrun.

'Jesus, don't come near me then, I can't catch anything now, not with the market next weekend.'

Shane rolls his eyes and tells me he'll be lucky if he has time for a cup of tea before next weekend never mind a trip home to Ballyclane.

'Does that mean you won't be seeing Amélie again?' I narrow my eyes accusingly. It was Amélie who told me about their trip out to Oakwood. There wasn't a peep out of Shane.

There's not a trace of guilt in his expression as his face lights up with a grin. 'She's lovely, isn't she?' he says, as if I need reminding of that fact.

'She is,' I agree, 'but what were you two doing cosying up out at Oakwood?' I move my face closer to my screen as if I can pull the truth out of his mouth with my threatening glare.

Shane only laughs. 'Just messing about.' Then he changes the subject right away. 'You know, Niall was in a really funny mood after you ran off on Saturday night.'

I almost interrupt to protest but it's true, that's exactly what I did, so I clamp my lips together and wait for Shane to say more.

'Dermot gave us a free round after we won and we were all in great form apart from Niall. He just sat there staring into his pint and didn't even seem to hear Amélie when she said she would love to see Oakwood as she'd heard so much about it from you.'

That's true, I did tell her how amazing it is and even promised to take her if ever she got around to visiting. I just didn't expect that to happen so soon.

'So, I offered,' he goes on. 'And she accepted, and we had an absolutely brilliant afternoon.'

I catch a glint of satisfaction in his eyes. I've known Shane long enough to know when there's more that he wants to tell me but he's holding back, waiting to be asked.

'Did something happen between you two?' I oblige.

His face lights up like all his best Christmases have come at once.

'It did. She kissed me.'

'She did *what*?'

'She kissed me. It was great.'

Hmph. Great. Not mind-blowing. Not spectacular. Not life-changing. Definitely not up there with me and Niall. But WTF? Amélie is supposed to be in love with Niall. Didn't she just tell me he is the love of her life? Bloody hell, she may be a sweetheart but she's doing my head in. I honestly can't keep up.

'And so… does that mean… are you two…?'

I can't see how a relationship could work between Amélie and Shane. She's off back to Paris soon and God only knows where else after that. Shane loves his job at the hospital. Would he really learn French, move to Paris, and give up his home, his career, and me, to follow Amélie wherever she decides to go next? I realise that I'm getting completely ahead of myself. It was only a kiss and I have less than five minutes to find out, so I get straight to the point.

'Are you two together now?'

'Nah, it was only a peck, unfortunately.' Shane gives a light easy laugh. 'She says I'm very cute but she's madly in love with someone else.' Then he shrugs. 'She didn't say who. Some French guy, I suppose. I think she's amazing but I knew from the minute I laid eyes on her that she was out of my league. I never expected anything more. I didn't expect that much, to be honest. I'm chuffed that someone like Amélie could even give me a second look never mind lean in for a kiss.'

'She definitely kissed you then, not the other way around?'

'She did, Jas. She did. And I'm never washing these lips again,' he says with a grin stretching out to his ears. 'But it's back to reality now and I seriously do have to go to work. I'll see you at the market on Saturday and I'm free Friday too. Make me a list of whatever you need. I'm all yours and happy to help out.' Then he gives me a big cheery wave and he's gone.

Maybe I need to be more like Shane. He looked absolutely smitten on Saturday night. Yet he seems to have completely accepted the fact that he could never keep Amélie and he's chalking it up to a sweet special memory and just pinning it somewhere in a corner of his brain like he might hang a pretty Disney decoration on a tree.

I decide to channel some of that energy and throw myself into my work and I spend the rest of the afternoon putting the finishing touches to more of my Christmas market hats. I only realise that I've forgotten to have lunch, and haven't even stopped for a cup of tea, when I hear a rap at the front window and look up to see Niall peering in. It throws me right back to that first afternoon and I remind myself again to *just breathe*. I'm not going to let myself think about what he and Amélie might have been getting up to in his garden, his cottage, and especially not up those gorgeous painted timber stairs.

I feel off-balance as I open the door. I'm not sure if that's down to lack of food, lack of fresh air, or lack of Niall. But I take as deep a breath as I can draw into my protesting lungs and I stare boldly into his eyes. I've got a life to live here, a market to organise, and a business to get off the ground. I don't have time for some smoky-eyed, smouldering, posh boy hell-bent on breaking my heart. The tingling, thrilling feeling that's coursing through my veins reminds me again that Niall is definitely not a boy. My mind spins with the memory of that kiss. Then I howl in my head for the hundredth time since I came home, that the last thing I need, messing with my plans and my heart, is a man.

Niall inches forward on the doorstep. He's so close now that we're almost touching and before I can stop myself, I'm picturing a scene skin on skin. I'm reeling with the warm woody scent of him and I don't know how much longer I can stand here, stand this, but I have to protect myself from falling apart and that means I absolutely can't let him in.

He's reading my mind again like he always seems to do and he pleads, 'Please, Jas, I need to explain about Mel.' There's something so honest and earnest about the way he's gazing into my eyes that I almost relent. But I don't. I know we've become close and he doesn't want to hurt me. And I'm sure he really does want to talk everything through and confirm that we can still be friends. But I don't have the energy to pretend.

If I didn't have so much to do and if it wasn't so important that I get a grip on my life, I'd walk past Niall right now and go home to Emmet Park and climb into my bed. And stay there for good. But I'm not ready yet to give up. I may have no choice but to give up on Niall but I still have my family, my hats, and this house. My heritage, my dream. And I'm nowhere near ready to give up on all that.

'You don't need to explain,' I tell him in as determined a voice as I can find. 'It's not really any of my business.' He blinks at me hard as I add, 'We barely know each other, it's not like we're even close friends.'

I'm being a bitch again, and a liar too, which I hate. But it's the only way I can find to protect myself. I have to spin a web all around me and try to create some sort of shield.

'How can you say that, Jas?' There's a shake in his voice and his eyes are searching mine like he's determined to root out the truth. 'How can you say we're not close?' He's shaking his head now as though he can't figure out what to do with me. I get it, I'm absolutely not cooperating. He should know that I've never been very good at that.

I take a step back and pull the door closer behind me. I'm hoping that he'll give up and take the very clear hint. This door is not opening any time soon and there is no way that I'm letting him in. I can't deal with hearing about his rekindled love affair with the wonderful woman of his dreams.

But he's not giving up and he exhales hard and carries on. 'Why can't you just listen for once, please?' He sounds utterly exasperated and I'm equally put out that he thinks he has any right to be pissed off with me. I didn't go giving him the kiss of his life and then back off and ghost him for weeks before flouncing off into the sunset with somebody else.

I don't say any of this. I just blow out a breath, fold my arms across my chest, and hold out.

'I didn't expect Mel, Amélie, to turn up out of the blue,' he says. 'I think I was in shock for the first couple of days. I'm not going to lie, we had something really special, and she is very important to me.'

Oh, for Christ's sake, I don't need to hear about how special Amélie is. I get it, okay. I close my eyes and keep them shut for a few seconds, half-hoping he'll be gone when I open them again. That never worked when I was a kid and it still doesn't now.

'Niall, I'm actually starving and I have an awful lot of work to do and I really don't have time for all this.' I press my fingers against my temples. 'You have no idea how close my head is to exploding. The last thing I need is you here on my doorstep, pouring your heart out. Go tell all of this to Amélie instead.'

He looks like I've just whacked him across the face with my fist. Which I would absolutely never do. No matter how much he's hurt me I know he never meant to and I really do understand that he still cares. Unfortunately, just not enough.

'I've told Amélie everything, Jas. We've been talking all afternoon.'

Yep, I'll bet you have, I think. In between lots of other stuff that I try hard to push out of my mind.

'I can't help how I feel,' he goes on and his eyes are charcoal now and burning into my soul. 'I've never felt like this before, not about anybody.' He looks close to tears now as he adds, 'I'm really struggling here, Jas.'

I'm close to bloody tears myself, huge big puddles threatening to flood down my face if I don't get out of here and away from this heartache right now. I don't know why he's so cut up. Maybe Amélie doesn't feel the same. She did just kiss Shane after all. Or maybe she just has that effect on him. Turning his everything to mush. Exactly like he does with me. Whatever the reason, I can't be his shoulder to cry on and I need to make that clear before he blows my heart wide open and tramples it to a wasted pile of dust.

'I'm sorry, Niall, I get that you're having a hard time with whatever all this is. Honestly, I do. And it's not that I don't care.

I really hope we can still be friends although I do need a bit of space before I'm ready for that.'

His face is falling now, his whole body seems to be sagging to the ground, and I don't think I've ever seen him look so lost. Maybe Amélie is having second thoughts and maybe that is breaking his heart but I can't help him with that when I'm struggling to hold together my own.

'I'm sorry, Niall,' I say again as I lean against the door and edge back into the hall. 'I can't be what you need right now. I have to focus on me.'

He hangs his gorgeous dark head and my heart breaks a little bit more. But somehow, I find the strength that I need and I nod as solemnly as I'm able and pull closed the door. Then I slump in a heap on the floor and silently weep until every tear in my aching body has drained out and I'm a dried-up wreck on the cold hard tiles of Gran's hall.

35

My face is a mess by the time I've cycled home to Emmet Park. Between the tracks of my tears and the rawness of the hard, biting wind, I look like I've been battered by a storm. Mam is in the kitchen so I head upstairs and splash my face over and over with lukewarm water. Then I shout down to her that I'm wrecked and I'm going for a lie-down.

I throw on my favourite PJs. Cathy bought them for me last Christmas – soft pale grey with a big blue Eeyore on the front. I climb under the covers and count my breaths in and out like Niall showed me the first day he took hold of my hands. I feel like I'll never sleep peacefully again. But when I wake it's nearly eight o'clock and Mam's sitting on the end of my bed with a hot-water bottle and a dinner tray with a big hunk of buttery garlic bread and a plate of spag bol.

'You're the best mother in the world,' I tell her, and I mean every word. I may not have loads of money and I don't have much hope of my own house or the perfect man. But I got the best start in life that anyone could possibly want. I got buckets and buckets of love from my mother, my sister, and my gran.

Mam smiles and sets the tray on my lap as I pull myself up. It smells like heaven on a plate and my stomach is growling before I even lift my fork. She stays put and watches me eat. She folds one arm across her stomach and lifts the other to prop up her chin.

Then she looks at me as though she's working on a puzzle and trying hard to make the pieces all fit.

'Are you okay, Jas?' she asks. 'You've been working so hard, and I'm really proud of you.' She glances over to the hats laid out across Cathy's old study desk and her face is a mix of wonder and awe. I can see that she's really impressed.

'But you've been through so much. And it can't have been easy over in Galway on your own. It doesn't seem like Gabe was any real support.'

I lower my eyes and chew the inside of my lip. I don't want to even think about him. He's last on the list of the things that concern me right now and it only reminds me of so many lost, wasted years.

Mam seems to pick up on this straight away. 'But Gabe's in the past and you're right to put him out of your mind. You're still so young, love, and nothing is wasted. Everything you go through is a learning and it helps to form who you are.'

I manage half a smile and tell her she's not just the best mother, she's clearly the wisest one too.

She smiles wistfully and adds, 'And I know you really miss your Gran.'

One stray tear falls down my cheek and I nod.

She squeezes the bridge of her nose and peers at me hard. She has that look on her face when she's nearing the end of her puzzle and she knows she's really close, but there's one or two pieces she still needs to make sure she fixes everything in exactly the right place.

'It really seems to be inspiring your work too, being back in Ballyclane, in the Square, in your gran's.'

More tears follow and it feels like this is all I do these days, crawl under my covers, wallow in my wounds, and weep.

'I'm sorry, Mam,' I say. 'Take no notice. I'm fine really, just a bit drained. You're right, I have been working so hard but I need to stop all this moping. I'm twenty-eight now, not eight, and I have a lot to be grateful for. I need to get a grip on myself and focus on that.' I lift my tray with my now empty plates onto the bedside locker. Then I pull back the covers and climb out.

'And I will,' I insist, as much to myself as to Mam. 'I have a market to organise and a whole pile of fabulous hats to sell.' I stand up tall or at least as tall as my fairly average five-foot-six frame will allow. And even though I'm absolutely faking it I feel another trickle of hope seep into my weary, washed-out heart.

'I haven't fully decided yet about Gran's,' Mam says as I pull on my fleecy dressing gown and follow her down the stairs. 'Nothing is set in stone. I just need to think it all through a bit more and make sure that whatever decision I make is definitely for the best.'

We're at the bottom of the stairs and I reach out to take the tray from her hands because, honestly, she's carried everything long enough. And I'm well able to carry my own. She tries to hold on, of course, and she laughs and says, 'Ah, Jas, let me mammy you for just a little bit more. You've been gone for so long and I'm so happy you've decided to come home.'

'I'm happy too,' I tell her. And it's true that I am. At least a small part of me is, the part that needed to find my way back.

'But whatever you decide, Mam,' I say as I set the tray on the kitchen table and pull open the dishwasher door, 'Cathy and I will be fine with it. As long as you do what's right for you.'

36

I'm in the Square this morning thinking I should add a few men's hats to my collection, but I don't know where to start. Most of the guys my age wear wool beanies if they wear hats at all. Christy is very attached to his tweed flat cap all right but apart from that I can't see much of a market here in Ballyclane. Focus on what you're good at, Jas, I tell myself. No point wasting time on notions that may not be wanted or needed at all. If I have a few spare hours next year, I can always learn to knit properly. I definitely don't have time now, even if I have just wasted the last fifteen minutes staring out on to the Square, half-hoping to catch a stray glimpse of Niall.

It's Amélie, though, that I see strolling towards my window, swinging a buttery brown paper bag. Looks like croissants for breakfast again. Yum. I switch on the already full kettle and scoot out to open the door.

'Oh, *chérie*, I have the most wonderful news.' Amélie's beaming as always and she's wrapped in a cream fake-fur hat and matching padded jacket like she's just crossed the plains of Siberia, not skipped over from Coffee Spot to my gran's.

'Don't tell me.' I grin as I pull the door wide and usher her in. 'Elena added chocolate to the croissants this morning, especially for you.'

Her face lights up even more. 'She did, she did,' she exclaims as I wince. I hope there's no chocolate in mine, I don't fancy eating dessert for my first meal of the day.

'But that's not my news,' she goes on as she follows me down the hall and into the kitchen. 'Della is coming tomorrow for our shoot.' She leans back against the white ceramic sink and watches my face go from stunned silence to half-unbelieving joy.

'But how?' I sit down on one of Gran's solid kitchen chairs. 'What about Viva Vintage?' I shake my head and consider giving myself a pinch. Della, here in Ballyclane? She seems almost too stylish and exotic for this place. Then I picture the Square in the evening with the Christmas tree glowing and all the gorgeous multicoloured lights. And the lane with its amber-lit lanterns and the prettiest walled garden for miles. And I see Della swirling her long wool cape and flinging her arms wide and declaring it all absolutely perfect, darling, and I relax.

'Her sister and her niece are going to look after the shop for the day. Her niece has been helping out since you left so everything will be fine.' Amélie claps her hands excitedly then. 'And Della will be here with us, and she's bringing winter coats and capes and jewellery and accessories... '

I wave my hand in the air to slow Amélie down, she's getting so carried away with her enthusiasm that she's almost running out of breath.

I pat the nearest chair and say, 'Sit down, Am, you're making me feel dizzy.' I smile as she flops onto the chair and I get back up to switch on the kettle again and sort us some plates and mugs. I open the butter-greased paper bag and tip the croissants onto the largest plate. Two chocolate and two plain, thank God.

I make us a big pot of tea. Amélie still hasn't gotten used to the idea that we Irish use tea as a universal balm and cure for all ills. But she's coming around and doesn't pull a face when I pass her a good strong mug of my best brew. She's chomping on her croissant and wiping gooey chocolate from her lips when I ask what time Della will arrive.

Amélie swallows down the last of her mouthful and smiles. 'Tomorrow morning, she hopes about eleven o'clock. I've sent her some photos of the hats I'd like to include and maybe later we can go back to your house and pick out some more.'

'Sounds good.' I nod.

'She says if we send her shots of the hats that you most want to feature then she'll go through the pieces she's gathered and decide what suits.'

I don't even question this. Della could be styling for *Vogue* she's that good. She just has an eye for exactly what goes with what. And I've never heard anybody complain. I have my own style that's for sure, but it's not to everyone's taste. Like Maura and Tracey Hamilton and probably plenty more.

Now that Tracey has popped into my head, I want to be sure the malicious cow won't turn up when we're working on our shoot. I haven't seen her since Saturday night. I know Amélie doesn't know her but she seems to have befriended everybody else in the few days she's been here so I decide it's at least worth a shot.

'Do you remember that girl that arrived and joined Maura at the quiz?' I can't call her a woman, she's too immature. I'm not even sure I feel comfortable calling her a girl. Sometimes I think she's not human at all. I feel my jaw tightening as I go on. 'The very thin girl with the cropped red hair and the permanent sneer.'

That last word seems to trigger recognition and Amélie scowls. 'Ah, yes. She does not seem very nice.'

It's the first time I've seen Amélie scowl and the first time I've heard her say a cross word, although her version of cross is a long way from mine.

'Have you seen anything of her since? I'm wondering if she's still hanging around.'

Amélie shakes her head. 'No, Nadia told me she went back to Dublin for a few days. I think she's coming again on Thursday with her husband and staying with Maura until Sunday night.'

I can't help but twist my face in a grimace and I'm sure Amélie must think I'm in physical pain. But the nightmare flashing before my eyes feels like I'm being ripped limb from limb. Tracey Hamilton swanning around my market, with some fat-cat man on her arm. Picking apart all my hard work, then pouring absolute swill on my hats.

Amélie eyes me with concern. 'Don't worry about her, *ma chérie*. She is nothing.' She flicks her fingers a few times as though she has just ground Tracey to dust in her palms and is scattering her now to the winds. Christ, I wish I could do that. Before the evil wagon takes her chance to grind *me* down yet again.

I finish my work about four and Amélie and I walk along the main street and take the bridge across the narrow river that cuts through Ballyclane. Then we turn and head out the road that leads to Emmet Park. I'm a bit embarrassed by the number of boarded-up windows and derelict houses that line the main street. It's a long way from Paris and I wonder again how I can possibly grow my business here. Ballyclane doesn't scream style and success. But then I look beyond the broken glass and peeling paint and focus on the bones. There are beautiful buildings still standing and a rich heritage that runs deep. If I can't believe in my hometown and back that up by trying to make something of myself here, how can I expect anyone else to do the same?

'This is so nice,' Amélie says as we turn into my street. And as I see it through her eyes, I realise she has a point. Most of Mam's neighbours bought their houses from the council and have lived here for years, just like Mam, and there's a real sense of community and pride in keeping their homes looking well.

Mam's door is painted sage green and the holly-berry wreath that I bought for her is proudly on display. The timber porch overhang is dripping in warm white icicles and the bare branches of the crab-apple tree are decorated with twinkling lights. It's a bit early in the day but I texted Mam to say I'd be bringing Amélie around later to take photographs of my hats. She was home having lunch at the time so she said she'd do a quick tidy and switch on the Christmas lights so that it would feel welcoming for Amélie when she arrived. Mam is like Cathy, she's obsessively neat and clean, so I'm guessing she was talking about my room when she said she'd do a tidy-up. It can be haphazard, to say the least, but I really don't think Amélie will care.

I wave at Mrs Flood as she passes by in her car. 'That's Shane's mam,' I say. 'You remember my friend who you met on Saturday night. And spent the afternoon out at Oakwood getting to know even better,' I add with a smile.

'Ah yes, Shane. He is very kind. And so cute,' she says with a definite twinkle in her eye. 'But don't worry,' she adds with a swift wave of her hand, 'it was just a little kiss. Everything is good with me and Shane. He is sweet and fun and everybody needs that now and then.'

I can feel my eyes still narrowed and I'm trying hard not to judge. Yes, totally, I get it, everybody needs a little fun. But don't go messing with the people I care about most even if you don't mean to hurt anybody at all.

I twist my key in the lock and open the front door to let us in. Then I show Amélie down the hall into the kitchen and fill up the kettle for more tea. We're sitting across from each other at the island and Amélie has admired just about every inch of Mam's house. I take a sip of hot tea and sigh.

'Amélie, look, I get that you and Shane were just enjoying some harmless fun. I was worried you might hurt him but he seems to have taken it all in his stride.'

Amélie laughs but I'm still feeling quite serious about all this so I add, 'I'm really more concerned about Niall. I'm not sure what's going on with you two but he's a really good guy, please don't mess him about.'

'*Non, ma chérie*, you have nothing to worry about. Everything is good with Niall and me. It is perfect, in fact.' She squeezes her hands together and it feels like she's squeezing every last bit of hope from my heart. Not fine, not getting there, not working things out. Perfect. Of course, it is. Well, I guess that's that.

'And I know you don't want to talk about all this, about love, about affairs of the heart, when you have so much to do.' She gets up from her stool and dashes around the island to give me a hug. Then she pats my hair as though I'm a confused little girl and she's happy to sort it all out. 'We had coffee this afternoon and he explained about your talk. He is very sad, of course, but he does understand. He is very special, Jas. And maybe later when you are ready to consider it all and to talk, I am here. And so is Niall.'

I haven't a clue how I'm supposed to respond to all that so I don't. I just sip my tea and take a bite of one of the cheese sandwiches I made for us to snack on and wonder if Amélie has any clue what I'm going through. She does seem to be aware that I have feelings for Niall but I doubt she knows how deep they run. She probably thinks it was just a crush and doesn't understand why I can't let go, move on, and stay friends. I'm sure that's what Amélie would do but I have a feeling my heart is more fragile than hers.

'You're right,' I say firmly and I hop off my stool, lift the plate of sandwiches, and add, 'Let's take these upstairs and get started on those pics. There's so much still to do and I'd better get back to my work.'

37

I stroll through the lane at eleven to wait in the garden for Della to arrive. We've given her directions and explained that she can park down the back and then we'll have everything to hand for our shoot. I'm passing Coffee Spot when I glance in the front window and see Niall and Amélie chatting together in our usual window seat. Amélie gives me a wave so I decide to be grown-up about all of this and I head in and pull up a seat.

Niall looks up and swallows hard as I approach. 'Amélie tells me you two are planning a photoshoot today. And your friend Della is driving down from Galway to help.'

I nod and mumble yes and do my best to return Niall's hesitant smile. I don't want him to feel awkward or guilty. It's not his fault that we kissed. He was only trying to comfort me and he did pull back before I could get carried away. He wasn't to know that the love of his life was about to reappear. I'm sure he wouldn't have kissed me at all if he had any inkling of that.

He goes on, 'You're welcome to use the cottage and my garden too if you'd like more privacy. Or even just variety for your shots.'

'That's a wonderful idea.' Amélie reaches over and gives Niall's arm an excited squeeze and my chest tightens like it's been gripped too hard as well. Then she turns her eager face to me and waits.

It's not easy watching the two of them all happy and chatty and relaxed but Niall and I never made any commitment to each other. All we had was a few heart-to-hearts and one brief encounter that he ended almost as soon as it began. They don't owe me anything, yet they are both doing their best to support me, so I need to try to accept this situation with some sort of grace.

'That would be great, Niall,' I say. 'That's really kind of you, thanks.'

'No problem. Anything I can do to help, just ask.'

Amélie spots Della's car driving past the window and she's up and out of her seat and running out of the door so fast she makes my head spin. I edge back my chair and I'm about to stand up when Niall reaches his hand across the table and almost touches mine, but not quite. I stare down at our hands just inches apart then I look up and his eyes are searing into mine.

'If we can't be anything more, Jas, I really hope we can still be friends.'

There's a crack in his voice and it's clear that he never meant to hurt me and he does really care, even if he has chosen somebody else.

So, I swallow hard and nod and manage to croak out the words, 'Me too.' I scrape back my chair and tell him I'll see him tonight at our last market meeting. Then I follow Amélie out into the lane.

Della insists on doing our make-up and fixing our hair before we start, so Amélie suggests using Niall's place as he has already given her a key and told her to work away. I'm not sure how I feel about this so I say that we could just as easily get ready in my gran's.

'But, *ma chérie*, then we would have to walk all the way across the Square every time we need to make a change.' She wiggles her hands and gives a conspiratorial grin. 'And anyway, I want to see this mystery cottage for myself.'

My jaw drops but she and Della are already making for the gate before I get to ask. How have you not seen it already? I know you stayed at Niall's family home the first night but seriously, is that still where you're based now? Not even one little detour to check out the cottage, Niall's bedroom, or that fake sheepskin rug. I know Niall well enough by now to know that he likes to take care and do things the right way. But Amélie's a passionate soul and Niall's ridiculously hot. This isn't making much sense.

I follow them up the gravel path and it's hard to get them to focus on the shoot as they are both so blown away by Niall's house. If Amélie hasn't pinned him down yet, it won't be much longer. By the look in her eyes as she takes in the downstairs, she can already picture herself moving in.

Her eyes flash to the stairs and she goes, 'Ooh, I'd love to see up there.'

I'll bet you would, Amélie, and if I'm being absolutely honest, so would I. But this is Niall's home and he has been really good to allow us in when he's not here and part of me feels really protective even though he's obviously not mine.

'So would I but that wouldn't be fair. That's Niall's private space and I'm sure he trusts us to respect that.'

'Of course, *ma chérie*.' Amélie beams. 'And he'll show you when you're ready, I'm sure.'

I shake my head in bewilderment. Amélie is so lovely but sometimes it's like she's from another planet. Why would Niall take me upstairs now that she's back? She may like to dabble elsewhere, like Shane, but that's definitely not Niall's style. And if she thinks I'm up for a threesome, she can bloody well think again.

*

We model three hats each and Della styles us for every shot. I'm in my dusky pink baker-boy, an enormous rust-coloured floppy, and my favourite green velvet bucket hat that I managed to rescue that awful afternoon. Della channels Twiggy in a stripey-coloured scooter hat, a paisley primrose headband, and a champagne cloche. Amélie's a Parisian angel in a raspberry beret, charcoal felt fedora, and scarlet pillbox with a delicate veil. We take some pics in the lane garden leaning against the pear tree and standing by the ivy-covered wall. But most of our shots are set up in Niall's. The backdrop is similar with gravel paths and ivy-covered stone but there are no prying eyes to make us feel self-conscious as we flounce and twirl and throw shapes. Or maybe that's just me, I don't think Della or Amélie really care. I'm grateful too for our crazy Irish weather: heavy floods in August, raging storms in October, and crisp clear sunshine on this perfect December day. It's looking good for the weekend too. At least some things are going my way.

Della borrowed her girlfriend's Volvo as her own Mini Cooper couldn't hold the volume of clothes, make-up and accessories she packed in. She makes us change outfits, jewellery, and even some of our make-up for each hat. It's half past three by the time we're finished and I'm glad I'm not modelling full-time. I'm so exhausted I want to lie down on Niall's bench and take a nap. But it's time for us to pack up. Della has to drive back to Galway and Amélie wants to tidy Niall's parents' house as they are due to fly back from Portugal tonight. She says she's had the place to herself since she arrived.

I'm thinking that sounds unlikely. I'm sure Lily and Jack have plenty of spare bedrooms with giant comfy beds for her and Niall. No wonder they haven't made it to the cottage yet. That thought drops a concrete brick in my stomach and banishes all notions of napping at Niall's. I need to get home to Emmet Park, wash off Della's movie set make-up, and get my head in some sort of shape to face the final market meeting tonight.

I say my thank yous and goodbyes and collect my bike from Gran's hall. I'm almost home when it occurs to me that Niall's parents seem to spend a lot of time in Portugal and I remember that Niall was there not long ago too. Maybe one of them has arthritis like Donal and needs the heat. Or maybe they just have so much spare cash that they have a holiday home out there as well as the mansion in the Square. My head starts to ache as I think about how hard it is for me and most of my generation to rent a basic one-bedroom flat, never mind buy a place of our own.

Then I feel a bit mean as I remember Cathy saying that Niall's parents used their own money to help people hoodwinked by Freddie. And Mam always said any property Jack had a hand in was solid and well-built and that he was a good hard-working man. But I'm a good hard-working woman and I'm still broke and crashing in my sister's old room. Where's the justice in that? I turn my key in the lock and go straight to the kitchen to fill the kettle. I need to lie down for an hour with a couple of Ibuprofen and a huge mug of tea to wash my headache away.

38

I have a nap and then get back up and make a chicken pasta bake so that it's ready for Mam when she comes in. She's still working full-time until she sells the house and I think she's starting to find the long days tough. We have a good laugh over dinner as she tells me about some of the scatty customers she had to deal with today. She says people lose their heads this time of year planning and preparing and buying up everything in sight. She's going to keep it simple she says. Turkey, ham and Christmas pudding and one present each. And she's told Cathy and Donal the same.

'You can give us each a nice hat,' she says.

'If I have any left.' I grin. 'If the market goes well, I might be sold out.'

'I wouldn't be the least bit surprised,' she tells me with a proud smile.

'I might stick with socks for Donal and Brian though. I'm not sure I can picture Donal in a powder-pink beret.'

She shakes her head with a laugh, and says, 'Ah, love, I'm so glad you're home.'

'Me too.' I glance at the kitchen clock as I start clearing plates. 'But I'd better grab my stuff and run or I'll be late.'

'Oh.' Mam looks disappointed. 'I forgot you had the meeting. I was hoping to talk to you about Gran's house.'

She looks serious now and I wish I could stay. I hate to see Mam worried or upset. But it's the last meeting before Saturday and I am supposed to be in charge, I absolutely can't be late. I won't give Maura Maguire the satisfaction for a start.

'Tomorrow night, Mam, I promise. I really have to go.'

'Okay, pet,' she says, as she waves me away from the dishes. 'I'm going to see the estate agent tomorrow afternoon to let her know what I've decided and we can chat about it all tomorrow night.'

I grab my duffel and tote from the hook in the hall and make for the door. I turn back just before I leave to reassure her. 'By the way, Mam, whatever you decide, it'll be okay. I'll be fine.'

I'm last in to the meeting and I'm waiting for a catty comment from Maura but all she gives me is a shy smile. I'm a bit taken aback but maybe spending so much time with Nadia is starting to rub off. Nadia has brought her mother along too so we're all introductions for a few minutes before we get down to business and Christy pours the tea. It's a full house tonight as Amélie and Niall are here too, so Christy goes to refill the kettle and make a second pot. He seems to thrive on keeping busy and doing his bit. I swear if this was the North Pole, he'd be Santa's right-hand elf.

It's a long meeting as we go over all the details and any last-minute additions. I've ordered extra outdoor tents as we did really well at the quiz and then the credit union offered us some sponsorship money to help out. I hadn't even asked them as I thought we were too late, but the manager was at the quiz and when she heard about all the free children's activities we have planned, she said it was exactly the sort of programme they want to support.

Nadia and her mother tell me they would like to have some games as well as story time and face-painting. And maybe some blowing bubbles as children always love that. They have a book with them from the library with all the old favourites but they're worried it will be too much for them on their own.

'We'll have some of Brian's students for face-painting,' I reassure them. 'And I have the perfect volunteer to help with the games – my friend Shane.' I see Amélie's eyes crinkle in a smile. 'He loves kids and he helps out at all his nieces' and nephews' parties. He's a big kid himself and he's always in charge of the games.'

Shane has three sisters, one younger and two older. The older two are married and I've lost track of how many children they have between them but Shane seems to dote on them all. And he did say he would do anything to help. Nadia is delighted and asks me if this is the friend who was sitting with me at the quiz. I tell her it is and it occurs to me then that I forgot to introduce her to Shane that night. I was so busy watching his reaction to Amélie, Niall's reaction to Amélie, and all our reactions to Tracey, and poor Nadia got lost in the mix.

We go over everything one more time and I'm happy that everything is on track. Niall says he has to go as he hasn't seen his parents since they got back from Portugal and they need to have a chat. Maura asks him to tell Lily to give her a call tomorrow morning about meeting for coffee as she would like a chat with her too. Then she shoots me a meaningful look. I have no idea what the meaning is supposed to be but something to do with Tracey is my guess. I feel my confidence start to fade and I catch Niall looking over at me as well. He's reading my mind again, I can feel it, and then he asks Maura straight out if his cousin is still staying at her house.

I already know she's gone home for a few days but also that she's due back tomorrow and will be here for the market. And here to mess with my head. Then Maura throws a curveball that I really did not expect.

'Hmph,' she starts as though she's talking about me. 'She's in Dublin, I think. But I believe she is due back for the weekend. She won't be staying with me, though. I have a full house with Nadia and Sofia and they are my priority now.' She gives Nadia's mum a warm smile. 'There's a perfectly good bed and breakfast over at Riverdale. I'm sure Tracey will be very comfortable there.' Then she starts to pack away her notebook and pens as if that's all there is to be said.

I've gotten used to my weekly wind-downs at Gallagher's and I'm a bit disappointed that Niall has ruled himself out. Even though I've accepted that nothing can happen between us, he did say he wanted us to stay friends. I ask Amélie if she fancies a drink and she claps her hands in an enthusiastic yes. It occurs to me then that I've forgotten about Nadia again.

'Would you like to join us, Nadia?' I ask. 'We won't stay late, just one or two drinks. Amélie and I can walk you back to Beechwood after.'

Maura looks at me as though she's ready to give me a hug and I take a step back just in case. She definitely seems softer tonight, whatever's going on with her, but I don't think I'm ready for that.

'That's a lovely idea. Oh, you must go, Nadia, it will do you good to get out. And just text me when you're ready and I'll drive over to collect you.' She turns to Amélie and me. 'I can drop you girls home too if you like.'

Bloody hell. 'That's okay, Maura,' I say. 'Thanks, but Amélie's only across in the Square and I have my bike so I'll be fine.'

39

I insist on buying the first round as I'm feeling flush for a change. Veronica was taking a break in the garden when we started our photoshoot yesterday and she fell in love with the stripey scooter hat Della was modelling. She says her teenage daughter will absolutely love it so she asked if she could buy it after we took our photos for the shoot. I was delighted but I hadn't a clue what to charge so Della stepped in. I'm still a bit shocked at the price but Veronica was more than happy to pay and she does do a roaring trade in that florist so I don't think she's short of cash.

I order a glass of Guinness each for myself and Amélie, and a white wine for Nadia, and we grab a booth down the back. There's a gorgeous fire in the stove across the way so we peel off our coats and settle in for a chat.

'Maura seems in a very good mood, for a change,' I say to Nadia as she sips her wine.

'You mean she's in a good mood with you?' Nadia looks pleased and it occurs to me again that this definitely has something to do with her, although maybe not in the way I first assumed.

'Have you said anything to her, maybe put in a good word?' I ask. 'She didn't bite my head off tonight. Not once. And she seems to have gone right off that cow, Tracey Hamilton, too.'

Nadia pauses a beat then looks at me kindly and says, 'I was in the toilet when Tracey was saying all those horrible things, Jas.'

She blinks slowly and adds, 'She is cruel and mean. I wanted to go after you but you left so quickly that I couldn't catch up.'

Oh God, oh God, oh God. I feel the colour rise in my cheeks and my eyes start to well up. I'm so bloody mortified that anybody overheard us that I just want to crawl under this table and die. Well, maybe not die, but at least take a very long break.

Amélie's gaze darts from Nadia to me and she wraps one arm around me and asks what on earth happened and tells me that whatever it was it will all be okay.

I really, really don't want to talk about it. Even if I did, I just can't. Whenever Tracey Hamilton comes into my head my whole body freezes up.

But Nadia is determined to get it out there. To tell Amélie what a bitch Tracey is and even though I hate hearing it all again, I listen to her recount Tracey's words and I hear her fury at what she overheard. And I hear Amélie's horror and her rage and I realise that nobody thinks Tracey is right in all this. Nadia tells us that Tracey was rude to both her and her mother and Maura noticed and was really annoyed. She asked Nadia what she thought of Tracey and Nadia told her everything, including what happened in Gallagher's toilets that night and how I was so upset that I ran straight home.

I'm still so embarrassed. I feel like a pathetic little kid. I should be well able to stand up to the Tracey Hamiltons of this world and, to be honest, I always thought I was. It's just with everything else going pear-shaped, all the snide comments and digs about me being trash and nobody wanting me really hit home.

'I just can't believe she's coming back for the market,' I blurt out. 'She's bound to diss everything, especially my stall. She'll do her best to put everybody off buying my hats.'

Amélie dabs the creamy Guinness from her lips, arches her eyebrows, and says, 'Ah, perhaps not.'

If you think you can get Tracey to switch personalities overnight and cheerlead my hats or at least back the feck off, go ahead. That's what I feel like saying to Amélie but I just ask, 'What do you mean?'

'The only person Tracey seems to be in touch with here is Maura. So, as long as Maura hasn't told her about your hats – ' Amélie pauses and looks over at Nadia – 'and as long as we make sure she doesn't tell her… ' Nadia nods and gives Amélie the thumbs up. It looks like she's on for that task.

'Then I will manage your stall on my own,' Amélie continues. 'And we can make sure that Tracey thinks the hats are my designs. Tracey doesn't know I am your friend. I was sitting with Niall on Saturday night so she will assume I am here for him.'

That makes sense, I assumed the same myself. But clearly, I was wrong. It's not *only* Niall that she's here for. Amélie has pretty much dedicated herself to helping *me* since the day she arrived. She's an angel, I tell myself again.

She flicks her golden curls and lifts her chin. 'I am working with an up-and-coming designer and we are going undercover for a feature in a top Paris fashion magazine. We are trying to test if Irish women have true style and fashion sense by seeing how they respond to these fabulous hats.' Amélie laughs wickedly and I tell her she may look like an angel but I can see now there's a bit of a devil in there too.

She presses one finger lightly to the side of her nose and adds, 'And I will whisper all this to Tracey in absolute confidence, of course. I can be charming, you know. Perhaps I will even offer to make her a very special price.'

'I'm not having that cow wear one of my hats!'

Nadia giggles and Amélie laughs even more. '*Ma chérie*, she won't wear it, not when we tell her it's yours. But wouldn't it be nice to hear her admit how beautiful it is and then hand over lots and lots of her cash? Surely, it is better in your pocket than hers.'

I lift my empty glass and clink Amélie's. Fair point, I suppose.

Nadia hops up and insists on getting one more round to celebrate our plans and we spend the next half hour chatting about her job at the crèche and Amélie's work for her magazine, which it turns out is mostly online. Amélie also gives me advice on the best options for promoting my hats when the market is over, and before we even finish our drinks, we're all starting to yawn and we agree that it's time to go home. Nadia texts Maura and Maura says she'll be outside in five. I haven't seen Nadia so cheerful since I met her. She usually has a kind smile but there's always sadness in her eyes. Despite all our talk about Tracey, there's a lightness to Nadia tonight and I resolve to make more of an effort in future and invite her along whenever we go out.

We say our goodbyes and I hop on my bike. And despite Tracey Hamilton's return, and the fact that I'm fairly sure I've lost whatever chance I might have had with Niall, I feel a bit more light-hearted too.

40

I feel a lot more able to face whatever comes my way as I sit at my worktable this morning. I have a few last-minute finishing touches to make to some hats then I'm going to take it easy for the afternoon. I'll text the stallholders one last time tomorrow morning to confirm that we're all good to go. Then Amélie and I are going to plan my stall and how we'll display my hats. The forecast for Saturday is good, considering it's the middle of December. Cold but clear and bright which is exactly what I've been hoping for all along. We're going to set my stall up outdoors. We've designated the wall between the whitewashed cottages and the garden for a row of tent-covered tables. And I'm going to place my table at the meeting room end so that it's perfectly visible to everybody coming in and out.

Amélie asked Della to bring some antique brass hooks from her shop and she's going to use them to hang a selection of hats on Gran's cream louvred screen. Della also brought two mannequin heads for us to use. Amélie says she'll rotate different hats on these throughout the day depending on her mood and any potential customers she sees hovering nearby. It feels a bit weird handing over so much control but I know my hats will be in the best hands. And it will give me time to make sure the whole market runs smoothly and the space to watch people's reactions to my designs.

Amélie has plans with Lily this morning. They're off to see an exhibition in the library called 'Navigation'. It explores the artist's quest to find her place in the world. As soon as this market is done and I have time to breathe, I'll be over to take a look at that myself. I could do with a few tips.

By eleven o'clock my hats are ready as they only need minor tweaks. I text Niall to ask if he's taking a break and if he would like some company for coffee. He and Amélie have been so supportive and they deserve to be happy so it's time for me to woman up and learn how to be a real friend. If Shane can get over two unrequited loves and still turn up on Saturday with a smile to help us both out, then I can at least try to forget one teeny heart-melting kiss.

Free for coffee anytime soon? I type and hit send.

Just finishing off a paint job on one of the lane cottages. Half past?

Perfect, see you in Coffee Spot in half an hour.

I make some toast and spread it with peanut butter to eat before I go. Elena's croissants and scones are fab but I can barely afford the coffee never mind all this eating out. I may have splashed a tenner in Gallagher's last night but that was medicinal for my mental health. I need to keep whatever money I make to use for building up my business. That's presuming I have a business to build. I'll have to see how Saturday goes.

Niall's scrolling through his phone when I arrive. His long black lashes shade his eyes and there's a trace of dark stubble along his jaw. I give myself a mental kick to remind me that he's Amélie's now and I need to erase the image forming in my brain. Or if I do have to picture him then I can at least give the poor guy some clothes.

I'm still staring hard when his eyes flick to mine.

'Hey, Jas, are you okay?'

'Hi, yeah, sorry, I'm in another world.' I pull out a chair and give Elena a wave. I need a glass of iced water fast to cool down.

I order the water and a latte and ask Niall how things are with him.

'Crazy busy. Bit like yourself,' he says. 'That's the problem with fixing up old houses, you're never finished. There's always another job to do.'

I don't mean to sigh quite so hard but it seems to pour out of me. I'm about to nod and sympathise when Niall leaps back in.

'But don't let that put you off. I'm just having one of those weeks. I love the work and it's definitely worth it in the end.'

I'm about to ask, *put me off what?* But then I spot the blob of paint covering the tip of his left ear and the rip running down the sleeve of his top, and I can't help but laugh.

'I'm sorry,' I tell him, 'but have you looked in the mirror in the last hour or so?'

His brows crease in a frown as though I've completely lost the plot.

'Hmm, well, let's just say you're not living up to the posh boy image I had of you the first time we met.' I reach over and lightly tap his ear then give his left sleeve a quick tug.

'Big daub of paint. Decent size tear.'

He glances down at his sleeve and grins. 'Christ, I am in a state.' He doesn't seem that bothered, though, as he rolls his eyes and adds, 'Ah well, all part of the job.'

Then he frowns again and says, 'Posh boy image? Is that what you think?'

'Ah, no. Maybe at first.'

He leans back into the window seat and his eyes are wide as he waits for me to elaborate. I'm trying hard to focus but all I can think about is how I never realised his eyebrows were so dark. I want to sound empathetic and reasonable and all those things a proper friend should be.

'Well, in fairness, your folks are hardly short of cash.' Aargh, no. That's not what I meant to say at all.

Niall's eyebrows nearly reach his hairline now and he looks a bit hurt. Or maybe annoyed. I'm not exactly sure.

'Sorry, sorry, I don't know what I'm talking about. It's just, you know, the huge house, the trips to Portugal. I presume they have a place out there?' There's a tiny sane voice somewhere at the back of my brain screaming, *Shut up*. But it's not bloody loud enough because before I can stop myself, I point out of the window at the lane and go on, 'And, all that.'

Niall leans one elbow on the table and presses his forehead hard into his palm. Then he looks up and straight into my eyes and slowly shakes his head.

'*All that* belongs to the banks as much as it does to me and Dad. And I'm working round the clock to try to make it worth our while. My parents don't own property abroad because my dad poured everything he made back into his business and most of his profits went into sorting out somebody else's mess.'

I swallow hard. I know exactly who he means. His bastard uncle Fred. I'm about to apologise again but Niall's not finished at all.

'Mam does want Dad to buy a place in Portugal. To take him away from all the stress. They've been looking at a house in a little fishing village and Mam loves it. But they can't afford to buy that and keep up the house in the Square. It's too big for them now and way too expensive to maintain.'

'Oh. Does that mean…?' I can't quite bring myself to ask.

'Does that mean my parents plan to sell? I don't know, Jas. We're going through all the options. But nothing has been decided yet.'

I almost say that sounds a bit like what I'm going through with Mam. But I think I've said more than enough and God knows what will actually come out if I open my mouth. I just reach out and take hold of his hand and hold it tight. He doesn't pull away and then his thumb gently caresses mine. He blinks very slowly and then gives me a look that makes me forget we're in a crowded coffee shop or even a world with anybody else but me and Niall.

Then I hear Amélie's sparkly laugh and I turn to see her and Lily coming through the door. I pull my hand back like I've been given an electric shock. Niall jerks his head and narrows his eyes as though I've done something odd and he's trying to figure out why.

Eh, the love of your life and your mother just walked in. That's why. I don't think they'd be impressed to find you holding hands and exchanging meaningful looks with me. Or maybe I'm inventing meaning in my head where there really wasn't any at all. I think I should steer clear of men and relationships for the rest of my days. This is all just too bloody hard.

41

I'm back at Gran's and I have a couple of hours to spare before I have to meet up with Amélie and Lily again. Niall introduced me to his mother as soon as she arrived and she and Amélie were buzzing about their plans for the afternoon. They've decided to decorate Niall's cottage for Christmas. And, somehow, I've been roped in. Not exactly chilling on the couch with a few episodes of *Friends* and a big pot of tea like I'd hoped.

I did tease him that it was a bit of a cop-out, and old-fashioned, to expect the women to fix up his house. He just held his hands up and grinned and said, 'Nothing to do with me, I wasn't planning to decorate this year. I don't have the time and, besides, I've only just moved in.'

Lily said she wants to clear out all the old decorations that have been clogging up the attic since Niall was a child. And, as she basically bought them for him anyway, he might as well have them now. Niall just shrugged and said, 'Grand.' But I wonder if he's concerned that she's doing a clear-out to get the place ready in case she does decide to sell. Maybe his life isn't quite as charmed as I assumed.

I'll be sick of decorating by the time Christmas comes. Maura has already donated lights, baubles, and a ginormous fake snow-flocked tree for the meeting room. She says her husband, Seamus, used to go completely over the top but she prefers the minimalist look. She's had the overflow stashed in the attic since he died but she couldn't face sorting them until now. I think having Nadia and Sofia to help made all the difference as she didn't have to go through it on her own.

Amélie and I have volunteered to decorate the meeting room tomorrow and Christy and his daughter are going to put up the outdoor lights. The tent rental crowd are due at some ungodly hour on Saturday morning and Niall has offered to oversee the tents going up. Then he and Brian are going to collect the extra tables from the school. And we'll all meet at ten to lay those out and sort the finishing touches before we open at noon.

All these thoughts about decorating make me realise I haven't put a single ornament up in Gran's. No tree, no lights, not even a candle in the window. I think I was subconsciously trying to keep the house less welcoming for any viewers eyeing up to buy. There haven't been any this week. I suppose it's not the time of year to consider a move. I look around the front room and think how disappointed Gran would be to see me sitting here without any trace of Christmas at all. I'm surprised she hasn't sent me a sign. Then I remember the robin at the back door this morning when I went to take out the bin. I even put out a small bowl of water and some blueberries in case it had come looking for food.

I go straight upstairs to the spare bedroom. I know Gran stored all her Christmas stuff in boxes under the bed. I drag everything out and choose a selection of lights, a miniature pine tree, some snow globes, and half a dozen pillar candles, and I haul my stash downstairs to decorate Gran's front room.

I finish my decorating and heat up some soup. Then I sit at the table by the window and admire my work. I've placed the miniature pine tree on the side table and lined up the candles and snow globes on the mantelpiece with holly sprigs and a string of warm white lights. I've arranged more holly and lights in the front window with a red pillar candle in the centre. It definitely looks more welcoming now.

I have my soup and brown soda bread and stroll over to the lane to see if Amélie and Lily are about. I'm making my way down to the garden when I see Niall sitting in his jeep. I wave and he rolls down the window and leans out.

'Hey.' He gives me what looks like a slightly mortified smile. 'I'm so sorry my mum has dragged you into decorating my house.' He winces and goes on, 'I would do it myself, but I have to meet with an architect this afternoon.' He points over to the cottages and adds, 'And between the lane and the market, and trying to figure out viable options for Mum and Dad, I honestly don't have the time.'

He does sound a bit overwhelmed so I laugh and say, 'It's fine, really, it'll be fun. I like looking around other people's houses. It'll give me a chance to have a good snoop.'

Niall laughs now too and bats me away with a wave. 'Snoop away, Jas. I don't have anything to hide.'

No, you really do seem to be an open book, I think to myself. I just didn't make it to the library in time and somebody else was lucky enough to check you out first. Although, the sample I managed to get my hands on was definitely five stars.

Niall's about to drive off when he pulls up, rolls down the window again, and calls out, 'Things should ease off after the market, though, so I was thinking of inviting everybody around to the cottage on Saturday night to wind down.'

'Everybody?' I didn't mean to but I know I've just grimaced and by the look on Niall's face, I'm an open book too. Unfortunately, in my case, that's a horror story at times.

'I don't mean everybody,' he reassures me. 'Just the committee and Cathy and Brian. And Bernie and Donal, and anyone else who helped out.'

Okay, that sounds more reasonable. I don't think I'd have the energy for a crowd after traipsing around the market all day. I definitely won't have the energy for his cousin but I don't feel like saying her name, so I don't ask.

'Sounds good.' I nod. 'Do you want us to bring anything? A bottle? Some food?'

'No, absolutely not. Just bring yourself.' Niall smiles. 'I'll get beer in. And Mum has offered to buy wine. She says it's a thank you to the committee as she loves the market and she's so glad it's happening after all. And Dad's going to make a veggie curry and beef stroganoff. He's been getting into cooking since Mum made him take a step back from the business. I think he wants to show off his skills.'

Niall drives away and there's a spring in my step as I carry on through the garden. I'm picturing the cottage and his pergola with the enormous picnic bench. I can see it all covered with warm twinkling lights and Niall standing by the porch with that gorgeous soft smile. Then Amélie appears in my vision and slots into place by his side and I'm roaring in my head, *No! No! Get out! That's not how it's supposed to be at all.* But she's definitely there now and it is how this story seems to end. And I wouldn't erase her, even if I could. She's been so generous and supportive and kind and I couldn't bear to break her heart even if she is breaking mine.

It feels like I've manifested her into place as the wrought-iron gate opens in front of my eyes and Amélie beckons for me to come inside. She's holding a cardboard box overflowing with tangled-up lights.

'Ah, *ma chérie*, come, come.' She looks over my shoulder and waves. 'I'm just waiting for Lily, and here she is. I forgot I gave Niall back his key.'

Lily waves at us both. She's carrying another cardboard box and as she reaches us, she passes this to me and hands Amélie the key. 'You go ahead and drop these, please,' she says, 'and then meet me back in the Square. The tree is still at the top of the stairs and I'll need help carrying it down.'

I smile and accept the box and say, 'Sure.'

I'm finally going to get a peek inside Niall's childhood home. Maybe see photographs of him as a kid on the walls, a glimpse of how he was formed. I probably sound like a lunatic stalker but for some crazy reason, anything that makes me feel closer to him gives me a warm, fuzzy feeling inside. Of course, Amélie will be right there with me looking at the same memories too. Yep, it's confirmed. I'm an absolute lost cause and I definitely am going nuts.

We collect the tree and more boxes of decorations and lights. I barely get to glance at the row of family photos lining the hall. Lily's all business and we're in and out in a flash and back down the lane. She can't wait to get to work on decorating Niall's place. She's so determined that the cottage will be Christmassy and welcoming when everybody arrives on Saturday night.

We set up the Christmas tree first. It's tall and slim and fits perfectly into the deep alcove to the side of the stove. It's in great condition and Lily insists on decorating in green, red and gold. I notice these are the only colours in the boxes anyway and then I remember that the tree in her hall was decked purely in various shades of gold. And she's dressed in classic camel and black. She clearly likes to keep things simple and I wonder what she'll make of the kaleidoscope of colour on my market hat stall.

By the time we've almost finished, Niall's kitchen-living room looks good enough to feature in one of those Christmassy photoshoots for some ideal home magazine. There are sprigs of holly everywhere. There's a basket of logs next to the wood-burning stove, and paper and kindling, and even firelighters ready to light. And every lantern, candle and bauble is white, gold, or garnet red.

I pop to the bathroom while Amélie fills the kettle and Lily empties the last cardboard box. By the time I return there's a range of Christmas-themed wooden signs hanging on the kitchen walls telling me to *have myself a merry little Christmas*, *don't get my tinsel in a tangle,* and, of course, *just believe*. I wasn't expecting these from Lily but they are all tasteful winter white, deep rich red, and beautifully made. Lily seems especially proud of her signs and I get now where Niall's fondness for those inspirational T-shirts was formed.

Amélie pours the tea and I tease her that her brew is so good she's an honorary Irishwoman now. Lily mentioned something earlier about having a snack. My stomach is growling now and I'm about to ask her if it's okay to root in the cupboard for a biscuit when the most incredible warm spicy smell wafts in. Cinnamon, ginger and cloves. My mouth starts watering and my nose is almost pulling me out of the door when Niall's dad, Jack, walks through carrying a foil-covered tray.

He's so like Niall I'm taken aback. I've seen him from a distance but I never registered who he was or got close enough to have a really good look. He has that same solid, grounded presence and the same kind eyes. Nothing like his brother, Tracey's father, at all. Not a trace of a sneer. I shiver as the toxic strain of the Hamiltons bleeds into my brain.

Jack seems to notice straight away that something's not right. He leans forward, sets his tray on the island, and looks at me with concern.

'Are you okay, Jas? You look a bit pale. Has my wife been overworking you?' he adds with a smile.

I try to pull myself together and straighten on my stool. 'No, no, not at all.'

Lily laughs and hands me a plate of gingerbread with a big dollop of cream. She insists that I sit down on the floppy blue couch and put my feet up to rest. Then she starts telling Jack how I've been working really hard, that I'm wonderfully talented, and how proud they should be to have such a gifted milliner in the town. I do as I'm told and move over to the couch. I don't actually lie down but I'm not far off. I have to lean into the soft, deep cushions for support. I don't know what has come as more of a shock – the fact that Lily thinks I'm gifted when I didn't know she was aware of my hats, or the realisation that Niall's dad actually knows my name. Maybe I'm not quite so invisible as I thought.

42

I managed to drag myself off Niall's comfy couch and Amélie and I are crossing the Square when I see Mam outside Gran's chatting to Jennifer O'Neill, the estate agent looking after the sale. My heart sinks in my chest but I force a tight smile and a wave. Amélie tells me to go home and get some rest and she'll meet me tomorrow morning in the lane.

When I reach her, Mam tells me she's on her way to Cathy's and she'll chat to me as soon as she gets home and we'll have a good talk. I feel my heart sag all the way down to the cracked worn footpath in front of Gran's house. As I approached, I overheard Jennifer say that she thought Mam had made the right choice and she wanted to wish her well. I suppose Mam is off to Cathy's to fill her in on this decision before she shares it with me. *That's okay, Mam*, I think. By the look of satisfaction on Jennifer's face, I already have a fair idea what it is.

I collect my bike from the hall and cycle home to Emmet Park. I fill a warm bath and throw in some lavender salts. I change into my Eeyore PJs afterwards and climb into bed. The lavender has made me sleepy and taken the chill from my bones, but it hasn't done much for the gnawing ache in my heart. I close my eyes and list all the things I have to be grateful for. My family, Amélie, Shane, this warm comfy bed. I know there's way more, and making myself do this does really help, but that's as far as I get then I'm asleep.

*

I reach for my phone when I wake on Friday morning and see that it's past ten o'clock. Mam will be long gone to work and I hope she doesn't think I'm avoiding our chat. I honestly do want her to make the best decision for her. And even though it will hurt like hell to say goodbye to Gran's home, if it means life will be easier for Mam, then I'll get over it and do my best to move on. I fill a flask with oat milky coffee and pack some of Mam's scones in my tote. That's breakfast sorted, at least.

I'm on my bike in the middle of the road indicating for the Square when I see Niall standing by the Christmas tree talking to Jennifer O'Neill and some woman in a long black puffer with a big furry hood. The guy in the tangerine Corolla who's been flashing at me to go ahead honks loudly on his horn. I turn into the Square and I'm about to give Niall a wave when the puffer turns around and I almost fall off my bike. And vomit on the spot. It's Tracey bloody Hamilton and she's staring straight at Gran's. Niall obviously hasn't copped me despite that idiot blasting so loud. He's shaking his head and pointing up at Gran's roof. Is he seriously giving that wagon advice? Tracey definitely has seen me now and the ice in her glare sends shivers down my spine. She can't, can't, can't seriously be thinking of buying my gran's.

Jennifer nods seemingly in agreement with Niall, then I see her fold her arms across her chest and look incredibly smug as she turns back to Tracey to give her some sort of speech. I try my best to lip-read but I can't make out the words. I presume she's justifying a high sales price as Tracey doesn't look too impressed. I'm still feeling queasy so I lean on my bike as I head for the lane. I turn one last time before I walk through the arch and Niall cops me at last and calls out across the Square. Then Jennifer gives me a big friendly wave. I don't wave or call back; I just return Tracey's scowl and face towards the lane.

My legs won't cooperate and I don't make much progress before Niall catches up. He's all cheeriness and smiles as he says, 'Hi, Jas, I suppose you can guess what all that was about.'

My throat aches as I swallow and blink back bitter tears. 'Yes, I'm sure I can. But I am a bit surprised, I didn't expect you to help.'

Niall narrows his eyes and it's clear he still doesn't get how much this hurts so I add, 'Especially not after I told you how I feel.'

'But I meant what I said, Jas. No matter what else happens I want us to be friends.'

'Friends don't betray each other, Niall.' I give him a look that could rival Tracey's glacial glare. 'Not to bitches like her. Although I suppose you are blood.'

Niall's jaw drops and his eyes widen as he stands in front of me, looking like I've just told him his world is about to end.

'Is that really what you think?' he finally says. 'Have you not spoken to your mum?'

'Leave my mam out of this,' I practically spit. 'She doesn't know anything about Tracey and I don't intend to spoil her plans.' Then my tears start to flow and I can't help but blurt out, 'I could have made something special with Gran's house. If anybody believed in me. But nobody does.'

I rub hard at my face to wipe off my tears and I'm about to turn away when Niall stares straight into my eyes.

'I believe in you, Jas. I've believed in you since the first time I saw you that day at your gran's.' Then he stares down at the frosty gravel and adds in a low choky voice, 'I just wish that you felt the same way about me.'

43

I told Amélie I'd wait for her in the meeting room but I drag myself down to the garden instead. Niall went straight to his jeep and drove off after my outburst and that odd stuff he said. What's the point of telling me he believes in me when he basically dumped me for Amélie, and now he's siding with Tracey against me and my gran? I know that doesn't make sense, Gran's been dead for more than two years. But I feel her with me in that house and I can't bear the thought of Tracey taking hold and wiping her out.

I'm huddled on a bench down the back, clutching my coffee, and feeling shattered to bits when Amélie appears. I don't see her approach. I'm staring hard at the ground, wishing I could dig a big hole and climb right in.

She doesn't ask me what's wrong. She just flops down beside me and gives me one of her lovely warm hugs. No wonder Niall went running right back. She's the sweetest person I've ever met and only an icy black heart could resist.

Speaking of icy black hearts, Amélie tells me that she saw Tracey just now in the Square.

'She didn't look very happy,' Amélie says. 'Did you two speak?'

'Nope. That's just her resting face. Miserable bitch.' I don't elaborate or say anything about Niall. I don't want to cause trouble between them and from what he said earlier he doesn't seem to think that he's done anything wrong. Maybe he does genuinely believe he's just helping Mam to make a good sale.

I remind myself that I also want whatever's best for my mam and there's no point moping about stuff I can't change. I slug back the dregs of my coffee and stand up. Then I give Amélie my pluckiest smile and say, 'Right, let's do this, let's decorate the hell out of that room.'

Amélie laughs. 'Maybe not hell.' She takes hold of my arm as we head back up to the meeting room. 'Let's think about heaven instead.'

I nod and pretend to agree but inside I'm thinking this Christmas may be heavenly for you, Amélie, but it feels more like hell now to me.

We're about to start sorting through fairy lights when Maura and Sofia appear. Maura's equipped with a speed mop and a pack of rubber gloves. And Sofia's wielding cleaning spray and an armful of cloths.

'We came to help,' Maura announces, as though that's the most natural thing in the world. She doesn't make catty remarks about hanging decorations on dirty windowsills or myself and Amélie not noticing the state of the floor. She just attaches her soggy cleaning pad to her mop and attacks the grubby floorboards instead. Sofia starts spraying the windows while Amélie and I hang decorations on the tree.

I can't stay miserable with all this support so I scroll through my phone for Christmas songs and by the time we've finished the tree, even Maura is humming along to 'Last Christmas' by Wham. Then Amélie and I channel Mariah, pointing at each other through fits of giggles as we belt out 'All I Want for Christmas is You'. We eventually manage to hang the lights and place all the candles and Christmas figurines in the right place.

Maura does a bit of rearranging of those but at least she does it with a smile.

Maura and Sofia leave just before lunch and Amélie and I trek over to Coffee Spot for some soup. We're tucking into leek and potato and crusty brown rolls when I get an urge to find out more about Amélie and Niall.

'So, tell me, what did you do before you came to Galway?' I ask as a way to lead in. 'Did you always work in fashion?' I'm hoping that's harmless enough.

'No. I always loved fashion but I began taking photographs as part of my job. I used to work in publicity for a charity. That's where I met Niall.'

'You were building houses too?'

Amélie shakes her head with a grin. 'No, *ma chérie.* Can you see me carrying bricks? I took photographs before and after the work. And I wrote articles about the difference it made to those poor people's lives. I tried to make people take an interest and donate their money to help.'

'And did you stay there, on-site?' What I really mean is, did you stay with Niall, but I'm not ready to come straight out with that.

'Only sometimes. I am from Paris, that is my home. I travel to places, take what I need for my work, and then I return to my own place.'

That doesn't sound as serious as I first thought and I start to feel a glimmer of hope. Della already told me Amélie plans to go back to Paris after Christmas. It certainly doesn't sound like she intends to settle here in Ballyclane. And she can hardly expect Niall to leave his family and business behind. Is she planning some sort of long-distance love affair or is she just taking what she needs from him and then moving on?

'But you and Niall were close?'

'Yes, we were *very* close,' Amélie smiles, 'but I was so young and my heart was in Paris so I was torn.'

God, she really does love the place. I must add Paris to my list of cities to check out if I manage to make any money from my hats.

Amélie stares down at her soup and for the first time since I met her, she looks sad. 'I was very upset when Niall said he had decided to go home. And that he didn't think we should stay in touch.'

I drop my spoon into my soup and stare at Amélie in shock. 'Niall broke up with you?'

I didn't mean to ask quite so bluntly but Amélie doesn't take offence. She just shrugs and smiles and her sadness seems to lift as she explains.

'I was young. A free spirit, not ready to settle down. Niall didn't understand my ways then. He likes to do things right.' She smiles contentedly and says, 'But I am ready now and the man I love is ready so I believe it will all work out.'

I feel every ounce of my Christmas cheer plummet to the floor. Amélie reaches out, lays a hand on my arm, and says, 'I hope soon you will be ready too.'

I'm not far off plunging my face into what's left of my soup. I love Amélie but she really is cracking me up. Seriously? Ready for what?

44

Amélie is off to Kilkenny for the afternoon, so I wander back down the garden to chat with Christy and his daughter while they hang the outdoor lights.

'I can't wait to see everywhere lit up, especially after dark,' I say. 'You've done a great job.' The pergola is strung with gorgeous vintage globes, and the apple and pear trees are wrapped in fairy lights.

Christy is standing on the top step of a ladder and holding onto one of the pergola beams. He starts to climb back down and I grab hold of the ladder to keep it steady as Mags emerges from the other side of the pear tree and marches towards us with a furious frown.

'Oh my God, Dad, how many times do I have to tell you? Leave the ladders to me.' She rolls her eyes at me and throws her hands in the air. 'Will you talk some sense into him, please?'

Christy laughs and tells her he's been climbing ladders since long before she was born and he'll be climbing them for plenty of years yet.

'Looks like you're nearly finished anyway,' I say.

'No rest for the wicked,' Christy chuckles. 'We're going to have a bit of lunch and then we'll tackle Niall's.'

Mags folds her arms across her chest and sighs. 'Only if you promise to leave the climbing to me. Otherwise, I'm going straight home.'

'Niall's?'

'Yes.' Mags nods. 'He asked me to put up outdoor lights in his garden too. Pretty much the same as we've done here. We're going to do that after lunch. If I can keep my dad on the ground,' she adds with a wry smile.

I think to myself that Niall's really going all out. He must want his place to look good for the party he's having after the market. Maybe it's not going to be as casual as I assumed. Then I remember I still owe Christy for the lights.

'Have you got the receipts with you, Christy? I can give you the money for those now if you like. Do you have Revolut?'

'Do I have what, love?' Christy frowns.

'No need,' Mags says. 'Niall told me to put all the lights on his account and to include the work here in my bill for his place.'

'Oh, right.' I was already feeling bad about being mean to him earlier. I feel even worse now. 'I'll fix up with him later so. We can work out a split.'

Christy chuckles again. 'Good luck with that, love. He won't take it; you know that yourself.'

I nod and smile and admit that Christy's right. But I have a surplus of funds building up in my Revolut and I don't want to be accused of making a profit on our community market so I'm not sure what to do. Then it occurs to me that we haven't spent all that much on activities for the kids so I send off a WhatsApp to Nadia and Shane. Shane's off for the rest of the weekend and Nadia was only working until lunchtime today, so they both agree to meet me for coffee at three. Then they can drive into Portville and buy what they need.

I should be claiming expenses for Coffee Spot with the amount of money I'm spending there holding meetings but I'm not sure

I can justify that. Hopefully, it'll all be worth it tomorrow if I sell some of my hats. Or rather, if Amélie does.

I bag my usual window bench as the lunch crowd has thinned out and Shane arrives almost as soon as I've sat down. I open my notebook and scan the pages for my list of his tasks.

'You're getting more like your big sister every day.'

'I wish,' I say with a sigh. 'She's happy and settled and successful. Definitely nothing like me.'

Shane tilts his head and asks me what's up. But before I get a chance to fill him in, a text beeps on my phone. It's from Mam. She wants me to come to Cathy's after work. She's going straight there for her tea and she wants the three of us to have a proper chat.

It's important, Jas, I read. *We seem to keep missing each other and we really do need to talk. Please come, xx Mam.*

I text back straight away. *I'll be there about five, xx.* Then I add a smiley face. Mam's a big fan of those and she's had more than enough to worry about over the years, trying to raise me and Cathy on her own. I don't want her to worry anymore.

I tell Shane about seeing Mam with Jennifer O'Neill and then about Niall and Tracey in the Square. He tells me again that I'm more than welcome to crash with him if I'm stuck and assures me that he really does mean just as friends. He's leaning across the table patting my hand and telling me it will all work out when he suddenly pulls back and sits up straight.

'Niall just walked past,' he says low, with a hand covering his mouth as if he's an undercover sleuth.

'So?' I've given up caring. Or at least that's what I'm telling myself now.

'So… If looks could kill.'

'Shit, he's really mad at me, then.' I shake my head. 'I went too far this time.'

'Not you. Me.' Shane frowns. 'Every time he sees us together it looks like I'm trying to make you hold my hand. I'm sure he thinks I'm into you. Or even that there's something going on.'

'You are into me.' I manage to crack a smile. 'Have you forgotten the serenading already?'

'I'm doing my best to forget.' Shane grins. Then he waves at the window and I turn to see Nadia walking across the lane. Shane registers the worry in my eyes and adds, 'Go after him, for God's sake. There's no shame in saying sorry, you know.'

I'm trying to figure this all out in my head as Nadia sits down beside me on the window bench. Why would Niall be annoyed with Shane? Should I go after him? Should I apologise for what I said?

Shane grabs the notebook from my hand, takes a pic of the open page, and waves towards the door. 'Nadia and I will have a look at your list.' He ushers me up off my perch. 'Go on, go after him before he's gone. Now.'

Okay, Shane has obviously decided to answer the last two questions for me. But I'm still no wiser as to why Niall would have any reason to be mad at Shane for holding my hand. It's not like *he* wants to. Not anymore.

45

I can't see Niall anywhere in the lane but his Jeep is still parked so I take a chance and wander down to the wrought-iron gate. It's open and I go straight in. Christy is, of course, up a ladder, hanging a mason jar from a hook in the high stone wall. Mags is beside him, holding on tight, muttering about grandchildren preferring their grandad all in one piece.

Then I hear Niall laughing and I turn to see him sitting on the picnic bench looking like he's FaceTiming his favourite person in the world. I'm almost all the way up the garden path when I hear him say, 'You know I love you too, Mel. Just make sure you're here on time tomorrow night.' Then he ends the call.

'Hey,' I say, trying hard not to choke on my words.

'Hey,' Niall goes in a much cheerier tone.

'Em, what I said earlier, it wasn't fair. I'm sorry.'

Niall looks at me for a beat and says, 'That's okay, I can see how it must have looked.' He sighs. 'But honestly, I was trying to help.'

I sit across from him on the other side of the long wooden picnic bench. It's taking all the strength I have to keep talking to him after what I heard him say on the phone. But I want to make things right.

'I know that. And I'm grateful to you for helping Mam. I just wish it didn't involve helping that awful wagon as well.'

Niall does a double take and shakes his head hard. 'I wasn't helping Tracey. I was trying to put her off in case she planned to make an offer your mother would find hard to refuse. I don't normally like to tell lies but I made an exception just this once. As far as Tracey is concerned your mum's house is a derelict wreck. Not that it matters now that your mum—'

'It does matter,' I interrupt. 'And I really appreciate it. I thought you were helping her because, well, she's your cousin after all.'

'She may be blood but it's pure poison that runs through her and her miserable parents' veins. And if it comes to a contest between Tracey and you, Jas… Believe me, you win every time.'

I do believe him and my arms are aching to reach out but I don't trust myself to stop if I touch Niall, so I stay put.

'Thank you,' I manage after a long slow breath and I force myself to meet those gorgeous grey eyes.

Niall bites his lower lip like I haven't seen him do for a while. Mostly because I haven't allowed myself to look. His eyes search mine like he's combing for clues and I blink and look away because I can't bear the heat from his gaze. He has the power to burn right through to my soul, but what's the point if I'm not the one who sets him on fire? All I want is to crawl under this picnic bench, curl into a ball, and give up. This 'staying friends' business is hard.

'You know, it would really help if you didn't assume things,' Niall says as I lower my head. He doesn't sound cross but he does sound hurt. 'You could just ask.'

The worst part is that I know he's right. So, I think, *Okay… Okay, I will.*

'So, you and Amélie?' I look back up again as I start. 'I heard you talking on the phone.' I shrug an apology but I couldn't help hearing. He did say it pretty loud. *You know I love you* I mean.

His face brightens and my heart squeezes tighter in my chest.

'Oh yeah, we're having dinner later, just the two of us.'

How romantic, I'm about to say, but the words congeal in my mouth and Niall keeps talking instead.

'I feel bad,' he goes on. 'I've hardly spent any real time with her without other people around. And so much has happened since we last met. So much has changed.'

Like Amélie being ready to commit. That's worth celebrating with a romantic dinner, I guess. And by other people, I presume he means me. I'm a gooseberry now. A third wheel.

'She's an amazing woman. I'm glad everything's working out and I want to make sure tomorrow night is as special as she deserves.'

'Tomorrow night?'

Niall winces as though he may have said too much. I almost say, just come right out with it, please, you can't make me feel any worse than I already do. But then I discover that's not actually true.

'That's why Christy and Mags are here. I want to make the garden look really special for the occasion.' His face turns a pale shade of pink as he adds, 'You've rumbled me, Jas, I'm a soppy romantic at heart.'

'What's the occasion?' I ask with a croak. I wonder if he's going to ask Amélie to stay. Or declare that he loves her so much that he'll follow her wherever she wants to go.

'It's all top secret. Her sister called me earlier in the week and we've been working out a plan. I don't know if Mel suspects but I have a feeling she does.'

Niall waits as though he expects *me* to give him an answer to this. Hasn't he met me? I'm always the last one to know. I just shrug; I seem to be doing that a lot.

'You two seem pretty close so you probably know what's on the cards. She told me she's been in Galway since the summer but anyone who knows Mel knows that her heart has always been in Paris and that's where she'll end up.'

'She does seem to love the place, all right.'

Niall grins as though I've made some hilarious joke. I'm back to being an amusement piece, it seems.

'She's thirty next week and I know that's a big milestone for her. She always told me she wouldn't settle down or commit until she was thirty at least. Anyway, everything hangs on tomorrow night. A guy can't wait forever, I guess.'

You guess? Seriously, you hardly need to guess. I'm thinking at this stage, Niall, you either know or you don't. I shrug and say, 'Wait for what?'

'An answer.' Niall's the one shrugging now. 'A proper commitment. I mean, if the guy arrives with a ring, that's a pretty big statement. He'll want an answer for sure.'

I almost hurl the dregs of my leek and potato soup all over his lovely picnic bench but I just about manage to keep it down. And if I wasn't so devastated, I'd pull him up on all this talking as if he's somebody else. *He'll* want an answer. What's with this royal *he*? I get that Niall's charming and handsome and his family's well off but he's not an actual bloody prince.

46

Niall asked if I would stay a while longer and help him decorate some more. He even suggested I give him a hand hanging mistletoe up in his porch. That was more than I was able to take. I may have accepted that Niall and Amélie have found each other again and appear committed to rekindling their relationship. And, yes, I have buckets of love and respect for them both. But I'm not ready to hold the mistletoe over their heads while they get up close and personal and finally seal the deal.

Luckily, I had a great excuse as I had already promised Mam that I'd call round to Cathy's so I didn't even need to lie. I'm lying enough pretending that my heart's not breaking apart.

I collect my bike from outside the meeting room and wheel it across the Square to Gran's house. I have almost an hour before I'm supposed to be at Cathy's and I might as well spend it with Gran while I still have the chance. I know this sounds mad and I definitely won't be saying anything to Mam, but I can't help the way that I feel. Mam goes to the graveyard at the far end of town once a week and spends ages tidying Gran's grave and saying little prayers. But I don't feel her there at all. To me, that's just a hole in the ground. I hear her here singing as she leans over her sink or humming as she threads her machine. My chest aches when I think that will be nothing but a memory soon and I don't feel anywhere near ready to tell her goodbye.

I stay about an hour in Gran's sketching out the market on my A3 pad. It feels overwhelming to be the person in charge of all these activities and tasks and I pray – I'm not sure to who, maybe Gran – that nothing goes wrong. Drawing it out really helps. I stare at my page to see where everything fits and I trace my tracks through the day. Then I realise I've drawn a stick figure in front of my stall with a droopy-down line for a mouth and two stick hands on her hips. I grab a red pen and scrawl over and over until I'm sure I have her thoroughly scratched out. There's no way I'm letting Tracey Hamilton anywhere near my hats. It's bad enough that she has her eye on Gran's house.

I cycle over to Cathy's and I see her and Mam through the kitchen window as I lean my bike against the back wall. Cathy's reclining in her armchair contentedly rubbing her stomach and Mam's at the kitchen table with the happiest smile on her face. I can't help but smile too at the way things are turning out for them both. Cathy's heart was broken over her miscarriages and she and Brian ache for a child. And Mam had to struggle for years, working and mothering and keeping a roof over our heads without any help from my dad. In fairness, Gran was her rock, and Mam and Cathy have been mine. Now it's time for me to step up and find some strength of my own.

Mam's face lights up even more when I walk through the door. She pats the chair next to her at the pine kitchen table.

'Sit down, love. I have some great news.'

I do as I'm told and return her cheerful grin as warmly as I can.

'I think I can guess, Mam. I saw you with Jennifer and she looked pretty pleased. I'm hoping you got a good offer on Gran's house.'

Mam gives a wave of her hand as though that's no big deal and

I don't want her to feel she has to downplay this for my sake so I go on.

'I want you to know that I'm delighted for you and I'll support you whatever you decide. As long as they give you a good price, I hope whoever buys Gran's place will be very happy in her house.'

I also hope Mam and Cathy don't notice that I've got my fingers crossed under the table and I'm chanting *Just not Tracey, not Tracey, anybody but Tracey* over and over in my head.

Mam reaches out and lays a hand on my arm and says, 'Actually, love, I've decided that I'm not going to sell.'

Oh God, oh God, oh God, this is all my fault. I'm an absolute bitch. If I hadn't gone whingeing to Niall, he wouldn't have put Tracey off. And even though I'm grateful to him for that and I don't want that wagon anywhere near my Gran's home, I can picture her bad-mouthing the place to everyone else in Ballyclane, and beyond. Now nobody wants to buy and it's all my bloody fault.

I'm spiralling now and I'm struggling to breathe and Mam grips my arm and asks me what's wrong.

'You've gone very pale, love. What is it? I thought you'd be pleased.'

'I'm so sorry, Mam. I'll fix this, I promise.' I feel my whole body start to shake as I confess, 'It's my fault that nobody wants to buy.'

Cathy's up now and she takes the chair on the other side of mine and starts rubbing circles on my back like she used to when I was small and I'd get panicky about the stupidest things. And she'd tell me they weren't stupid at all and to take my time and let it all out and everything would turn out okay.

Then Mam reaches under the table for my hands and holds them tight in her own.

'Jas, love, I don't know what's put that silly idea in your head. But you can put it right out. I've had two offers,' she says. 'Good ones too. But it's made me realise how valuable the place is and I'm not just talking about the money. I don't want to sell my mother's home. I never really did.'

'But you need that money, Mam.' I'm shaking my head and wishing the rest of me would stop shaking too. 'What about all your plans?'

'My plans will be fine, love.' Mam squeezes my hands. 'I'm still going ahead with selling Emmet Park, though not for another few months. And like I told you, I don't want to give up work completely, sure I'd miss all the craic. I talked to Grace, the manager, about cutting back and maybe taking a month or two off after Christmas when things are quiet. She's big into family-friendly and flexitime and all that so she said not to worry about it, she'll sort it out.'

I let out the breath that I've been holding hard for what seems like forever.

'But what are you going to do with Gran's house?'

Mam eases one of her hands from around mine and reaches over for Cathy's instead. Then she says, 'What are *we* going to do? That's more to the point.'

Cathy laughs, points to her expanding front, and says, 'Well, I might not be much help for a while.'

I look from Mam to Cathy and back again and I still can't get my head around whatever it is that they mean.

Then Mam says, 'I couldn't cope with tackling the house all on my own. All those memories that I didn't know what to do with, and so much work. Or at least that's what I thought.'

I've stopped shaking at last and Cathy stops rubbing my back. And I ask, 'But what's changed your mind?'

'You, love. You've changed my mind.' She traces a finger soft across the side of my face. 'Seeing the beautiful hats that you've made from Gran's old clothes. The dearest memories you've taken and created something even more special from. And seeing you there at the front window. You're so like her, you know.' Then she laughs. 'And listening to you chatting to her when you think I've gone out back and can't hear.'

Oh God. My eyes flit from Cathy to Mam to check if they think I'm stark staring mad.

'It's okay,' Cathy says, 'I talk to her too.' Then she chuckles and rolls her eyes. 'Just not out loud.'

Then Mam gives me a look that makes me scared she might cry and she says, 'The most important reason of all is knowing that you really do plan to stay.'

She tells me how Cathy told her about our talk and that I really am happy to be back in Ballyclane and want to base my new business here in my home town. Then she tells me about Niall, how he called her and explained he had exaggerated the problems with the house because Cathy told him she was worried about Mam taking it on by herself.

'He met me at your gran's last week. You were tired and I think maybe a bit upset about something and you'd gone up to bed.'

I know the evening she means. The day Niall showed up at Gran's door wanting to explain about Mel, or Amélie as she'll always be to me. I don't share this, though, I just nod.

'He walked all around the house with me and talked me through what we could do. And he explained about the grants and said he'll help us apply. And give us as much help and advice as we'd like. He says there aren't any major structural issues and the work needed, like insulation and damp-proofing and replacing some of the slates, is straightforward.'

'That was really good of him,' I say.

'He said something else.' Mam gives me a look that I can't quite figure out.

'Oh?'

'He said he's glad I've decided to take this chance. That he knows how much it means to you. And if I have you on my side

I can't go wrong because you can do anything you put your mind to. He really believes in you, Jas.'

It takes every ounce of strength I have left not to bawl.

47

'What I can't figure out,' I say to Shane, 'is how Niall plans to help us on the house if he's going to be in Paris with Amélie.'

We're in my room, panned out on the double bed watching *Sex Education* on Netflix. Otis and Maeve are tangled up in crossed wires again and it makes me feel better that I'm not the only one whose heart is a mess. I do have ten years on those guys, though, I should have things sorted by now.

Shane hits pause on my laptop screen and gives me a look.

'I don't know, Jas, do you not think you're assuming a lot? How can you be so sure that Niall's planning on leaving everything behind and trailing off to Paris after a woman he hasn't seen in years?'

'Because she's Amélie, for God's sake. I bet you'd trail after her too if she gave you the nod.'

Shane just laughs but then he turns serious again. 'I've never seen them kiss. And I've never seen Niall look at Amélie the way he looks at you.'

'What? Don't be stupid.' I give him a shove. 'They're just being kind. They're both my friends and they don't want to hurt me so I suppose they're trying to be discreet.' Then I sigh. 'Which is awful, now that I think of it. They've found each other again after all this time and they can't even relax and enjoy that because of me. I have to make more of an effort to be supportive and let them know I'm okay with it all.'

'Are you? Okay with it?'

'I will be.' I nod. 'I have to be.'

'And he definitely has a ring?'

'Yep, he told me so himself.'

Shane slides down on his pillow, stares at the ceiling, and says, 'It all seems very fast. Amélie's only been here a week. And they're not even sleeping in the same house. Do you not think that's a bit strange?'

'He lost her once. I suppose he wants to make sure he doesn't lose her again. And Niall likes to do things right. He probably feels it will be more special if they wait until they've made that commitment. It sounds like Amélie wasn't ready to commit before. Maybe he wants to make sure this time round.'

My chest aches as I think about tomorrow night and how I'm going to have to watch Niall give Amélie his ring and then probably sweep her upstairs to his bed.

'Do you think Amélie will say yes?'

'Well, she did say Niall was the love of her life.'

'Seriously?'

'Yep. She said she had two great loves in her life. Niall is definitely one. I assumed fashion was the other but maybe it's Paris. Amélie told me herself her heart is still there. And Niall said the same. And now that I think of it, Della said Amélie is definitely going to stay in Paris for good after Christmas as she's missing it so much that she knows it's her forever home.'

Shane clasps his hands behind his head and blows out a breath. 'But why would Amélie kiss me if she had just found the love of her life the night before?'

'One last fling.' I shrug. 'Before she settles down for good. That's the impression she gave me. Although, maybe she thinks you're so irresistibly hot that she couldn't help herself.'

Shane clicks his tongue. 'I wish, but to be honest, it was barely a kiss at all. I think she just thinks I'm nice.' Then he elbows my arm and grins. 'Amélie might be able to resist me but I'm not sure Niall can resist you. Maybe he and Amélie do have some scorching love affair in their past. But I've seen him looking at you, Jas, especially when you're not looking at him and I'm not convinced that Amélie is the one that he wants. Or if he does want her, he definitely wants you too.'

Feck, I think Shane might have a point. Maybe Niall does have feelings for me as well. There have been quite a few of those smouldering looks. And times when I can feel him wanting to reach out as much as I want to reach out and touch him. Maybe if Amélie hadn't turned up last week to help me everything would be different and Niall and I would have a real shot. But Amélie did arrive. And she came as my friend. She's been kind and supportive ever since that day she followed me down the stairs. What sort of a friend would I be if I tried to take away the love of her life when all she's ever done is try to help me chase after my dreams?

I sit up and press play. I'd rather watch Otis and Maeve mess with each other's heads than try to cope with the mess that's in mine.

'I'd better head home,' Shane says as he eases himself up off the bed. 'You have a long day tomorrow. And so have I if we get half the number of kids that Nadia's expecting to show up.' Then he adds as he walks through the door, 'She's very sweet, isn't she?'

'She is,' I agree. I think about saying, 'Be kind to her tomorrow, she's had a really hard time,' but Shane is already halfway down the stairs. He's been hanging out in my house for the last twenty years. I'm long past showing him to the door.

48

The yellow haze of street-lights filters through the blinds as I reach for my phone and see that it's almost eight o'clock and time for me to get up.

I stretch my arms wide and whisper my list. Not my market list. Not yet. I've been writing a gratitude list before I go to sleep and then running through it out loud before I get out of bed. I started after that evening with Niall when he told me how he tries to see his glass half-full. It seems to work for him so I decided to give it a go. Apart from my disastrous love life, I think it's working for me too.

I list all the good things in my life yet again: Mam, Cathy, their plan for Gran's house, and the fact that they really do seem to believe in me and want me to stay. And the best, most supportive friends anyone could ask for: Shane, Amélie, Della and Niall.

Okay, things have gotten a bit mixed up, especially when it comes to friends and romance. But I should know by now that I can't have it all. Even Santa lists have to be scaled back. I learned a long time ago that someone like me can't expect the moon and I should be grateful to have so many bright twinkling stars.

I remind myself again that I need to be supportive of Niall and Amélie today no matter how much it hurts. And to let Niall know somehow that I do believe in him too, even if that can only be as a friend. Then I drag myself up and search through my wardrobe for something warm and cosy to wear.

I had notions of dressing up in Gran's velvet-trimmed coat and my gorgeous bottle-green hat but I'm going to be lugging tables and cleaning up mess. And it's not like there's anyone special that I'm trying to impress, I'd only be wasting my time. I pull on my thickest black jeggings and my navy snowflake Christmas jumper over a plain black top. I add winter socks, my black lace-up boots, and a navy wool scarf. I pile my hair up with a scrunchie, grab my duffel from the back of the wicker chair, and I'm ready to go.

I have breakfast with Mam and we pack all my hats into the back seat of her car. I've wrapped them in tissue paper inside and out and laid them carefully in lined green crates that Mam brought home from work. She made a batch of scones last night and she's got those wrapped in tinfoil in the boot. She says she makes them every year for the committee to munch on before the work starts and she's happy to do her bit this year as well.

Christy and Niall are chatting outside the meeting room when we arrive at half past nine. The outdoor tents are in place and everything looks great. It's a crisp sunshiny day despite the biting cold and there's no threat of rain or much wind, so it seems like all my Christmas wishes have come true. Except for one. And, let's face it, Niall was always out of my reach.

'This looks fantastic,' I tell them. 'What time did the tent crowd arrive to set up?'

'Six o'clock,' Niall says with a yawn.

'You haven't been here since then, have you?' Dear God, this guy is a saint.

'No, no.' He shakes his head. 'I know the lads well, so I left them to it while I collected the tables with Brian. I checked everything was okay before they finished and headed back home.

Christy just texted me to say he was here so I came to give a hand to set up.'

'There's no need, honestly. The others are coming at ten so we've loads of help. You go and get some rest.' He looks like he could do with a few more hours' sleep and with everything he has planned for tonight, I feel bad taking up so much of his time.

He just laughs. 'Do I look that rough?'

I smile and give a noncommittal shrug. He looks bloody gorgeous but I'm not about to tell him that.

'I'll give you a hand to get the tables sorted and I might have a quick nap after that.' He rubs at his cheek and gives another weary yawn. 'I haven't been sleeping as well as I normally do.' It feels like he's about to say why or at least give a hint but he pulls himself up. I presume he's excited about his big proposal tonight and anxious whether Amélie will say yes. I don't think he has much to worry about. How could she not?

'You can give me a hand to bring in the Burco boiler so,' Christy says. 'We'll have to have tea before we start. It's tradition.' Then he spots Mam coming towards us with her tinfoil-wrapped tray and his eyes light up and he throws us a wink. 'We'll need something to wash down Bernie's famous scones.'

Mam, Christy, Niall and I are tucking into tea and scones when Maura and Nadia arrive just after ten. Shane and Brian are only a few minutes behind. With so many helpers it's no time at all before we have everything set up. Amélie arrives at half past with a tray of freshly baked sausage rolls from Jack. We'll all have put on half a stone before the market opens at this rate but it does feel amazing to have so much goodwill and support.

Shane and Brian give me a hand to collect the screen and mannequin heads from Gran's and when we arrive back in the lane, I see Amélie walking down the garden with Niall. She's linking his arm and nuzzling her head into his shoulder and I feel my heart pinch at the sight.

It's the first time I've seen them so close and I think again how considerate they've been not rubbing their rekindled love in my face. I know Niall had a long talk with Amélie before he came to see me to ask if we could stay friends. So, I'm sure she knows I have feelings for him and we've both been tiptoeing around that but it's time I let her know that I'm okay and I've moved on.

Amélie links arms with me and Della all the time. She shouldn't feel that's all she can do with Niall when I'm around. If they want to hold hands or kiss or hold each other close, it's not fair if they think they can't because of me. As soon as this market is over, I'll have a proper talk with them both. This is a special time for them and it's not okay for me to get in their way. Besides, Niall's porch is heaving with mistletoe and they can't let all that go to waste.

The other stallholders start arriving after eleven and by the time we're due to open at noon, the meeting room and lane are full of festive cheer. Maura and Christy have pride of place at the top of the room with Maura's fresh holly wreaths and Christy's wooden cribs. There are stalls with everything from handmade cards to silver snowflake jewellery and there's a gorgeous citrus and spice aroma from the table by the door laden with puddings and mince pies. I give everybody a Santa hat to wear and Christy sets up his CD player and speakers in the corner by the double doors.

'The grandkids have me deafened with that hip-hop pop,' he says. So, it's Judy, Bing and Frank on a loop for the afternoon. Everybody seems happy, though, and I catch Mam humming along to 'Have Yourself a Merry Little Christmas' as she clears away the crumbs from her scones.

I'm glad I decided to set my stall just outside as I can watch everyone pile in and out. Niall secured some hooks to the wall this morning and Amélie attached an A2-sized board with photographs of my hat-making process, including the original garments, Gran's Singer 201, and a range of shots from our photoshoot modelling the finished hats. She's perched on a stool between this board and Gran's louvred screen and I'm going to flit back and forth between here, the garden, and the lane. We've hung some of my hats on Della's brass hooks that we attached to the screen. The mannequin heads are holding my charcoal fedora and scarlet pillbox for now and Amélie says she might switch these for others throughout the afternoon. There's an assortment of bucket hats, berets and cloches laid out on the cream linen tablecloth. And my favourite green velvet bucket hat rests on the top corner of Gran's screen. I've already told Amélie that's purely for display and is definitely not for sale.

49

It's almost half past two and Amélie has sold eight of my hats, even though she's asking an arm and a leg. I did try to tell her that she can't charge prices like that in Ballyclane, but she says I have to understand how special my hats are and she's determined to make sure everyone appreciates their value from the start. I'm at the mulled wine stall next to ours inhaling the spicy woody smell when Hannah Armstrong and her cousin Laura emerge from Coffee Stop and dash over to my stall. They must be visiting their grandparents for Christmas. Hannah and Laura live in Edinburgh but they've been coming to Ballyclane at least three times a year since Hannah's mother, Claire, married her gorgeous Scottish James and moved over there. Laura's parents were already based there so the girls grew up together and have always been close.

'Oh my God, Han, these are fabulous. What do you think?' Laura picks up a cornflower blue baker boy hat and tries it on.

'It's beautiful. They all are,' Hannah says. She runs her hand slowly over the selection laid out across the table. Then her eyes flick up to Gran's screen and Amélie's photo board. 'This is wonderful.' Her chocolate-brown eyes widen as she points to the photographs and then back to my hats. 'These are works of art.'

My stomach flips as I take the paper cup of mulled wine that Elena's sister, Zosia, holds out. Hannah Armstrong just called my hats works of art. Her dad, James, is a well-known artist and

Hannah's starting to make a name for herself too. I've seen some of her work online and it's beautiful and interesting and real. I'm blown away that she seems to feel the same about mine.

'This is my favourite. How much?' Laura pulls out a wallet stuffed with notes. These girls have been coming to Ballyclane's Christmas market for years so they know we haven't gone contactless yet. Amélie names the price and Laura parts happily with her cash and proudly places my cornflower creation back on her lovely blonde head.

'How about you, Han? See anything you like?'

'I love them all but that one is really special,' Hannah points to my favourite, perched on the top corner of Gran's screen. I'm still standing a few feet from my stall and I'm not sure if Laura and Hannah realise that the hats are mine.

'Are you the milliner?' Laura asks Amélie. Amélie turns towards me and raises her hand as if to point but before she has a chance to reply, Tracey Hamilton marches out of the meeting room and makes straight for my stall. How did I not see that wagon go in?

Hannah and Laura followed Amélie's gaze and Hannah's eyes narrow as she watches my face fall. Tracey breezes past the girls as if they don't exist and lifts the red pillbox from the mannequin's head. I feel like ripping it right out of her hands and telling her it will clash rotten with her tomato-red hair. But my feet have frozen on the spot so I take a slug of my mulled wine and thank God that Zosia added a decent splash of port from her below-counter flask.

'You're that French girl, aren't you?' Tracey calls out as though Amélie has trouble hearing and should be grateful that Tracey is aware of her at all.

Amélie stands up and peers down her nose and Tracey swallows, clearly regretting her faux pas.

'These are exquisite,' she says and reaches past Hannah to finger the charcoal fedora. 'I take it they're yours?'

Amélie's eyebrows shoot up and her eyes flick to mine. I stare at her hard, give the tiniest shake of my head, and try to impart my thoughts. We've been over this, Amélie – do not let Tracey Hamilton know that these hats were made by me.

'They are by a designer friend of mine,' Amélie says. Then she lowers her voice. 'I work for a Paris fashion magazine and we are doing a feature on how Irish women respond to couture.' Tracey gasps and mouths, '*Vogue*?' and her eyebrows arch as high as they can possibly go. Amélie just pouts. 'I really can't say, I've already said too much.'

Laura is watching Amélie and Tracey and hanging on every word but Hannah turns her back on Tracey and looks over at me. I see a question forming in her eyes and I let a half-smile play on my lips. She gives me the tiniest nod and turns back again to my stall.

'I was just commenting how these are obviously works of art,' Hannah says as she turns to face Tracey. 'Wasn't I, Laura?' She nods at her cousin to agree.

'Absolutely.' Laura points to her hat with a grin. 'I'm wearing art on my head.'

'I'm an artist myself,' Hannah quips in a haughty tone that I doubt she has ever used in her life before. 'And this is my cousin, Laura. Laura works in PR.'

Laura seems to pick up the vibe immediately. 'Hannah and I know couture when we see it. I snapped this up straight away.' She flicks her long blonde locks. 'I'd advise you to do the same before the prices go through the roof.' I almost give the game away with my snort as Laura adds, 'That red would be stunning with your hair.'

Tracey cocks her chin and holds the pillbox at arm's length with one hand. Then she spots my green velvet bucket hat and points towards that.

'How much for the two?'

'Six hundred for the pillbox but the green one is not for sale. That's only for display,' Amélie says breezily.

Tracey scowls but Amélie ignores her and carries on, 'And I do ask you to be discreet about the price. We can't have everybody expecting to buy designer pieces for next to nothing. I'm making a special arrangement for you ladies because you clearly understand couture.' She smiles at Hannah and Laura as though she has just given them the same deal and they smile back as though they wholeheartedly agree that Tracey is a very lucky woman indeed.

Tracey takes it all in her stride. She's already sporting a handbag that was probably twice as much as Amélie is asking. And I doubt that she works for the money herself so it won't cost her a thought to splash out. She pulls out a cheque book but Amélie shakes her head and points her towards the top of the lane.

'We don't accept cheques. There's a machine across the road from the Square. But hurry, I've sold most of our best pieces already and I wouldn't want you to miss out.'

I start backing around the side of Zosia's mulled wine stall. I can't trust myself not to crease up at the thought of Tracey racing across the Square to take out more money than I've earned in a month so that she can pay for my hat. I'm almost out of sight when Tracey catches a glimpse out of the corner of her eye. She turns her nose up and sniffs, 'Well look who it is, lowering the tone.' Then she turns to Amélie and says with her trademark sneer, 'Don't let that one put her filthy fingers on your lovely hats. She wouldn't know couture if it landed on her head.'

Amélie goes deathly pale and I'm terrified she's going to give me away. But Tracey doesn't give her a chance. She turns with a flounce and strides up the lane clearly determined to make sure she gets back before anyone else makes off with her prey.

50

'What a bitch!' Laura says as Hannah stands, shaking her head in disbelief.

I just shrug. *You have no idea, girls,* I think to myself. I decide to disappear down the garden before Tracey arrives back as I don't want to deal with her anymore. Amélie's doing such a great job of winding her up, I'll leave it to her to get my revenge. It'll take more than six hundred euros to erase years of vicious remarks but it's not a bad start.

'We're going to drop these to Granny Angela,' Hannah says to me as she holds up a paper bag of mince pies. 'Is it okay if I come back later to take some photos? When that horrible woman has gone.'

'Of my hats?'

'Yes, if that's all right. That's if there are any left and they're not all sold.' She smiles. 'I might take a few shots quickly before I go. But I want to take my time capturing the green velvet as I'd like to paint that if you don't mind.'

Mind? Oh my God, I'm thrilled that Hannah Armstrong wants to paint one of my hats but I'm also worried that Tracey will land back before I make my escape, so I just give her a thumbs up and say, 'Absolutely, no prob, see you later,' and dash off. I've already told Amélie not to sell my favourite hat so that will be still there for sure. I'm delighted that it's Hannah's favourite too.

I wander through the garden to see how Nadia and Shane are getting on. The last time I checked, Nadia was reading from a giant-sized storybook about Rudolf the Red-Nosed Reindeer and Shane was prancing around the pergola with a pair of felt antlers on his head and sporting a shiny light-up nose. Now Nadia's wearing a long blue cape decorated with silver snowflakes and singing 'Let it Go', in the most beautiful voice that she never mentioned she had. And Shane is dressed as Olaf the snowman, helping enchanted children blow bubbles, and pretending to catch bubble snow. The kids look like they are having the time of their lives and Nadia and Shane seem to be enjoying it just as much.

I'm about to go closer to see if I can help when I see them share a secret sideways smile that tells me they've got this and are happy to be left to themselves. It occurs to me now that Nadia and Shane would be good together and I can't believe I didn't see this before. But I guess neither did they. They certainly seem to be getting on well and it looks like they might be thinking of more. If not, I'll make sure to give them a nudge. My own love life might be a disaster zone but I'm doing a great job of matching up everybody else.

I haven't seen Niall since this morning and I've been all over the market for the last few hours making sure everything is okay. It's not like him to stay away, especially if he thinks anybody might need his help. But now that I think of it, things are running smoothly and the market is a resounding success. Okay, we ran out of mince pies by three o'clock and I had to tell Christy not to let Maura add any more of his port to her mulled wine. There's a tell-tale flush to her cheeks and she keeps waving at me whenever I pass. I've just about gotten her on my side so I don't want to be responsible for her having a hangover in the morning and deciding that it's somehow my fault. But apart from that, it's all good.

I make my way down to the end of the garden and push at the wrought-iron gate. It opens. Niall normally locks it when he leaves, so I presume this means he's inside. He seemed a bit down this morning. I'm not sure if there's anything I can do but I can let him know that I'm here as a friend if that's any help.

I don't see any sign of him in the garden so I walk up the path to the porch. There's enough mistletoe hanging over the door to ward off every evil spirit around and bring him as much love as he could possibly want. I wonder if that's what's getting him down. Does he know if Amélie will say yes? And what will it mean if she does? He's put so much work and care into this cottage and the lane. It's bound to be hard to contemplate leaving all that behind.

And even though I want them both to be happy, I can't help feeling that this is all happening way too fast. They may have been in love once and they may well feel they still are, but they've only been back together a week. And Amélie kissed Shane the day after they reconnected. Niall can't be happy about that. If he even knows. My head is messed up just thinking about it all so I can imagine how confused he must feel.

I press the doorbell for a couple of seconds and wait. I'm already starting to doubt myself and question why I'm here. If he doesn't answer immediately, I'll take that as a sign and leave him alone. Before I have a chance to change my mind and retrace my steps Niall pulls back the inner porch door. He seems taken aback to see me but he does manage a smile.

'Hi, Jas, what can I do for you?' He has the outer door open now but he's hovering in the porch and doesn't seem inclined to invite me in. I get that, of course, the last time he welcomed me into his home, I turned into a blubbering wreck and then threw myself at him when he was clearly just trying to be kind. I need to make it clear that he has nothing to worry about this time around.

'Hi, I haven't seen you all afternoon and I wondered if you're doing okay. You seemed a bit down this morning and I thought maybe you could use a friend.' I raise my palms and add, 'And I do mean just a friend.'

He sighs and looks unsure but I'm not taking no for an answer and I move a step closer to the door, and to Niall. I get that warm woody scent again and my head reels as I breathe him in. I'm here as his friend, I remind myself. And Amélie's too. I care too much about them both to let my crazy unrequited lust get in their way.

'I'd love a coffee if there's one going.' I offer him my breeziest smile.

He's far too polite to refuse and moves back to make way for me to come in. The first thing I notice is that the island is covered with drawings and plans. Architectural plans. Not what I expected Niall to be wrapped up in on our Christmas market afternoon. With a party to organise and a girlfriend to propose to as well. I wonder if he's feeling overwhelmed and trying to escape into his work to take his mind off it all. I know that feeling, it's exactly what I've been doing myself.

'Another project?' I ask, and I wonder how he's going to oversee that if he moves to Paris.

He blows out a breath and starts to clear the drawings away. 'No, it was something I was working on but I don't think it's an option anymore.'

I notice the catch in his voice. He must love Amélie very much if he's willing to give up everything that he's built here over the past few years. I don't say that. It's not my place to judge or try to put him off. Maybe he can restore beautiful old buildings in Paris instead.

'Is it okay if I take a look?'

He hesitates for a beat then says, 'Sure. But can we keep this between you and me? I haven't shown these to anyone else, especially not Mum and Dad.'

He opens out one of the drawings and I see detailed plans for reconfiguring his parents' house. I pore over these while Niall makes us coffee and I'm very impressed by what I see. The drawing shows three separate apartments, one on each floor. Niall's parents' house is enormous so each apartment is the size of an average townhouse and the side of their house faces on to the lane so the top two apartments each have their own separate entrance and a designated parking spot, also in the lane. He has clearly put a huge amount of thought and time into the plans and I can't imagine anyone not being over the moon to live somewhere like this. If they could afford to, that is. This sort of location and luxury wouldn't come cheap.

'This looks amazing.' I run my hand across the drawing. Then I look up and see Niall's worried frown. 'Why haven't you shown this to Lily and Jack? Surely, this is exactly what they need? They could live on the ground floor and rent out the top two floors. Or sell them if they prefer. And the house is in such good condition, it doesn't even look like it would take that much work.'

Not that I have a clue about these things but I have been thinking about renovations and building work a lot these days because of Gran's. I've been watching that *Cheap Irish Homes* programme and picking up all sorts of tips. Lily and Jack's definitely won't come cheap, these apartments will be worth a fortune. But two beautiful apartments in the centre of town will free up two houses somewhere else so they'll be doing their bit to help with the housing crisis too. I'm not sure why I do this but when Niall turns to get the coffee pot, I take a sneaky pic with my phone.

'I don't want to put any pressure on them. I think they've already made up their minds to sell.'

'But you've put so much work into this.' I hold out my hands towards his drawing and it's all I can do not to reach a bit further and take hold of his arm. He's sitting directly across from me staring down at his abandoned plan and I can't believe he looks so lost. I decide that I'm going to get to the bottom of this and do whatever it takes to help. There's no way Niall should be looking so anxious and depressed on what should be one of the happiest days of his life.

'Did they tell you this? Did they say they have definitely decided to sell?'

Niall leans on the counter and pinches the bridge of his nose. 'Not exactly but they've been talking about it for a while and I found out last night that someone is planning to make them a really good offer. One that they'll find very hard to refuse.'

'You have to at least show them your drawings first.'

Niall sighs. 'No, Jas, I don't. Dad has already had one serious heart attack. Mum's main concern is making sure he doesn't have any more stress. I don't want him to feel he has to take on a big project like this for my sake. I want them to make the right decision for them, on their own terms.'

'Okay, I understand that.' And it's true. I do. I felt exactly the same way about Gran's house and Mam. But now she knows I really do want to stay here and I'm willing to work hard for my dreams. And that's changed everything for her. And for us. I think Lily and Jack deserve the same. They should at least have the chance to look at Niall's plans and see how hard he has worked to come up with a viable option for them. And a fabulous one too.

But then I wonder if maybe Niall wants them to sell. If he is planning to move away with Amélie maybe he thinks it's best if the whole family cuts their ties with Ballyclane. Then they can wipe out any bad memories of that awful business with Freddie and make a fresh start. But it seems like Niall only heard this news recently and that means Lily and Jack can't possibly have made up their minds.

'Do your parents know about this offer yet? I presume it was Jennifer that got in touch?'

Niall takes a sip of his coffee, puts down his mug, and starts biting his lip. I know by now that means he's feeling something intensely. I can't always figure out whether it's good or bad but it seems clear that he can hardly bear to spit out the words.

'Tracey came to see me last night.'

I stare across at him with my mouth hanging open and I'm sure it's not a good look. But Niall doesn't care what I look like and neither do I right now. All I can think about is how the hell am I going to make sure Tracey Hamilton does not get her claws on that house.

'I'm sorry, Jas, I'm sure it's the last thing you need. Having Tracey living across the Square from you. But her husband is loaded and they're willing to outbid any offers Jennifer might get. And it might be that Mum and Dad will be glad to keep it in the family too.'

I'm still in shock and silently shaking my head so Niall carries on. 'I don't think they ever had any issue with Tracey, she's well able to charm when she wants. I doubt they realise how two-faced she is. And it's not like they can blame her for what Freddie did. That was all him.'

'But *you* know what she's like. Can't you tell them? They won't want to sell to her if they know she's an out-and-out bitch.'

'I'd be doing it for all the wrong reasons,' he says with a wince. 'To get the outcome that *I* want. That's not fair to Mum and Dad. And besides, I'm not sure they will get another offer. Certainly not anything close to what Tracey can come up with. There aren't many people in these parts with that sort of cash.'

'But if she wants to buy your parents' place then why was she looking at my gran's.'

Niall's shoulders sag and I can almost feel his heart do the same.

'She was just being nosy. She never had any real interest in buying it. She knows it was your gran's and that you're working there now. I think she just wanted to get in for a gawk.'

Oh God, I feel sick at the thought of her creeping around and pawing through my hats. Although she can't have seen my hats, otherwise she'd know that they're mine.

'Don't worry, Jennifer didn't let her anywhere near the place. But I really messed up. I thought she was genuinely interested and I was worried she'd keep trying to persuade your mum to sell. So, I said the house was practically falling apart. I thought I was helping to put her off but all I've done is give her more ammunition to taunt you with. I'm so sorry, Jas.'

I can't believe that with all Niall has going on he seems more worried about how this will affect me. And how to do what's best for Lily and Jack. He doesn't seem to be considering what he wants at all. I can't stop myself anymore. I climb off my stool, walk around the island, and wrap my arms around him to give him a hug. I'm not trying to make a move but I can tell he's in a bad place and I want him to know that I'm here and I care.

He trembles in my arms and lowers his head. Then he reaches out and pushes back a strand of hair from my face. His eyes move to my mouth and I feel the heat of his gaze on my lips. And, oh God, if I don't pull away this instant, I'll never be able to again. My arms ache as I draw back like I'm rowing against an invisible tide. 'I'm sorry,' is all I can give.

Niall looks more lost than ever as he peers into my eyes. 'You know how I feel about you, Jas.'

I have no idea how I'm supposed to respond to that because really, I don't have a clue. If he wants to marry Amélie – and it seems that he does – then how can he possibly expect any more than friendship from me? I can't believe he's the type of guy to cheat but maybe this reunion with Amélie has happened so fast that he's having second thoughts. I don't want to be his bit on the side or last final fling or whatever the hell this is turning out to be. And I won't betray Amélie. She's out there fighting my corner, building me up, and being the best friend anyone could want. The least I can do is make some bloody effort to be the same.

I swallow and try to keep the shake from my voice. 'You've been a great friend to me, Niall. And I want to be a good friend to you too. I'm sorry if I haven't always acted as though I believe in you. But honestly, I do.' I take a deep breath and go on. 'I can see you're going through a tough time right now and everybody has a moment of weakness sometime. Like I did when I got upset about Gran. I'll always be here if you need to talk or anytime you need me as a friend.' Then I summon every last ounce of strength I possess to tell him, 'But I think we both know that's all I can ever be.'

I wonder if I'm imagining things as he mouths the word *ever* as though he can't believe I mean what I say. For Christ's sake, Niall, you made your choice. It's breaking my heart seeing you in pain but I have no idea what is going on in your mind and if I don't get out of this cottage right now my own head is going to explode.

'I think I'd better leave.' I start to move towards the door. Niall presses his face hard into his palms then sighs and looks up at me again.

I have no clue what parting words to expect but I certainly don't anticipate what I get.

'Would you do me one favour, please.'

'Sure,' I say quietly and wait.

'Well, it's more for Mel.'

'Okay,' I'm waiting for, *Don't say anything about this,* or *let's just keep what nearly happened here between ourselves.*

But instead, he says, 'She's not expecting Jules to appear tonight. It's meant to be a surprise. So, could you suggest she dresses up and makes a special effort?' He pauses as he sees my eyebrows rise. 'She always looks beautiful, I know, but considering the occasion, her sister asked me to make sure she looks her best. She says that's what Mel would want if she knew.'

Wow, that was some turnaround. One minute you're devouring me with your eyes. The next you're asking me to make sure your perfect woman looks even more perfect when you ask her to be your wife. That's not confusing at all.

'Okay, sure.' I suppose I did vow to be a real friend to them both. Might as well start straight away. 'What time is Jules getting here?' This sister of Amélie's seems to have more of a say in the proposal than Niall does himself.

'I think about eight. I'm not exactly sure. I've done my bit, the lights, the mistletoe, keeping everything under wraps. The rest is up to Mel.'

I think about saying, *Well, you might have a bit more of a role*, but it's none of my business so I don't. I should be long gone by now but I finally get around to asking one more question that's been bugging me all week. 'Why do you keep calling Amélie Mel?'

Niall shrugs, 'I never knew her as Amélie, only Mel. That's who she told me she was, way back when. She wanted to keep her life outside Paris separate, to feel like a different person when she was with me. She thought it would be fun to use a shortened version of her name. And I'm sure it was. It just wasn't as much fun for me when I found out why.'

There's a flicker of hurt in his tone and I wonder if he means that Amélie was with other men when she was with him. Was that what he found out? I wouldn't be surprised considering what happened with Shane. And she did say she wasn't ready to settle down, until now. Is that why Niall almost kissed me? To even the score? Dear God, for two people who seem so wise and grounded and kind, their relationship is completely messed up.

'I'll do my best,' I finally say as I make for the door. 'And I won't mention Jules. I'll tell Amélie I feel like getting dressed up myself and I'd love it if she'd do the same. Don't worry, I've go this, I won't let you down.' I walk out through the porch and one last thought occurs to me before I leave, so I turn back to Niall. 'You know with everything you have planned for tonight, and after that, I think you should start calling her Amélie now.'

51

It's almost four o'clock and I run through yet one more list as I make my way back to my stall. I'll have a quick look in the meeting room to see how things are going then I'd better let Amélie go for a break or maybe even finish up. She's been perched on that stool for most of the afternoon. Mam covered for a while and I tried to take over a few times, but Amélie seems to be relishing her role as my undercover fashion agent. She keeps waving me away and telling me to leave it to her.

When I get to my stall, I find Cathy on Amélie's stool. 'I sent her over to Coffee Stop for a rest.' She smiles at me. 'You go ahead and join her. I'll keep an eye here.'

'I'll just take a quick look inside and see how everyone is doing, then I'll be back to take over if that's okay?'

'Absolutely not.' Cathy pats her bump. 'I'm feeling great at the moment and I miss being involved. I couldn't help out earlier and I definitely can't help with cleaning up. But I've already gone around the meeting room for a chat with everyone and they're all good. And now I'd like to sit here for a while and take it all in. You go and have a hot chocolate and a nice sticky bun and take a break. You deserve it, you've been running around all day and working hard on your hats for months.' Then she looks at me as though I'm a favourite child and says, 'I'm so proud of you, Jas.'

I could use some sugar. And a chat with Amélie to work out if she has any inkling about what Niall has planned for tonight. I'm worried that he's moving too fast for both of them because he's afraid of losing her again. Maybe he thinks giving her a ring will make her commit and stop her having any more of those flings. But it won't unless that's what she wants anyway. And even if it is, I'm still concerned that this is out of character for Niall, he seems so confused about it all, and he doesn't seem to be thinking things through. What happened to the wise solid soul who helped me to slow down and breathe and steadied my feet on the ground? Maybe now I need to do the same for him. I can't believe I'm even thinking this way, it's like I've finally grown up.

Nadia and Shane have finished their story time and they're ensconced in the window seat, looking smiley and pleased with themselves. And with each other, I hope. I give them a wave and leave them to it as I've just spotted Amélie down the back. But she's not on her own. She's chatting animatedly with Maura and Lily and before I can make up my mind about joining them, Maura shoots a hand in the air.

'Jas, come and sit down,' she calls. I can't exactly refuse so I order a hot chocolate from Elena and pull up a chair.

'I sold out by half past three.' Maura beams at me. 'And it's all thanks to you.'

I'm baffled as to how I've gone from arch-villain to local hero in her eyes and I try not to look as though I think she's losing her mind.

'Your idea of holding it here in the meeting room and the lane was perfect,' she goes on. 'With the garden for the children and the decorations and lights it's our very own winter wonderland here in Ballyclane.'

She's looking a bit misty-eyed and I try to sneak a sniff of her coffee to check if there's something stronger in there. She seems sober enough, though, and her voice takes on a serious note as she says, 'I owe you an apology, my dear. I misunderstood you at first.' Then she gives a sharp cough. 'No, actually that's not quite correct. In fact, I was misinformed. But I know the truth now and I hope you can forgive me and that we can be friends.'

That was some speech and in fairness to Maura, it took guts. I know Nadia set her straight about Tracey but I wasn't expecting her to admit that she was wrong. I haven't always been easy on her either so I take another gulp of hot chocolate and do my bit to make amends.

'It's all in the past, Maura. I'm famous for getting the wrong end of the stick so I'm no one to judge. I'm glad we're okay now and I'd like us to be friends.' I smile at her warmly and add, 'Because I'm not going anywhere, we have plenty more markets ahead of us, and I think we make a great team.'

Maura beams. 'That's exactly what I was hoping you would say.' Then she spots Christy and Lizzie taking a table near the door and excuses herself to go join them for a chat.

I sip my drink and try to figure out how to broach the subject of Niall with Amélie while Lily is still here. But Lily seems to have an agenda of her own. She folds her hands under her chin and says, 'I found out some interesting truths myself this afternoon.'

My head starts to spin and my breath catches in my chest as I picture Lily outside Niall's kitchen window watching him run his hand through my hair and lower his head to meet mine. I'm not sure which troubles me more – the thought of Lily thinking that I would betray Amélie and try to seduce her only son, or the memory of Niall's eyes on my mouth. Then I pull myself up. Lily was probably nowhere near Niall's this afternoon. I close my eyes for a beat, take a deep breath, and remind myself that everything is working out fine and I need to stop winding myself up. I'm beginning to realise that Tracey Hamilton is not the worst head wrecker I face. I do an even better job on my own.

Lily gives me a look of concern and pats my arm. 'Is everything okay, Jas? You look pale.'

Amélie puts an arm around my shoulder, gives me a squeeze, and tells Lily, 'She's been working too hard.'

'Just like my son.'

Amélie laughs, 'Yes, they both work too hard and worry too much.' Then she winks at Lily and adds with a gleam in her eyes. 'Tonight, when the party is over, I am going to lock them in the cottage and not let them out until they take a proper break and talk everything through.'

I stare wide-eyed at Amélie and I almost say, 'What the hell?' but I don't get the chance as Lily laughs too and says, 'That sounds like a very good idea.' She immediately adds, 'But I need to discuss something else with you first.' She goes quiet and serious and looks me straight in the eye. 'I had a visit from Jack's niece, Tracey, this afternoon.'

I swallow hard and steel myself as best I can. If Niall won't fight this battle for himself then I'm going to have to take Tracey on.

'I know why she came to see you,' I say. 'I understand that she's his niece but you may not know who she really is. And you don't know how hard Niall has worked to come up with a plan for your home. It's a wonderful plan too, I have a sample here on my phone.'

I pause to catch my breath and scroll through my pics. Lily lays her hands in front of her on the table and says, 'I know exactly who Tracey is and I would love to take a look at my son's plans. I knew he was working on potential options but I didn't want to put him under pressure, so I was waiting for him to come to me.' Then she holds out an open palm and nods towards my phone. 'But if it's all right with you, I would appreciate a look.'

I'm not sure what she means about Tracey but I get the impression that Lily knows her own mind and won't be easily fooled. At least if I show her the photo I took of Niall's drawing then he'll be in with a shot. Hopefully, Lily will follow up on her plan to visit him and ask to take a look at the rest.

Her face softens as she stares at the image and I see a tear in the corner of her eye. 'You should go and see him,' I say. 'He's home now.'

Lily nods and rises to leave. But before either of us gets to say another word, Amélie jumps from her chair, roars '*Merde,*' and dashes towards the door. Coffee Spot is directly across from my stall and I stare out of the window and see exactly why Amélie tore off. Tracey Hamilton is back and she's pointing at my green velvet bucket hat and Cathy is carefully climbing down from her stool. I'm rooted to the spot watching all this play out in slow motion and praying Amélie gets there before Cathy accepts the wad of cash that Tracey's holding out. But before Amélie can make it or Cathy lays a hand on my hat, Hannah Armstrong runs behind the table clutching a camera around her neck and stands directly in front of Gran's screen.

I race out through the door and pull up a few feet from my stall. Tracey has her hands on her hips and she's chanting, '*I want that hat*,' like a tantrum-throwing three-year-old child.

Then Amélie calls out, 'I told you that's not for sale.'

Tracey spins on her heels. 'Everything's for sale.' She sneers and waves her wad of notes in the air. 'I'll ask the designer myself. Anyway, what is so special about that hat?'

Amélie narrows her eyes and I can almost see steam blasting from her ears. 'Only the designer wears that hat.'

Tracey's eyes flick from Amélie to Hannah to my hat as if she's weighing up her chances of a snatch. But Amélie and Hannah have their hands on their hips mirroring Tracey and daring her to even think about making a move. Then Tracey spots Amélie's photoshoot board and she leans forward with her eyes wide and her jaw hanging down.

'You let *her* wear it. You let Jas McAdams put your precious couture hat on her ugly, scraggy head.'

Amélie, Cathy and Hannah open their mouths to protest but I stand behind Tracey shaking my head and I press my finger to my lips to tell the three of them to stay quiet. That bitch is all mine.

I keep my voice steady and my feet planted firmly on the ground. Tracey can throw all the tantrums she wants. I'm not listening to her anymore. I've moved on.

'That's because I *am* the designer, Tracey. That is my hat. Those are all my hats, including the one that you bought.'

Tracey twists very slowly to face me, as though every inch that she moves is causing her pain. 'You' is the only word that comes out.

'I wasn't fond of that one anyway, I almost threw it in the bin.' I smile as if I've swallowed a full bag of sugar. 'But I can't sell you any of my real collection. I only cater for customers with taste.'

'You,' she says again and I almost say, *Come on, Tracey, you can do better than that.* But I'm oddly enjoying this and I'm not in any hurry so I wait.

'You've been making those hats in the Square,' she spits. 'I won't have it. You can't set up business in the Square. I'll object.'

I fold my arms across my chest and laugh in her face. 'Go right ahead. Let's see how far you get. A young up-and-coming designer, featured in the best fashion magazines, opening her business in the heart of Ballyclane. I'm exactly what this town needs.'

'But *I'll* be living in the Square.' She rocks on the balls of her feet and pouts for all that she's worth. 'I won't have you lowering the tone.'

'Pah, it's you that would be lowering the tone.' I swivel my head to the side to watch Maura fume. She and Lily stare hard at Tracey with absolute disgust in their eyes.

'But you won't get the chance,' Lily says with a note of steel. 'You certainly won't be buying the Hamilton house. Our home is not for sale.'

'But. But... ' Tracey can't seem to think any further than that so I follow up.

'You might want to look further afield. I don't think you're welcome in this town.'

Tracey opens her mouth but shuts it again as Lily, Maura and Cathy chime in to let her know that she is definitely not welcome at all.

She fires one last desperate shot, telling me she'll find a way to target me online.

'Don't even think about it.' I hadn't realised that Hannah's cousin, Laura, had arrived until now. 'My mother is one of the most influential public relations specialists in Europe,' she says. 'And I'm not far behind. If you even think about going after Jas, we'll know exactly who we need to take down.'

'Nobody will listen to you anyway,' Amélie adds. 'Not after they read my piece about Jas overcoming a nasty childhood bully in order to believe in herself and her hats.'

'I'll definitely be retweeting that,' Laura quips.

'And I'd love to feature these hats on my blog,' Hannah says.

A puce-faced Tracey finally gives up and storms back out of the lane. And I know it's been a long day and I may be losing the plot but I swear I can hear Munchkins singing in my head, *Ding Dong! The Witch is Dead. Ding Dong! The Witch is Dead.*

52

It only takes an hour to clear up because everybody gives a hand. Brian's transition-year students have been on litter duty all day as well as their face-painting task. Elena kept them topped up with hot chocolate and gingerbread cookies and Brian and I will write glowing references for their President's Award so they're happy out. The meeting room won't be in use again until after Christmas so we'll leave the floor and window washing until next week. We all need an hour or two now to catch our breath before Niall's party. After that, I think we'll need to sleep for a week.

Mam drives me home for a power nap and a quick shower to revive before I go to meet Amélie to get dressed up at Gran's.

'You made a wonderful job of the market, love,' she says. 'And your hats were an even bigger success. Everybody's talking about you, you know.'

Those words would have been a stake through my heart a few months ago. I'd have been imagining ridicule and pity and God knows what. Now I just smile and allow myself to bask in the glow of Mam's pride.

I've arranged to meet Amélie at seven and we have an hour to get ready before her sister is due to arrive. I promised Niall we'd be at his place by eight. He looked like he had the weight of the world on his shoulders when he came to help us clear up. But I saw

Lily approach him as he was walking back to the cottage, so she should at least ease his mind about the house. The rest I presume is just nerves, worrying if Amélie will say yes. I told him to go home, have a hot bath, and down a glass of something strong. And do some of those deep-breathing techniques. He started all that smouldering eyes stuff again, though, so I had to make an excuse and run off before my own breath gave up the ghost.

Amélie arrives at Gran's still in her Christmas jumper and leggings like myself. She has an armful of garment bags folded over her left arm and she's carrying a black Chanel cosmetic case that she tells me was a present from Jules. Her sister must have plenty of cash.

'Let me do your make-up, please, *ma chérie*.' Amélie lays her case on Gran's kitchen table and puckers her rosebud lips in a pout.

'That's okay, I'm just going to throw on a bit of lippy and I'm done,' I tell her. Tonight is Amélie's night and nobody is going to be looking at me.

'No, no, no,' she says. 'If I am going to make myself beautiful then I am going to make you beautiful too.' I'm about to tell her she already is when she says pretty much the same to me. 'But with your big brown eyes and that beautiful mouth, you barely need my help.' Then she laughs. 'But it will be fun to paint such a pretty face.'

I throw my hands up and smile. 'Looks like I don't have a choice.'

I suppose if I'm going to be standing on the sidelines watching the man of my dreams sweep you off your feet, I might as well look good while I'm there.

I'm going to wear my navy Kooples dress and Gran's bottle-green coat. And my velvet bucket hat, of course. Amélie has her gorgeous cherry-red Chloé dress, a mix of wool, cashmere and silk. And over that, an elegant black wool coat that belonged to her great aunt. I can barely afford the price of a pint and I don't think Amélie is overly flush, but we've managed to pull together outfits that would look well on the cover of any fashion magazine with a bit of creativity, family wardrobes, and Della's pre-loved designer haul.

'When do you fly back to Paris?' I ask as Amélie buffs my face with her brush.

'Monday.' She beams. 'I can't wait. I've loved my time in Galway but I miss Paris and I miss Jules. It's time for me to go home.'

'You're really close to your family?'

'Oh yes, of course,' Amélie says as she glides her Touche Éclat pen across the top of my cheekbones. 'But I will miss you, *ma chérie*, and Della too. She has been so kind.'

Della and Amélie clicked so well that within a week Amélie moved out of the flat next to Gabe and into Della's spare room. She's driving from Galway on Monday morning with Amélie's stuff loaded in her girlfriend's Volvo and taking her on to the airport from here.

'We both feel the same about you,' I tell Amélie, 'I'm really going to miss you when you go.'

'Well, no tears tonight.' She laughs as she draws her pencil across my eyebrow. 'You'll mess up my work.' She waves her hand in the air with a flourish. '*Voilà*, you're done.'

I gasp as I peer in the mirror because I don't think I've ever looked this good. I'm not exactly ugly but I usually seem like I've just crawled out of bed. Most days I'm happy with my natural look but tonight is going to be hard. I'm glad that even if I feel miserable on the inside, on the outside I'll look radiant and strong.

53

The Square looks great with the crib, the tree, and all the houses lit up and decorated with wreaths. But when we step through the arch it's even more magical and Amélie coos. 'It's perfect.'

And I think, yes, it is. With lanterns and string globes running the length of the lane and the trees wrapped in warm twinkling lights, it's the perfect romantic atmosphere for everything that Niall has planned. The magic continues as we go through the gate and it hits me again that I can't believe he could be happy leaving his beautiful cottage behind. I think about asking Amélie if he's definitely moving to Paris and when. But I don't want to spoil the surprise or sound like I'm judging and I can't trust myself not to let that come across in my voice. I absolutely believe Amélie should settle in her beloved city and it's great if Niall is willing to try and make that work. But it's a hell of a major life decision to make in the space of one week.

We walk up the gravel path and I see Cathy and Brian through the front window sipping from mugs with giant marshmallows floating on top. I've had more than enough hot chocolate today. I won't be hitting the wine or vodka tonight but I could really do with a beer. Brian opens the door and Michael Bublé floats out crooning 'It's Beginning to Look a Lot Like Christmas'. It definitely is but Phoebe Bridgers reassuring me that things will work out 'If We Make It Through December' would be a lot more in tune with my mood.

There's a roaring fire in the stove and the cottage is toasty warm. Amélie dashes over to give Niall a hug and tells him the place looks amazing. 'Mostly thanks to us.' She laughs as she points to herself and then me. Niall gives her a thumbs up and asks what we'd like to drink. As he hands me my beer, I think this is all very friendly and polite but I'm really not seeing any sparks. For two people about to commit to love each other for life, I'd hope for a bit more oomph. If they don't want to kiss or hold each other close with me watching they could at least chance a lingering look. I've already made it clear to Niall that we can only ever be friends. Maybe I need to reassure Amélie too that I'm over whatever it was. I can't keep raining on her dreams.

Nadia and Shane arrive next. I wonder if they travelled together and I ask Nadia if Maura's on her way.

'She said to apologise, she needs an early night.' Nadia stifles a smile. 'I think she had a little too much of the mulled wine.'

'But it's non-alcoholic,' Cathy says with a frown. Then she remembers and grins. 'Don't tell me Christy was passing around his flask.'

Shane and Nadia settle on the couch and when Christy and Lizzie arrive Shane insists on scooching up to make room for them too. Nadia's practically sitting on his lap and neither of them seem to mind in the least. Shane seems to have forgotten all about Amélie's kiss and his crush on me is clearly well in the past. And for some reason, I'm not the least bit worried that these two have only known each other a week. They seem easy and comfortable together but there is also most definitely a spark. Shane's sporting a bright blue Christmas jumper with *Happy Holidays* across the front and I have a good feeling this is one holiday romance that will last.

Niall leaves us to it for a while and heads out with Brian to help Lily and Jack bring in the food. It's only when he comes back through the door carrying a cast-iron casserole dish that I think to myself he's not very dressed up. Considering the occasion and the fact that he asked me to make sure Amélie looked good, he might at least have thrown on a special shirt. He's wearing dark navy jeans, sneakers, and a navy Christmas jumper with a white smiley penguin on the front. Not exactly classic proposal attire. But he's clearly had that bath or a shower at least. He looks clean and fresh and as he sets his casserole down beside me on the island I can't help leaning in to his smell. Maybe I'll sneak an old T-shirt under my coat before I leave. Then when he's off loving it up with Amélie in Paris, I can tuck it away under my pillow and drag it out every now and again for a sniff. I drain my bottle of Peroni and ask if there's anything I can do to help. Anything to get me out of my own head.

Lily passes me a ladle and asks me to start dishing out food. There's vegetarian curry and beef stroganoff and mountains of garlic bread and basmati rice. Mam and Donal arrive just in time and soon everyone is tucking into a plate and sipping a glass of wine or a beer.

'Should I put some aside for the guest,' I ask Niall. I almost say Jules then I remember that Amélie's sister arriving is supposed to be a surprise. Although, Amélie is over the far side of the living room chatting with Cathy and it's unlikely she'd hear. Niall keeps hovering beside me as though there's something he really wants to say but he can't seem to get it out. He's probably feeling bad about what almost happened this afternoon. But I've reassured him often enough that I know we can only be friends so he needs to get over himself and move on. And let me do the same.

'That's okay, Dad made backup, there's no danger of running out.' He checks his phone and says, 'I thought I'd have an update by now, we're running a bit late.' He barely lays his phone on the counter when it beeps with a text and he blows out a breath. 'Okay, we're on. I have about twenty minutes before Jules gets here. I'll go out and get things ready, turn on the patio heaters, and fire up the pit.' He takes a gulp of his Guinness, leans his head to one side, and says, 'Maybe you could help?'

Part of me feels like telling him to feck off. He nearly kissed me again this afternoon and I know he doesn't mean to but he's completely messing with my head. But I look over at Amélie and see her gorgeous warm smile and I want this to be perfect for her so I nod and say yes.

The pergola is strung with vintage globes and there's a stone-paved area over to one side with the firepit already stacked with wood. Niall adds a firelighter and sets it alight as I switch the patio heaters to high. Amélie looks so lovely in that dress I want to make sure she doesn't need her coat when we all start taking photos once Niall seals the deal. There are rows of tea lights along the deck railings waiting to be lit. Niall passes me a candle lighter and we start at opposite ends and work our way around. Neither of us has said a word since we came outside but as we reach the last candles, we face each other just a few feet apart. I look up and see yet one more bunch of mistletoe hanging overhead. This universe is messing with my mind. I'm all for believing in signs but I'm not great at figuring out what they mean. Am I the evil spirit here that needs to be warned off? Because that mistletoe is definitely not bringing me luck and I've absolutely given up on love.

Niall's eyes lock with mine. 'You look lovely tonight,' he says low and hoarse and I feel like a puddle of melting snow. Don't *you look lovely* me I want to howl. I'm not able for this anymore. But his phone beeps again and he says 'Shit, I have to go. Will you bring Amélie outside? On her own.'

One minute he's staring into my eyes and saying things that he shouldn't and that I can hardly bear to hear. Then he's swearing and giving me orders, which is not like Niall at all. The stress must be getting to him too. I guess the countdown to this proposal is on.

I walk through the porch and hear the whole gang singing along to 'Fairytale of New York'. It wouldn't be Christmas in Ballyclane without Kirsty and Shane. I'm on my way through the kitchen doorway when my own Shane steps forward and stops me in my tracks.

'Well?' he says as he stands in front of me and arches his brows.

'Well, what?'

'You and Niall, I saw the two of you go outside. On your own.'

I close my eyes for a few seconds but when I open them again Shane is still standing there with a hopeful grin on his face.

'Niall is not interested in me,' I say with a sigh. 'It's the beautiful French angel that he wants.'

Shane covers his face with his hands and shakes his head really slow. Then he looks straight at me and says, 'Seriously, Jas, you need to get out of your own way.'

I set my hands on my hips and face him down. What kind of a bloody best friend says something like that? When I've already told him Niall has a ring. 'You're the one in the way,' I tell him now. 'I need to get Amélie outside.' Then I lower my voice and groan through gritted teeth, 'Because Niall's about to propose.'

Shane steps back, clearly in shock. Well, I guess I won that battle even if I did lose the war. But I can't even call it a war, I care about Amélie too much. I focus on that as I call out her name and beckon her to come over to where I wait by the door. She skips up with a smile. That's basically her resting face, happy and sweet. Mine is more of a scowl. At least these days that's how it feels.

'I've had so much fun this week, *ma chérie*. And I've made so many good friends. I can't wait for you all to meet Jules.'

I nearly say *that might happen sooner than you think* but I need to stick to the plan. Her sister is meant to be a surprise. I take Amélie's arm and lead her through the door and out through the porch. 'Come outside for a while,' I say. 'We don't have much time left before you go back home.'

She oohs and aahs at the lights on the pergola and the candles all along the rails. 'We must bring everyone out, it's so perfect, like a dream.'

I can't say, *All your best dreams are about to come true*. So, I say, 'It's peaceful now, just the two of us, let's wait.'

We sit facing out onto the garden admiring the glowing mason jars and fairy lights when the wrought-iron gate swings wide and Niall strides through accompanied by a mesmerising vision in a sharp blue suit. I don't know who this friend is or where the hell Jules is. But I need to tell Niall that if he's planning to propose with this guy standing nearby then he seriously needs to up his game. Sneakers and smiley penguins won't cut it. Not when the Duke of Hastings from *Bridgerton*, or as close as I've ever seen, has walked on to the set of our ordinary little lives in Ballyclane.

But I don't get to utter a word. Amélie leaps from her seat before I've barely had time to draw breath. She races down the path with a screech of delight and flings herself into the hot stranger's arms. I've had plenty of my own illicit fantasies watching that show but I do know it's not actually Regé-Jean Page. And even if it was, there are still rules about this sort of thing. I get that Amélie's impulsive but this really isn't okay.

But now he's holding her close as though he can't bear to let her go and then he starts kissing her like he wants to do it right there against the wall. *This is not fecking* Bridgerton*!* I almost shout out. *Her boyfriend's right there and you've only just met.* I have heard of love at first sight and I'm sure it can happen but this is seriously taking the piss.

Then a lightbulb flicks on in my brain and it hits me with a force that this is Jules. I was expecting Amélie's sister but there is nothing sisterly about what this guy is up to right now. This must be who Amélie was talking about when she said she had two great loves in her life. I know one of those is Niall and I assumed the other was fashion or photography or Paris. But it's clear now it's Jules and it looks like Amélie has just made her choice.

Poor Niall.

My eyes flick to Niall and he's walking away, strolling up the path towards the pergola and leaving Amélie and the sharp-dressed hottie to carry on getting it on. Bloody hell. He brought this guy here and he's not even putting up a fight. Does this mean Jules was *the guy* all along and the lights, the mistletoe, the magic, it's all for him?

It's only a few days since Niall told me how special Amélie is to him, how he's never felt like this about anyone else, and how much he's struggling with it all. And I told him to go tell it to Amélie instead. She must have told him about Jules. No wonder he was so upset. And after all the support he's given me, I couldn't get over myself and listen to his problems for once. God, I feel such a bitch.

54

I stand up straight and hold out my palms as Niall reaches the deck.

'What the hell?'

He presses a finger to his lips and shakes his head. Then he takes his phone out of his jeans pocket and swipes. Suddenly, 'Love Story' by Taylor Swift wafts from the outdoor speakers and the first thing that occurs to me is that it's Shane and Amélie's song. Then I remember that's just in my head. And it was barely a kiss. But whatever is going on down that garden is a hell of a lot more than one kiss. Those two look like they're smitten for real.

They walk towards us now, holding hands as they practically float up the path. Hot guy mouths *Thank you* to Niall and I feel a hand on the small of my back as I'm directed into the porch. Niall closes the door, turns to me, and says, 'That's Jules.'

Yeah, I think I figured that out. I don't say that, of course, this is not the time for rubbing it in. I just nod. We're still staring through the side window of the porch when Jules leads Amélie to the pergola, gets down on one knee, and produces a ring. Amélie squeals one more time and flings herself into his arms. I'm guessing the answer is yes.

I lean my head against the misted-up glass and peer out at the fairy tale scene.

'What is the deal with this guy?' I turn back around and study Niall.

'I told you, that's Jules.' He pinches the bridge of his nose. 'I thought Amélie would have told you all about him by now.'

'Um, no, we've been wrapped up in the markets and my hats.' I wince as I realise how selfish that sounds. 'I thought you were talking about Amélie's sister when you said you were texting someone called Jules. Who is he to Amélie and what's he doing here?'

Niall shoots me a puzzled look. 'He's her boyfriend, of course. He was going to surprise her in Galway then she told him she was here in Ballyclane. Amélie's sister found me on Facebook and put us in touch.' He goes quiet for a moment and adds. 'I think he was worried at first that Amélie was here to see me but I set him straight and we've been working on his plan ever since.'

I wonder what he means by 'set him straight'. That Amélie was only here for me? That she had no romantic interest in Niall anymore? That he was prepared to bow out and help Jules if that would make Amélie happy? I think about how to ask this but I'm exhausted trying to get my head around it all. I flop down on the bench that runs along the timber wall of the porch and start with a hesitant, 'I thought…'

Niall peers down at me with a frown. 'You thought what?'

I thought Amélie and Niall were a done deal. But I don't get to reply as the outer door opens and Amélie and Jules stand beaming big happy smiles, waiting to be welcomed inside.

Niall gives Amélie a hug and shakes Jules' hand as though he's genuinely happy for them both. I take my cue from him and do my best to manage the same. We go back inside and I lean against the wall and watch as everybody congratulates them and Amélie introduces Jules to them all. Niall sits on a stool by the island watching on as if he's a proud parent and couldn't be more pleased for them both.

I get that he wants Amélie to be happy. But to be so graceful about it and actually help the guy take the woman of his dreams from literally under his nose. Then sit there smiling through it all. He must *really* love her to do that. I've said it before and I'll say it again, the man is an absolute saint. Well, in real life at least. He's definitely no saint in my dreams. Christ, I have to stop thinking about that. Be a friend, be a friend, be a friend.

55

Christy and Lizzie and Mam and Donal head home and everyone else moves outside to the deck. The firepit is blazing and the infrared patio heaters radiate warmth. Jack brings out extra bottles of wine and Peroni and cans of Guinness. Lily passes around merino-wool blankets that she pre-warmed by the stove. I'm achingly tired and could easily curl up on Niall's couch and drift off to sleep. But the others are all chatting and smiling and full of Christmas cheer. I don't want to be a killjoy and point out the elephant in the room but, seriously, am I the only one who gives a damn about Niall? Don't they remember how cut up he was the first time? He told me about the girl who broke his heart. He must have told his parents and Brian. Don't any of them care?

But the spotlight is firmly on Amélie and her stunning new man. All anybody seems interested in is how long they've known each other and how they got together and where he found such a beautiful ring. Hello, Niall's sitting right there. Do you think this is what he really needs to hear?

Although I have to admit, I am dying to know more. Where did this guy come from and when? Amélie and I only got to know each other when she helped rescue my hats and I was back in Ballyclane by the end of that week. She was the most incredible support to me but I was a wreck and I barely registered that Amélie had a life beyond me. I started to follow her on Instagram but she posts about fashion and never about personal stuff. She told me once, laughing, that she only talks about her private life with real friends. Some real friend I am. If I had asked anything about her life before Galway I might have heard more about Jules. And about Niall.

And even when she came to help with the market, it was mostly about me and my hats. I feel bad now that she didn't think she could talk to me about her relationships. It must have been so hard having to make up her mind. Jules is all sexy and French and seems to adore her but Niall is Niall. He's across from me now and it's like he senses that I'm thinking about him and his gorgeous grey eyes lock with mine. He's sitting directly in front of the firepit and I know he never feels the cold but as he peels off his jumper and his T-shirt pulls up underneath, I swear he's doing it on purpose to see how I react. I have to swallow and hold myself still but I'm sure he can see the heat in my eyes. I don't care if she's got the Duke of Hastings, or close enough. As far as I'm concerned, Amélie's making the mistake of her life. How could any woman not want Niall?

Jules starts to explain that he and Amélie have known each other for more than eight years. He was a male fashion model when they met. Yep, that makes sense. Amélie was starting out as a photographer and they were both travelling all the time. So even though it was love at first sight they agreed to give each other space and not cramp each other's style but he knew they would end up together in the end. Then Jules gave up modelling and studied philosophy at the Sorbonne and now he's writing a book. I wasn't expecting that. Probably something about the meaning of life. He seems to have that figured out.

But that means *he* was with Amélie before Niall. And Niall was the affair on the side. Not Jules. Oh God, this is all starting to make sense. That's what Niall meant when he said it wasn't much fun for him when he found out. That Mel was Amélie and Amélie had Jules. His heart was broken and now it must be happening all over again.

Cathy says that her back is beginning to ache and it's time for a lie down so she and Brian say their goodbyes. Then they're followed by Lily and Jack. So now it's just Nadia and Shane, Amélie and Jules, and me and Niall. Or rather me. And Niall.

I look around the table and I think how hard love is to understand. Jules said he and Amélie fell in love at first sight yet it's taken them eight years to commit. And Shane thought he was in love with me and then Amélie, although in fairness he did admit that was just a crush. It took him a while to notice Nadia but now he barely has eyes for anyone else. I thought Niall and I had a real spark and the more I get to know him the more I can feel myself losing my heart. But he pulled away and then Amélie arrived and I can't blame him if old feelings resurfaced. I think he has feelings for me too but I have no interest in being some sort of second-best substitute when she's gone.

Jules whispers something to Amélie in French and Amélie laughs and tells us she and Jules are going home and she'll see us tomorrow for brunch. Jules had planned a hotel but Lily insisted he stay with them as Amélie already has the guest wing tucked away at the top of the house.

Shane stands up too and holds out a hand to Nadia. 'Yeah, it is getting late.' He yawns. 'It's time I walked Nadia home.'

It's only half past eleven and Shane doesn't look the least bit tired to me. That was definitely a fake yawn. When I left for the market this morning, I didn't even think about arranging a lift or bringing my bike. I assumed I'd be walking home from Niall's party with Shane. But that's obviously not happening now, I'd be an awkward third wheel.

'I'm sure Niall will walk you home,' Shane adds with a grin.

I'm going to have serious words with that boy tomorrow. Just because he's all loved-up doesn't give him the right to meddle when he really doesn't have a clue. 'I'll crash in Gran's.' I scowl at him hard, firing daggers with my eyes. 'It's only across the Square, I'll be fine.'

Then I look over at Niall. He's resting his chin on his hand and staring down at the table looking lost and alone and my heart breaks for him again. I can't bear to see him hurting so much. Then he looks up through those beautiful dark lashes and I can't read the look in his eyes but I don't think he wants me to go. I'm in dangerous territory here. I can see he's not ready to be left alone and I know he really needs me as a friend. And I want to be. But I also want so much more.

'You two go on.' I wave Shane and Nadia away. 'I'm going to use the bathroom. Then I'll give Niall a hand to tidy up before I head off.'

That sounds harmless enough. Nothing to read into there. Nothing to suggest that I'm hanging around hoping for a shift or offering myself up as a way to mend his poor broken heart. I'll help him clear things away, say a few comforting words, and promise him it will all work out. Like it says on that T-shirt he wears.

He's wearing a T-shirt now too; he hasn't put his jumper back on. He must have infrared blood. I was too busy taking in the broad angular line of his shoulders and the lean hard muscle on his arms to notice the lettering etched across the grey: *Believe*.

I smile to myself as I walk back into the cottage. The guy doesn't own a single plain shirt. Then I feel a tug at my chest as I think how ironic it must seem to him now. I always thought Niall wore those T-shirts to pass on a message to the rest of us. But maybe it's himself he's been trying to convince.

I do some deep breathing while I'm in the bathroom and I remind myself of all the great things that have happened this week. Mam deciding to hold on to Gran's house, the market going so well, and my hats being such a success. And wiping the sneer off Tracey Hamilton's face. I look in the mirror as I wash my hands and I tell myself I just need to get Niall to do the same. He's worked so hard at seeing the glass half-full. And I'm finally getting there too. I won't let him slide back down.

He's loading the dishwasher as I stroll back into the kitchen and I give him my cheeriest smile. 'Lily seemed really impressed with your plans,' I say. That's safe enough ground, might as well lead with that.

Niall smiles back and his face softens. 'Yes, Dad too. They love them. It's such a relief. I know they'd be sorry if they sell.' He closes the dishwasher and pulls up a stool. 'And thanks for your help.'

'Hey, I owe you, after all you've done for Mam.' *And me*, I want to add but I don't want to cross any lines. I'm not even sure where the lines are anymore.

'Will you have one more beer before you go?' Niall tilts his head. 'I'm going to, and you can't leave me sitting here drinking on my own.' His eyes crease in a smile and I feel an ache in my ribs. I had two beers earlier but I've been drinking water since then. One more won't do any harm. And I owe it to him to keep him company for a bit. It can't be easy thinking about Amélie tucked up with Jules in Niall's family home.

'I'd love one,' I say, 'but do you mind if I take the couch, I'm starting to flag and I'm not sure I can stay up on a stool.'

'Sure, work away, I'll bring over your beer.'

I pull off my boots and curl up on one end of the couch.

Niall grabs two beers from the fridge, passes me mine, and perches on the arm at the far end.

'Mum was very impressed with your hats,' he says. 'She's going to tell all her friends how good they are.' He takes a sip of his beer. 'And Amélie's convinced you're going to be famous. Sounds like you're shooting for the stars.'

I'm baffled as to how he can drop Amélie into the conversation so casually and I'm about to ask if he's okay when he adds, 'I hope you are starting to believe in yourself now, Jas.' He lifts his beer in salute and there's a catch in his breath as he says, 'You're amazing, you know.'

I reach over and clink his bottle with my own. I'm careful not to meet his eyes when I lean in, I don't trust myself that close. 'Thank you. I am,' I say. Then I look up and laugh. 'Is that why you wore that T-shirt tonight? In case I need more convincing to believe?'

His eyes go dark as he holds my gaze and I want to look away but I can't. I guess he's hoping for a distraction, some sort of consolation prize. I can't be that. I need to be strong but the way he's looking at me now, it's like all he can think about is tearing off my best dress. And it's all I can think about too.

I blink and lower my eyes to his chest and I see that lettering again, *Believe*. Then I remember Mam's words, *He really believes in you, Jas.* And Niall's *I believe in you. I've believed in you since the first time I saw you that day at your gran's… I just wish that you felt the same way about me.*

And something settles inside me: a feeling, a wish, a spark of hope. The way he looked at me that day when he said, *I've never felt this way about anyone else…*

I was so wrapped up in Tracey, and Gran's house, and everything I thought was wrong with my life that I never dared to dream he could be talking about me.

'I'm not giving up, Jas.' His voice is low and hoarse. 'I'm not ready to give up.'

My stomach dips. Is he talking about Amélie again? Or could he possibly be talking about me? I could let these questions swirl around my mind but I've come too far to keep making that same mistake. I still don't feel sure but I want to be brave. I take a slow deep breath and I let my head fill with all the positive voices that have supported me these last few weeks, especially Niall's. And I ask him straight out, 'You're not giving up on *who*?'

'On you, Jas. On *you*.' His brows crease in a frown. 'Who else would I be talking about?'

I need to be sure of exactly what he means so I decide to come clean. 'I thought you were still in love with Amélie. I thought you were planning to propose.'

His jaw drops then he stands and starts rubbing at his head as though he's trying to shake up his brain. He takes a gulp of his beer and stares down at me again. 'How could you possibly think that?'

'Because it felt like you told me so.'

'I most definitely did not.'

I take a long swig of my own beer and tell myself I can do this, and I go on. 'You said Amélie was really special to you. Then you said you had never felt like that about anyone else. I thought… I thought you were telling me you were still in love with her.'

Niall takes a step back and stares at me now like I'm the craziest person he's ever met. He chokes out a shocked laugh and my eyes blaze. I can't bear to think he might be laughing at me. It's like we've gone back to the start.

'Stop laughing. That's not fair. You said you loved her once. You said she broke your heart.' I stand now too and face him as tears stream down my cheeks.

His face falls and he sets his beer down on the floor. He steps forward and looks into my eyes. I close mine because his gaze makes my head spin and I need to slow down my mind.

He takes hold of my shoulders, gently, carefully, and presses his lips to the top of my hair. 'I don't love Amélie. I thought I did once but that was years ago. And I'm not even sure that I ever really did.'

'But how could you *not* love Amélie?' My voice comes out as a whimper but I turn my face up towards his and open my eyes.

'Because she's not you, Jas. She's not *you*.'

*

He closes his eyes now and it pulls at my heart because that's exactly what I do. When I don't want something to be happening or when I want it so much and I can't believe it is and I'm scared if I keep my eyes open, I'll have to watch it all disappear. There's so much I could say but this moment needs more than words.

I reach up and wrap my arms around his neck, thread my fingers through his hair, and ease his head down towards mine. Then I kiss those dark silky lashes and the tip of his nose. I glide my fingers along the side of his face. He has that classic chiselled jawline thing going on but his skin is so fucking soft. His eyes are still closed and he gives a low moan as I trace one finger across that delicious full lower lip. Then I hold his face in my hands and I kiss that beautiful mouth as if my whole life depends on this kiss. Because the way I feel now it absolutely does.

He kisses me back as if his whole life depends on this too. Then his hands are on mine and I'm pressed against the wall and every inch of my body is screaming, *Now, now, everything, please.* But Niall draws back and even though he's still holding my hands I think, *No, not again, don't pull away from me.* But it's clear that's not what this is. He gazes down at me and his eyes are blacker than the dark December sky. It feels like he wants to swallow me whole.

Then he says, 'I need to know that you're sure.'

My voice barely sounds like my own as I let out a low groan. 'I've never been more sure of anything else in my life.'

He presses his forehead to mine and says, 'I think it's time we took this upstairs.'

Fireworks explode beneath my skin and every inch of me thrills at the thought of what that means. But I smile and keep my tone light. 'Yeah, it's about bloody time. I was beginning to think nobody would ever get to see that sacred space.'

Niall laughs into my neck and whispers something about my sacred space and heat sears up my thighs and melts my insides. He takes my hand and leads me up those painted oak stairs.

He lays me down on his bed and pulls off his T-shirt as I start to unbutton my dress. My fingers are trembling and I don't get very far, I'm too busy staring at his chest.

'You're going to have to help me with this.'

He smiles and eases himself over me and starts to kiss me again and my body arches against him. But then he breaks, goes all serious, and says, 'I want you to promise me one thing.'

I press my head back into the pillow and narrow my eyes. I'm not gone on all these interruptions and I'm not into rules. Just kiss me for God's sake and we'll take it from there.

But this is Niall, and he looks so earnest, so I shrug. 'Depends what it is.'

'Talk to me, please.'

I want to say, *I have other things on my mind, we can talk in the morning if that's all right.* But I know he's only getting started, so I wait.

He traces circles down the side of my face. 'Whatever crazy stuff is going on in your brain, let me know. And if you're worried about something or you think I'm thinking something you're not happy about, just ask. I don't want us to go through this again. Because, honestly, I'm all yours.'

I feel my eyes well up because I know he means every word and just being here with Niall, hearing his solid, grounding voice, makes me feel like everything's right with my world.

I nod and hold his gaze. 'I promise I will. If you will too. Because I'm also absolutely yours.'

He smiles down at me and he's about to say something else but I don't give him the chance because my body aches for him and I don't want to hear another word unless he's telling me all the ways he's going to take care of that. I drag one hand along his shoulder and bury my face in his chest, breathing in that warm woody smell. I slide my other hand down his lean hard stomach. I slip my hand beneath the waistband of his jeans. 'Take. These. Off.'

His mouth quirks in a smile. 'So, this is what's been going on in that crazy brain of yours all this time.'

I dig my hands into his back and pull his body hard down on mine. You have no idea of all the crazy stuff going on in my head.' I skate my tongue along his lower lip, tasting cinnamon and beer. 'All the ways that I want you.'

He kisses me slow and deep then keeps his eyes wide open as he says, 'You have no idea how much I want to spend the rest of my life finding out.'

Acknowledgements

To my wonderful sisters, Anne, Sharon, and Michelle, and their husbands and families for their kindness and support. My best friend and early reader, Fiona, and her hubby, Mark, for helping me to breathe again and picture good things. Kathleen in West Cork for red wine and so much laughter through tears. To my darling daughter, Kate, who lights up my life, and her lovely partner, Leo, who lights up hers.

My agent, Nicky Lovick, for believing in my writing even when I didn't myself. My editor, Carolyn Mays, and copy editor, Kay, for helping to make this a much better book. Laura and the cover design team for my gorgeous cover. All at Bedford Square for choosing my story and working on my book.

Vanessa Fox-O'Loughlin, Maria McHale, and all the gang at Writers' Ink for sound advice and encouragement. The Romantic Novelists' Association for being such a welcoming, supportive group. My writing friend, Seána (aka Catherine Tinley), for her encouragement and advice.

The staff at Mountmellick Library for being so warm and welcoming, and all my writing and creative friends there. All those who give so much to the community in my home town, especially those who gave us such wonderful Christmas memories growing up.

The Frames for kind permission to reference their brilliant

songs. Claire Leadbitter for her help with this. Glen Hansard for his powerful (and definitely not godforsaken) lungs.

To the readers and writers and dreamers. Here's to the mess we make. And here's to doing it all over again.

Bedford Square Publishers is an independent publisher of fiction and non-fiction, founded in 2022 in the historic streets of Bedford Square London and the sea mist shrouded green of Bedford Square Brighton.

Our goal is to discover irresistible stories and voices that illuminate our world.

We are passionate about connecting our authors to readers across the globe and our independence allows us to do this in original and nimble ways.

The team at Bedford Square Publishers has years of experience and we aim to use that knowledge and creative insight, alongside evolving technology, to reach the right readers for our books. From the ones who read a lot, to the ones who don't consider themselves readers, we aim to find those who will love our books and talk about them as much as we do.

We are hunting for vital new voices from all backgrounds – with books that take the reader to new places and transform perceptions of the world we live in.

Follow us on social media for the latest Bedford Square Publishers news.

@bedsqpublishers

facebook.com/bedfordsq.publishers

@bedfordsq.publishers

bedfordsquarepublishers.co.uk